"YOU WILL HAVE TO WAIT."

"I—"

She angled her chin. "In case you have overlooked the fact, I am in an indecent state of dress." As soon as she uttered the words, she wished them back. Seathan's hard glare of moments before darkened, a potent reminder he was not only a warrior but a man.

A very virile man.

A man assured of his abilities.

A man confident he would always leave a woman satisfied.

Sweet Mary! "I meant . . . you will depart so I may dress."

He stepped toward her as if a predator stalking its prey. "I will depart?" His gaze moved over her with excruciating, seductive slowness before pausing on her face. "You are quick to command those around you, my lady."

Shivers of awareness slid through her. "Nay twist my words. Any other man would not have dared intrude upon a woman alone in her chamber, much less barge in and issue orders."

"On that you are correct. Any other man in my position would have secured you within the dungeon until he had gained the truth . . ."

Books by Diana Cosby

HIS CAPTIVE

HIS WOMAN

HIS CONQUEST

HIS DESTINY

Published by Kensington Publishing Corporation

His CONQUEST

DIANA COSBY

ZEBRA BOOKS
KENSINGTON PUBLISHING CORP.
http://www.kensingtonbooks.com

ISBN-13: 978-1-4201-0991-7
ISBN-10: 1-4201-0991-X

First Printing: November 2010
10 9 8 7 6 5 4 3 2 1

Printed in the United States of America

This book is dedicated to my parents,
Sam and Jean White,
who have always believed in me.

ACKNOWLEDGMENTS

I am truly thankful for the immense support from my family and friends. My deepest wish is that everyone is as blessed when they pursue their dreams.

My sincere thanks and humble gratitude to my editors, *Kate Duffy* and *Megan Records*; my agent, *Holly Root*; my critique partners, *Shirley Rogerson* and *Michelle Hancock*; and to *Mary Forbes* for the extra brainstorming, all of which made Seathan and Linet's story breathe life and allowed the magic of story to infuse their journey.

Special thanks to my children, *Eric, Stephanie*, and *Christopher*, as well as the *Wild Writers* for their continued amazing support!

Kate Duffy was an amazing editor and friend who made such an immense difference in so many lives. God bless you, Kate. I miss you.

Chapter 1

Dangerous.

The cold, moor-swept air hummed with the ominous warning. Stark. Foreboding. Like the captive rebel who prowled in his cell only paces away from where Lady Linet Dancort hid. His each step predatory. His each breath cast out in a ragged hiss.

Though hidden in the shadows, with distance and iron separating them, like the storm howling outside Breac Castle this night, the threat exuded by this man was very real.

Draped within her thick wool cape, she regarded Seathan MacGruder, Earl of Grey. Only a fool would dare cross her brother's prisoner.

And she was far from a fool.

An ache built in her chest that her life had crumbled to this moment. She wished the years back, wished her father and mother still lived and that her brother, Fulke Dancort, Viscount of Tearlach, had not betrayed her. But as the cool, storm-fed wind rattled across her skin in a macabre caress, her wishes crumbled one by one.

Linet swallowed hard. Hopes, like fairy tales, were for the innocent. For those who had something left to believe in.

How dare her brother betray his promise of allowing her to choose her husband? This night, Fulke would regret the arrangements he'd made for her to marry a neighboring earl to strengthen his ties, an earl known for his abuse, an earl whose brutality had left his last wife dead.

At the rattle of bars, she focused on the Scot who stalked his cell like an animal caged. Here was a man who represented truth, not lies wielded for a self-serving purpose.

Thunder smothered the bells of matins.

Through the carved window, she scanned the midnight sky battered by hard, spring-fed rain. She must hurry. With a steadying breath, Linet pushed back her hood and stepped into the torchlight. A slight scrape sounded as her slipper touched the stone floor.

The Scottish rebel whirled to face her.

Lightning split the sky. Thunder snarled in its wake. Through a tangle of black hair, Lord Grey's eyes, feral like a wolf's, locked on hers.

A tremor rocked her as potent as the next blast of thunder. Her mind commanded she retreat.

She held.

Like the air pulsing with energy, her every sense

grew charged with awareness. The urge to shield her face from his unapologetic glare stunned her. Throughout her life, her father had given her the freedom to study alongside her peers, and he'd encouraged her to speak her mind.

Never had a man's presence, much less his gaze, incited her interest to a mind-spinning degree. It was illogical this prisoner could make her feel anything with a mere look.

But standing paces away, with his warrior's dark gaze burning into hers, her body trembled. She owed her reaction to nerves. And rightly so. By the rebel's formidable height, scathing look, and arrogant stance, there was little safe about the Scot. And with orders for him to be hanged at first light, he must be desperate.

As was she.

Fulke's demand that she cede to his dictates and marry the neighboring earl echoed through her mind. She welcomed the anger, embraced the emotion that for the last month since her brother's return had kept her sanity intact.

Enough pondering the past. She would ensure that her brother paid for his greed. He would lose not only the powerful alliance her arranged marriage would have brought, but also this prized Scottish rebel, a noble high in William Wallace's ranks. A loss that would earn her brother naught but King Edward's wrath.

Head held high, she stepped within a hand's length of the cell door.

Lightning illuminated the chamber.

He'd shifted, hands on hips, his feet now braced in an aggressive stance.

"I have come to set you free." Thunder rumbled, this time closer, an ominous backdrop to her quiet offer.

The earl remained silent, his expression raw with distrust.

The rebel doubted her. She'd expected as much. God forbid if he discovered that Lord Tearlach, his sworn enemy, was her brother.

At the jangle of keys, his eyes narrowed.

Linet lifted the heavy iron ring into the windswept torchlight. "I will set you free. In return, you must agree to escort me to my mother's clan in the Highlands."

In silence, Lord Grey scanned the corridor to where the guards lay slumped against the wall.

"I have drugged them."

Eyes as black as the devil's own sliced to her. "You do not fear me, lass?" His voice, dark and deep with threat, curled around her like a fist.

"No," she lied.

"Then you are a fool."

"Nay, determined." She drew in a slow breath, refusing to betray how his presence unnerved her. She'd dealt with his type of arrogance before, warriors who appraised their enemy, then used their opponent's weakness to attack.

In this confrontation, she would decide her own fate.

And in this instance, his.

Linet lifted the key that would unlock his cell.

Torchlight caressed the hammered length of iron. "Have I your agreement?"

"How do I know this is not a trick?"

"You do not," she replied. "You know nothing about me except that I hold the key to your freedom."

In silence, shrewd eyes assessed her as he debated her offer.

The Scot's arrogance amazed her. He was imprisoned inside her brother's dungeon without hope of escape, his hanging set for dawn, yet he hesitated.

Again the image of a wolf flashed through her mind. A predator. A man who protected his own, whatever the cost. What he didn't understand, and never could, was that she had as much to lose as he, including her life.

"Your vow," she demanded, wincing inwardly at the desperation that slipped into her voice. "I hardly think you have an option."

He drew himself to his full height. "You have my vow, the vow of a Scotsman."

Unease rippled through her. His declaration echoed as more of a threat than a promise. As if she had time to debate the wisdom of freeing the rebel. They must leave before another guard appeared.

Before she could convince herself her ill-conceived plan was indeed foolish, she motioned the dangerous Scot back. "Move away from the door."

Seathan MacGruder held still, intrigued by this mere slip of a woman who dared issue him orders. A muscle worked in his jaw as he studied his unlikely rescuer. She was beautiful. Like a fairy forbidden to leave the Otherworld, she stood before him with proud defiance.

Her amber-gold hair secured behind her head in a harsh knot served to frame the fine curve of her face, a mouth that promised passion and confident eyes shadowed by secrets.

Why would this lass dare free him to escort her to the Highlands? Did she not realize he was Lord Tearlach's prize prisoner? Was she unaware that if the viscount learned of her scheme, she would be hanged?

God's teeth. Something was amiss. But whoever she was, he would sell his soul for a chance at freedom.

And revenge.

Dauid's image burned his soul. His most trusted friend, a man whom he'd grown up with, a man who'd been knighted at his side—and his betrayer.

Had he not witnessed Dauid standing alongside Lord Tearlach as the viscount's men had hauled Seathan away, he would have defended Dauid's honor against any accuser.

As well, Seathan had witnessed the viscount's knights mercilessly slaughtering the Scots who hadn't a chance to escape. Then the English had left them to rot.

Fury rippled through Seathan. He could forgive Dauid of many things, but not this. Once free of Breac Castle, he would warn William Wallace and his clan of Dauid's treachery.

Then, he would find Dauid.

And kill him.

Shaking off the dizziness from the torture served to him by Tearlach's men to discover where William Wallace hid, Seathan pressed his face against the bars and scanned the corridor for any sign of a trap.

The guards, as this mysterious woman claimed, remained slumped against the wall.

Seathan withdrew into the shadows and gave the cloaked woman a distance he believed she would consider safe.

For a split second, the woman hesitated, as if debating the wisdom of her decision. Only the slight tremble of her breath belied her outward calm.

Unlock the door, he willed.

Hesitant eyes flicked to him. On an exhale, she focused on the door.

As the forged key scraped in the lock, the room began to blur. He fought to clear his vision.

She pushed open the door.

Seathan lunged forward.

On a cry, the woman shoved the door back.

He ripped the iron bars from her hands, hauled her inside, and pinned her body with his own against the stone wall. Before she realized his intent, he jerked her dagger from its sheath.

Outrage cloaked her face. "You gave me your word!"

"Quiet!" he growled, working to catch his breath and ward off the throbbing wound in his right side. A sticky warmth oozed down his flesh. Bedamned. The gash he had staunched with cloth had broken open. Seathan scanned their surroundings.

The corridor remained empty.

"Release me!"

Though she was clad in a thick cloak, it couldn't hide her slender frame or her tempting curves beneath. His fevered body stirred with interest.

"I said quiet," Seathan warned, owing his body's response to exhaustion. Well he understood the turmoil incited by desires of the flesh. Needs clouded one's keen judgment and left rational men with the common sense of an ass. Once lust cleared, a man's emotions lay ravaged and the woman was gone.

Many years had passed since a lass had stirred this depth of awareness within him. And with each, a cold reminder of the penance for poor decisions made.

As if she sensed his wayward thoughts, fear flickered in her eyes. "I said release me!"

"Lass—"

She dug her nails into his arms as she fought to break free.

Seathan caught her hands and pressed them above her head against the wall, his body trembling from the effort. "I will not harm you," he ground out, silently damning her actions, which left their bodies splayed in an intimate press.

"If you do not let me go, I will scream!"

He clasped her wrists with one hand, moved his other to muffle her, but at her partial freedom, she jammed her elbow into his bruised rib. On a curse, he recaptured her wrist and held it back, his face inches from her own.

She opened her mouth to scream.

Bedamned. In a purely tactical decision, he covered her mouth with his own.

The shot of lust inside him was immediate.

Hot.

Destroying.

The lass froze as if stunned by his boldness, then she twisted to break free.

He held her tight. By God, she'd not raise the guard. Seathan angled his mouth and deepened the kiss.

Her struggles weakened. She held, not kissing him back, but not resisting.

He touched his tongue to hers, soft, seducing, wanting her totally lost to sensation. And he'd guessed correctly. Her mouth was sin itself. Her taste, a softness that lured a man back for more.

He rolled with the tide of sensations, a mixture of heat, of his own desperation and need. The cell around him faded, the aches pounding through him fell away as he sank into the kiss. On a soft moan, she leaned against him and began kissing him back, hesitant, unsure, as if a flower daring to open beneath the first rays of the sun.

The fumbling inexperience of her efforts, the tiny gasps of pleasure as she moved her lips against his own, seduced him as effectively as if she were a seasoned courtesan. His mind blurred as his body took full control. Wanting to touch her, to savor the velvet sweep of her skin beneath his fingers, to drive her over the edge before he sank deep into her silken depths, he released one of her wrists.

A guard's call echoed in the distance.

Seathan broke free, his pulse racing, his blood pounding hot, and recaptured her hand. He stared at the beguiling woman, stunned, amazed, and still wanting her.

What in bloody hell? He'd meant to silence her. To keep her from bringing every knight within the castle from rushing to the dungeon. But need had poured through him in a blistering wash, smothering even his pain, and for a moment he had willingly drowned.

Neither did he miss the desire still burning in her eyes, flames that ate at his control and invited him back.

The pulse at the base of her neck raced. "Our bargain," she hissed, "was for you to escort me to the Highlands, nothing more."

If the situation weren't so dire, he would have laughed. Here she stood trapped by an armed warrior twice her size and she dared to argue?

But in this she was correct. He had given his word. To her good fortune, he was a man of principles.

Gritting his teeth against the pain and willing his body to calm, Seathan released her and stepped back. He wasn't sure what reaction to expect from her, but her wiping her mouth with the back of her hand as if she found his taste foul wasn't one that suited his pride.

He caught her shoulders and dragged her to within a hand's breadth of his chest. The male in him demanded she acknowledge the heat that had surged between them. Regardless of her initial rebuke, if he touched her now, with her willing response of moments before, he might seduce her.

Another guard called in the distance.

Eyes wide, she glanced down the corridor. Her worried expression convinced him his instincts proved right; she was involved with something more than a simple plot to ensure their escape.

The last of his desire fled.

"Who are you?" Though softly spoken, his words were laced with menace.

Silence.

"Tell me or I swear I will secure you within the cell and depart."

Panic flashed in her eyes. "Your honor rests on your word."

"Aye, to take you to the Highlands, but not to be used as prey for one of Lord Tearlach's twisted games. Your name!"

At the mention of the viscount, her face paled. "Linet." She shot another nervous glance down the dungeon. "If we are discovered . . ."

Another guard called out, this time closer.

"'Twould seem he is searching for his drugged counterparts." Seathan caught her hand. "Come."

"Wait!"

He tightened his grip and hauled her down the eastern corridor.

The lass fought him. "Not that way! We must use the secret passage."

Seathan rounded on her, winced at the pull on his wound. "If you value your life, this had best not be a trap."

She shook her head. "I want my freedom as much as you."

And for an unexplainable reason, be it the stubborn lift of her chin, or the desperation in her voice, Seathan believed her. Not that he would tell her. Or let down his guard.

"Which way?" he demanded.

"Toward the stairs."

He looked past the unmoving guards and the steps leading to the keep, to the remainder of the dungeon beyond. Then he pinned her with a skeptical glare. "There is naught but the dungeon's end."

"The passageway is known to but a few."

"A few?"

"There is no time for debate."

"Or treachery." The lass held his harsh glare. She had brawn, he'd give her that. Seathan nodded. "Lead the way."

She tried to pull her hand free.

He held tight.

"Release me."

"Not until we are safe."

Frustration flashed on her face. "I am helping you escape."

"Aye, for reasons you withhold."

She shot him a cold look, then turned and started forward.

The cool breeze melded with the stench of the dungeon, providing a hint of fresh air. But to him it was heaven, cutting through the nausea threatening his every breath. He pushed forward. Adrenaline kept him upright as did his thoughts of revenge.

They kept to the shadows as they moved along the corridor. Errant flickers of torchlight cut through the murky gray, periodically illuminated by another slash of lightning.

They moved past unconscious guards slumped in the narrowed hall, the men's breathing even, their bodies tangled in haphazard positions. The lass had claimed she'd drugged them. In this, she'd told the truth. Still, a nagging doubt of her intentions persisted. Why did the lass flee the castle in the dark of the night?

Several paces farther she stopped. "Here."

Sweat covered his body as he braced his legs to steady himself. He scanned the wall. Illuminated by a torch set within a sconce, each crafted stone lay wedged into place with expertise, not a crack or any fault to suggest an entry.

"I see no door."

At Lord Grey's gruff claim, Linet laid her hand upon a nondescript stone about waist high. With a slight push, the hidden stone panel swung inward.

Stale air rushed out. The candle she'd left burning inside sputtered in a mad dance. Then the flame steadied and embraced the opening within its soft glow.

A muffled rumble of thunder echoed as she glanced at the earl, whose gaze lay fixed on her with suspicion. As if she expected anything different? Since he'd first seen her, he'd watched her with nothing but predatory doubt.

Except for when he'd kissed her. A subtle edge

of arousal had darkened his gaze, an element as basic as the need for air.

Memories of his heated look poured through her, an urgent pull that demanded a response. His dark taste, a sheer male essence that overrode every other thought.

Unnerved, she willed his effect on her away. Lord Grey was too dangerous a man to relax her guard. God forbid if he learned it was her brother who had imprisoned him, tortured him, then sentenced him to hang.

She needed to keep her wits. Though he was weakened from his beatings, his eyes smoldered with intelligence, that of a warrior trained to notice the smallest detail, a man who wielded his mind as deftly as his sword.

She should have anticipated his asking her name. Shaken, she'd given the rebel her real one. Thank God he hadn't recognized it.

That she attributed to his deteriorated condition. Though a seasoned fighter, several times she'd caught him weaving since they'd departed the cell. The sheen of sweat on his face betrayed the effort of his each step.

After the brutal beatings he'd endured since his arrival at Breac Castle a fortnight past, she was amazed he could stand, much less walk. Another testament to his strength.

And proof the Scot was dangerous.

Had she erred in freeing him to seek revenge against her brother? Aside from not trusting him, with his injuries, he was going to slow her down.

No, Fulke's loss of his valuable prisoner more than compensated for any challenges ahead.

How long before Fulke realized she was behind Lord Grey's escape? Caught up in his search for the Scot, surely he wouldn't think of her, nor would her brother notice if she didn't appear in the morn to break her fast. She'd told her maid that she felt ill, to inform Fulke that she would remain in her chamber to rest, which would buy her more time.

Time enough to be a league away from him and his despicable edicts before morning.

Lord Grey urged her forward. "Go."

Followed by the Scot, Linet stepped inside the secret tunnel.

The earl closed the door behind him with a soft thud. Candlelight flickered into a steady pulse; his gaze never wavered from hers. Neither did she miss how his body trembled from his effort.

Disgust filled her at Fulke's cold-hearted abuse. "Can you make it out?"

A breath of a smile touched the earl's mouth, but there was nothing warm or friendly in his expression. "Aye, with or without your help."

Anger sliced her. "After all that I have risked, you think I would abandon you?"

Black brows drew into a harsh frown. "Exactly what have you risked, my lady?"

"My life to free you."

His grip tightened on her hand. "Why? Or should I ask, for whom?"

She angled her jaw. Though an intimidating man, he'd soon learn she was not a woman swayed by threats. "My reasons are my own. Rest assured, I do not plot against you. All I wish to gain is my escape from Breac Castle and to reach my mother's clan in the Highlands." He opened his mouth to speak, but she shook her head. "I will not tell you anything else. If you wish to ask more questions, you will but waste time we can ill afford."

The Scot watched her as if a hawk appraising its prey. Then, his grip loosened. "Time will reveal if indeed you speak the truth." His somber words reverberated in the fractured darkness.

A shiver stole through her. He was a man who achieved his goals, regardless of the means. But was he a man who gave with his heart for that which he believed?

A man like her father?

Linet stared at the strong lines of his face framed by the flicker of candlelight and shadows, at the curve of his lips still pressed into a hard line, and at the anger that never quite left his eyes.

Even facing the certainty of a sentence of death, Lord Grey had held his own. He was strong. Powerful. Defiant.

A rebel until the end.

However dangerous his presence, she couldn't help respecting his self-reliance, his confidence honed from years of facing, and more important, overcoming adversity in his fight to win Scotland's freedom.

And God help her, neither could she forget her body's response to his touch, or the utter devastation of his kiss. No, she refused to think of either. Once she escaped Breac Castle, her life would be guided by her own hand. Not by men, like her brother, who held and wielded power for their own gain. Or by this Scot, who possessed the ability to stir her soul.

A distant shout rang out.

Lord Grey jerked her into his arms and clamped a hand over her mouth. Candlelight wavered at the quick movement. Another shout had him glancing toward the door.

The clunk of men's boots on stone sounded with a muted echo. Footsteps pounded opposite the door, then faded.

He spun her around, glared at her with a ragged curse. "You lied!"

She shook her head. "They have only discovered you have escaped. They will not expect you to know of this tunnel."

"No?" Candlelight glinted off the dagger he'd taken from her in the cell. He pressed the honed blade against her throat. "If you value your life, my lady, you had best pray they do not."

The rebel secured the dagger in his belt, snatched the candle, and turned toward the dirt pathway. With the guards' echoed shouts filling the dungeon beyond, he hauled her into the darkness.

Chapter 2

Adrenaline pumping, Seathan dragged in another gulp of the stale air permeating the tunnel as he hauled his captive alongside. He ignored the pounding in his head and how at times his vision blurred. With each step, the muted din of guards scouring the dungeon for him faded.

Candlelight illuminated the aged pathway cluttered with cobwebs and trickles of moisture edged with growth. He pushed forward. Naught mattered but achieving his goal.

Revenge.

By God, he would have it.

Images of Dauid's stoic silence as he'd stood beside Lord Tearlach, the memory of the other Scottish rebels being dragged from the secret meeting, savaged his mind. Like blasted sheep led to a slaughter.

Thank God his brothers, Alexander and Duncan, had split off from him the day before the attack and had ridden with William Wallace to meet with

Robert Wishart, the Bishop of Glasgow. If not killed in the slaughter, they, too, would have been tortured for rebel information and sentenced to hang.

Disgust rolled through Seathan as he thought of the Parliament held by King Edward at Berwick the summer past. He'd ordered prominent Scottish landowners, burgesses, and churchmen to swear fealty to him, then sign and affix their seals as proof. The Ragman Roll was naught but parchment scrawled with names of those without the backbone to fight for their country's freedom or those who signed under duress.

Numerous nobles embroiled within the rebel cause had signed without intending to support the English crown, including Bishop Wishart of Glasgow and Robert Bruce, Earl of Carrick. Then, there were those like himself and William Wallace, who refused to sign, consequence be damned.

Rumors of King Edward's gloating that day as he'd watched each Scot sign the parchment fueled Seathan's anger. As if to rub salt in a festering wound, before he'd headed south to England, the king had installed the Earl of Surrey as governor of Scotland and Hugh Cressingham as treasurer.

Confident he'd quashed the last of the rebels' resistance, King Edward had ridden home to deal with the turmoil wrought by Flanders.

The English bastard believed he'd conquered Scotland, destroyed its people's will to fight. He'd ridden from Scottish soil, leaving them naught more than pawns to be ordered about.

But he was wrong.

The Scots would never cease in their battle to reclaim their freedom.

The woman at his side gave a weary sigh.

Seathan glanced toward her, and a new thought came to mind. "You said you wished to go to the Highlands to be with your mother's clan?"

In the flicker of candlelight, wary eyes met his. "Yes."

"You are English."

She hesitated. "Half. My father was."

"Was?"

"He is dead."

Suspicion flared at her claim, but her grief-stricken expression proclaimed her words true. "I am sorry." She shrugged, but he saw the emotion she tried to shield from his view. He understood all too well the pain of losing a parent, and of the responsibilities arising from such a loss. "Your mother?"

"Dead as well."

"How?" he asked, his heart softening a degree.

"It matters not."

From the coolness of her reply, it did, but to disclose the reason to him would splinter the tough exterior she carefully built. A facade he, too, had forged out of sheer necessity. Any similarities between their lives, however, ended there. The challenges he'd faced were far from the pampered existence this noblewoman had enjoyed.

Her fingers curled within his palm. Seathan tried to ignore the softness of her flesh, how the velvet of her skin pressed against the roughness of his calloused hand, and how too easily he could imagine her fingers upon his body in a silken caress. Though she'd kissed like a siren, he'd tasted her innocence.

Who was this noblewoman? More important, what had prompted her to free him?

Or rather, who?

Though she was cloaked in a cape of worsted wool, her serviceable garb hid neither her refined quality of speech, nor her regal bearing.

Unease crept through him. Even as he'd accused her of having a part in Lord Tearlach's twisted game, mayhap to free him for the thrill of the chase, his charge made no sense. Not that he'd put such past the Sassenach, whose amusement at Seathan's capture had eroded to fury when he'd refused to divulge any information under torture about William Wallace or the rebels' plans.

Which had led to Tearlach's order for Seathan to hang at first light.

If the viscount wasn't behind her actions, then who? Her request for an escort to the Highlands rang sour. A noblewoman needing protection would not seek out a man beaten to the point of near collapse. She had chosen him for a distinct purpose.

"Linet?"

"Yes?"

"Naught, I but wanted to know if indeed that is your real name."

Red streaked her cheeks. "Proof I am not lying to you?" She shook her head. "Worry not. I expect nothing more from you than your vow given to escort me to the Highlands." She faced forward and continued walking at his side.

If only it were so simple to believe her. Lives of thousands lay at stake. He would be a fool to accept words easily given. No, he'd watch her, listen for her to stumble and expose her true motive.

As he walked, a chill shook his body, then another. He forced himself to continue, each step punishing muscles long abused. He released her hand. The last thing he wished to do was reveal his deteriorating condition to her, but he needed to prepare for the worst. If possible, to make a plan before he passed out.

"Once we are safely away from Breac Castle," Seathan said, "we must hide."

Linet studied him a long moment. "Your injuries are slowing you down. For that I am sorry. How much longer do you think you can continue?"

The sincerity of her words caught him off guard, but he needed not her sympathy. "Nay doubt my ability to travel if need be."

"I never doubt men like you."

Unsure whether she paid him a compliment, he ignored her claim. Her opinion mattered little. After he delivered her to the Highlands, he would never see her again.

The candle sputtered.

"Halt." Seathan shot her a warning look, shielded the candle with his free hand. The flame trembled, then grew. The wavering light barely illuminated a foot before them. Though he didn't want her to see his weakening, his need to ensure she didn't bolt swayed his decision.

He reached for her.

She stepped out of range. Within the cast of yellowed light, outrage sparked in her gaze. "You believe holding me is necessary?"

"Aye." Her defiance intrigued him. He stepped forward, caught her hand. "I will take no chances until the castle walls are far behind us." Then, when it came to her, he would still use caution. Though truth rang in her words, questions about her motive sat ill within his mind.

On a frustrated sigh, she relaxed her hand within his. "There are several dangerous twists ahead. They must be taken with care."

He raised the candle. "Lead the way."

An order given, Linet mused, by a man comfortable with taking the lead regardless of the task. But in this, they shared the same goal—to escape. She started forward, and Lord Grey kept pace at her side.

A rat scurried before them, then disappeared into the darkness. They skirted shards of pottery strewn around the next bend.

"Breac Castle is a Scottish stronghold. Or was," Lord Grey said.

"So I was informed," she replied, well aware the Scot but probed for information. Linet neglected to add that the transfer had occurred twelve years past, when King Edward had seized Breac Castle and bestowed it upon her father for his staunch support of the crown.

Except a year later, with the death of Queen Margaret, the Maid of Norway, who was pledged to marry King Edward's heir, Edward of Cavernarvon, division had cut through Scotland.

She remembered her father's disgust for those of unworthy lineage who had come forward claiming 'twas their birthright to gain the throne. Then, how her father had placed himself within the English king's eye by backing Robert Bruce, lord of Annandale, in his bid to claim the Scottish throne.

Linet was proud of her father's stand, for supporting what he believed was just. The past few years had exposed King Edward's true ambition, not to ensure that Scotland gained a king, but to become its sovereign.

After the capture and sack of Berwick, the Battle of Dunbar, then King John's submission to King Edward, the English ruler had achieved his goal.

Her father believed in a fair hand, something the English sovereign seemed to overlook.

Sadness swept her as she remembered the people slaughtered for King Edward's self-serving goal. Thank God her father and mother had not lived to see the town of Berwick razed, including every man, woman, and child. And once the massacre had ended, English knights had torched the tragic heap.

The senseless slaughter still burned in her heart. How could any man lust for power enough to take a life, especially that of an innocent child? She might forgive many things, but never that.

King Edward had dared claim the sack of Berwick

a victory, but in her heart, he had delivered much more than war against the Scots.

But desecration.

Had her father suspected King Edward's dark plans to conquer Scotland? If so, it made sense that he'd kept his belief a secret.

A secret he'd never shared with Fulke—a son who held in esteem the English king and his caustic methods of gaining power, a son who shared the English king's trait of greed. Characteristics she despised.

She slid a covert glance toward Lord Grey—a rebel who opposed King Edward's carnage, a Scot who dared risked all for his beliefs.

Though dangerous, this man possessed the qualities she'd admired in her father. But neither his qualities nor his similarities to the man she'd looked up to changed the hard fact.

In the Scot's mind, she was the enemy.

How he viewed her mattered little. Once she arrived at her mother's village in the Highlands, she would be free to live the life she chose.

Linet's heart ached as she took in the sturdy walls of stone offering a path to escape. She would miss Breac Castle, the memories made over the years, the laughter shared.

But not her brother.

After Fulke's treachery, he no longer held her respect.

Or her love.

Lord Grey shoved forward with predatory intent. "They will search the tunnels for me, will they not?"

"Eventually," Linet conceded, staring straight into his suspicious gaze. Once her brother had discovered her absence along with the Scot's, Fulke would search every nook of the castle for them, including the hidden passageways. "But not because I am in league with the Viscount of Tearlach," she added, surprised to find it important that the Earl of Grey believed her.

"No? Then why?"

As much as she wished to explain, for her safety, she would tell him nothing more.

At her silence, a smile as cold and dangerous edged his mouth. "You have secrets, my lady, but you have chosen the wrong man to deceive in this game you play. Before our journey is over, I will know each and every one."

Tension wove through her. "The only game played is one you conceive within your mind."

He grunted. "Should I not find your appearance on the eve before I am to be hanged an unlikely coincidence?"

"Should you not give thanks that I risked my life to save yours?"

Eyes alive with suspicion studied her. "You risked your life, but not for my sake."

"Perhaps," she admitted, inwardly shaken to discover that she was no longer motivated solely by her determination to halt her brother's plans. Despite the meager time she'd spent with this powerful Scottish lord, she was drawn by his strength, his tenacity to fight for what he believed in. She understood why men followed the earl without doubt.

And more unnerving, she found herself caring that he lived.

Around the next turn, candlelight exposed a haphazard pile of rocks that formed a wall. Linet halted. A cave-in. Sweet Mary. Their most direct route to escape was ruined.

The earl turned to her with an ominous frown. "The tunnel is blocked."

"I did not know. I swear it."

He studied her for a long moment, glanced toward where the pathway had split several steps back. "Where does the other tunnel lead?"

"To the cliffs. But the route weaves through the castle and would take hours to travel. With but one candle to guide us, we must choose a shorter route."

"And that would be?"

"We must pass through the stables, sneak past the guards, and enter yet another tunnel that leads to the cliffs." She paused. "But I caution you, it is a treacherous path."

"More treacherous than returning to the dungeon? Nay, I will take the risk." His hand trembled as he turned, the candle held high.

She caught the sheen of sweat dripping down his face, the stiffness of his gait. She couldn't worry about him, nor the feelings he inspired. For each of them, fate held a different path: Never could Seathan represent more than revenge against her brother.

"I will make it," he said as if sensing her doubt.

The edge to his voice warned her not to argue. But determination wouldn't push muscles exhausted or a mind fevered. With his hand firm around hers, she kept pace as he headed back toward the other tunnel, and prayed they'd make good their escape.

The fresh scent of hay infused the cool rush of air as Seathan inched the plank open, the faint tinge of smoke from the extinguished candle fading.

A horse whinnied, another shifted. Rain pounded on the wooden roof. He frowned at the next blast of thunder. The storm would make their travel more hazardous, but its rumbles would provide them cover.

Had his brothers found the meeting place where he and his men had been betrayed by Dauid? Were they now braving the harsh weather in search of him? Or had Alexander and Duncan yet to return from their meeting with William Wallace and Bishop Wishart?

Bedamned.

He hated the not knowing. Until he had traveled at least two days by foot, he could learn naught. Worse, once he and Linet escaped Breac Castle, Tearlach's men would be scouring the forest for him, increasing the danger to his brothers.

Seathan searched the stalls through the slats. No one worked within. "Come." Seathan tugged her forward. Keeping to the shadows, he crept through the well-kept stable.

"You are trembling."

The worry in her voice had him damning his body's weakness, and her keen eyesight. "Keep moving." He inched forward, careful to keep out of sight of anyone within the bailey.

Lightning flashed. Thunder rolled in its wake. The rain of moments before increased to a downpour.

"Post extra men upon the wall walk," a commanding voice ordered from nearby.

Seathan stilled. Tearlach. A damnable voice he would recognize to his grave. The woman's hand tightened in his. "You know him?" he demanded in a rough whisper.

"Of course. He is lord of Breac Castle."

Aye, but the nerves in her voice indicated a much closer tie. "Is he your lover?"

Delicate nostrils flared. "I despise him."

Truth spilled through her words, but instinct assured him that she concealed more from him. Still, a part of him found comfort that she knew not Fulke's touch.

"Keep low—and quiet." Careful not to startle the horses, he eased forward, using the distant torchlight as a guide as they wove through the stables.

"I want every corner of Breac Castle searched again," Fulke's voice boomed, this time closer. "They must be here!"

Christ's blade. Tearlach had discovered his escape. He'd wanted to have traveled several leagues before his absence was discovered.

Seathan stilled. The full impact of the viscount's words slammed home. He turned toward the noblewoman. "They?" he asked, the softness of his burr laden with threat.

"You could not have escaped alone," Linet whispered.

Which made sense, but far from soothed his instinct that something was seriously amiss.

"We have searched all of the buildings, my lord," a man's voice called out.

"I care not," Lord Tearlach yelled. "Search them again. By God, they will be found this night!" The slap of footsteps faded as his knights scattered, rushing to do their lord's bidding.

The splat of water sloshed in a puddle nearby.

"Someone is coming. Hurry!" Seathan dropped, then rolled into a stall.

Linet followed.

Once inside, Seathan lifted a pile of hay. "Get in." She crawled beneath the heap and he joined her.

The bay within the stall stamped its feet and snorted.

Footsteps grew louder.

Seathan clamped his hand upon his dagger.

"Ho, Blanchard," a deep male voice rumbled. "Not liking the storm?"

Torchlight flickered over the pile of straw above Seathan as he sheltered Linet with his body. He put a finger over her lips.

She nodded.

Through the wisps of hay, he caught sight of the knight as he rubbed the bay's neck. After a pat on the withers, he began making his way down the line of stalls in a slow, methodical sweep.

Long moments passed, each one stealing precious darkness they needed to make their escape. More disturbing, with each passing second, heat from Linet's body melded with his. The soft warmth, infused with her woman's scent, was designed to seduce.

Seathan gritted his teeth in disbelief. With his body screaming from its torture, one would think he could ignore her scent, how well she fit against him, or the lingering memory of their kiss. But sheltered by the backdrop of falling rain and caught within the blanket of the hay's warmth, he was all too aware of her presence.

A bloody curse.

Soft footsteps crunched on hay as the knight slowly made his return. He stopped one last time outside of the bay's stall, lifted his torch in a slow sweep. As if satisfied everything was in order, he exited the stable into the downpour.

"All clear," the knight called once outside.

From far away, Lord Tearlach ordered him to help search the dungeon again.

Other guards' voices echoed in the pounding rain as they reported in from around the castle.

Seathan exhaled. They were safe—for now.

"That was too close," Linet whispered.

Her soft breath upon his face assured him her lips were but a whisper from his own. Awareness burned through him, and he hardened. The situation would be funny if it were not so serious. Beaten and barely clinging to consciousness, his body seemed not to care.

He swallowed hard, trying to ignore that if he but leaned forward, he could again taste her, the alluring essence of woman, and for a moment forget the pain washing through him.

"We must make it into the tunnel before the guard returns," he gritted out.

"We will." The conviction within her words inspired his own. She pressed her hand to his chest.

He stilled, too aware of her, dangerously so. "What is it?" he asked, not needing his thoughts clouded by desire.

"Nothing."

But he heard the tremble of her words, her desire to say more, and damn her, her concern. He wanted no woman worrying about him. Let her care for a man who wanted a woman in his life for something more than a night's pleasure. He'd learned well of a woman's deceptive ways, a lesson Iuliana, his former lover, had impressed upon his mind with devastating clarity.

Seathan caught the noblewoman's hand and shoved to his feet. The stall blurred around him. He braced his feet and sucked in a deep breath.

"Lord Grey?"

"Seathan," he hissed out.

Seathan? Linet stilled, surprised at his offer of familiarity. As if she would ever understand him.

He glanced past her. The rain was beginning to slow. "Move." He took a step forward, then another.

"No. It is too far. We must return to the tunnel before you pass out."

"We cannot go back. Too dangerous."

The stubborn man. "As if your falling on your face in the middle of the stables is safe?"

Obsidian eyes bore into hers. "I am well enough to travel."

Far from it, but she remained silent. They would need all of the Scot's arrogance to keep him moving.

Torches illuminated the upper bailey, an open expanse where Fulke and his men trained during the day.

She pointed toward the stone tower farthest away. "The next tunnel is through a door inside the arsenal tower." He nodded as they continued along the path.

They stole through the shadows, keeping the curtain wall to their backs, the fresh scent of spring rain filling her every breath. Both were soaked, but at least the rain would erase their tracks.

She shot a worried glance at the Scot, who was visibly struggling. Let him make it!

"Lord Tearlach," a guard called from the wall walk above.

With a muttered curse, Lord Grey flattened himself near her against the curtain wall, his chest heaving.

Hidden within the deep shadows, Linet peered out.

In the distance, her brother came into view, then halted.

She held her breath. Had Fulke seen them?

Long seconds trod past, then he turned and headed toward a nearby guard, his stride lengthened by his too familiar fury. The heavy rain fractured his words. ". . . see her, tell me!" Fulke demanded.

"Yes, my lord," the guard replied.

Fear tore through her. Had Lord Grey heard her brother's reference to her? Terrified, she glanced over. His eyes were shut as if he was focused on fighting back the pain. Linet glanced toward Fulke.

Her brother whirled and stalked toward the keep.

"Go," Seathan ordered in a soft command.

She shot him a quick glance, shaken to find him watching her with unsettling interest. No time remained to wonder the reason. She nodded, thankful when moments later they entered the arsenal tower, then slipped into the tunnel and closed the door.

"We have no candle," he stated.

"The tunnel is short and straight," she assured him. "I know it as if the back of my hand." At his light touch indicating she should lead, she headed into the blackened passage.

Shrouded in darkness and embraced by his male scent, she found the setting strangely intimate, despite the danger. Unsettled by her thoughts, by his muscled body straining at her side, she focused on her goal.

Silence punctuated the darkness as they traveled. In the distance, Seathan caught the growing sound of rain.

"We are almost there," she said.

He heard her worry, doubts that he could reach the safety of the forest, concerns that tormented him as well. But he'd be damned if he'd give up.

Clenching his teeth, he lengthened his stride.

Through the opening ahead, hints of purple touched the sky. "Sunrise," he hissed as if it were a curse.

She looked at him, her eyes laden with worry as well as hope. "They will not expect us to depart the castle through this tunnel."

True, but it did not remove the danger of their being seen. At the tunnel's rim, in the pale light, Seathan surveyed the steep slope broken by boulders and shrubs. He released her.

She glanced at her freed hand, then toward him. "You trust me now?"

"Nay, we are out of Breac Castle." He ignored her flash of irritation and started down the steep slope. Loose rock had him catching a nearby bush; his body screamed as he jerked to a stop. He held tight.

Behind him, Linet made her way down with caution.

Each step led them closer to safety, but with the purple hues growing lighter in the sky, before long the sun would break the horizon. Even with the shield of rain, if a guard looked down, they would be seen.

He gritted his teeth, swore, but step by step, descended the damnable rocks. At the bottom, sweat covered his body, and his mind swirled with dizziness. Dragging in a deep breath, he steadied himself.

A gentle hand caught his arm. "Seathan?"

He ignored her and glanced up. Dawn sifted across the sky, its exposing light spilling upon the forest around them. "Move." He stumbled forward.

She caught him, fighting to steady him. "Lean against me."

He hesitated.

"Your pride will not save your life!"

Damning his weakness, Seathan leaned against Linet as they continued. His life and possibly his brothers' lay in the hands of this slip of a woman. A woman who held secrets. A woman who called Tearlach her lord.

A woman he could never trust.

Chapter 3

With care, Linet walked across the leaf-and-needle-strewn ground scattered with patches of snow. The rich fragrance of earth and spring offered a soothing mix but did little to ease her worry. Since they'd entered the forest, Lord Grey was leaning more of his weight against her, and his arm around her shoulders was losing its grip.

He started to slump forward.

"Hang on to me!"

Ire flashed on his sweat-streaked face. His grip tightened. His steps, however shaky, kept pace with hers. "I will."

He would, but for how long? With the way he was trembling, the pallor of his face, and his sluggish movements, the only question left was when his legs would finally give out.

She scanned their surroundings void of the fall of rain. The fragile morning sunlight spilled over the treetops, dawn's warmth meager against the cool mist clinging to the air. But with the Scot's fevered body leaning against her, she was hardly cold.

They needed to find somewhere to rest and, if possible, build a fire to dry their clothes. Frustration brewed within her. With the woods soon to be swarming with Fulke's men in search of them, they couldn't take the risk.

The land angled upward.

Seathan halted, his breathing rough.

"We need to keep moving," she said.

"I . . ." He closed his eyes, then slowly opened them. Piercing green eyes glazed with pain stared at her.

Beneath his intense stare, she caught her breath. Within the dungeon she'd believed his eyes black, but she was wrong. Exposed by the sun, they reminded her of emeralds beneath a storm-filled sky.

Where had that foolish thought come from? As if it mattered. Linet tried to push him forward.

He didn't budge.

If he stopped now, there was no way she could carry him. God forbid if he passed out. "I said keep moving!"

Teeth clenched, he started forward.

Step by laborious step, they ascended the hill, each movement taking a visible toll on the earl.

Please let him reach the top of the knoll. Linet rolled her eyes at the absurdity of her thought. Here she was silently pleading they'd make it several more paces when days of arduous travel lay ahead, their path cluttered with mountains that made this rise of land look like a poor-told jest.

A journey that in Lord Grey's condition, he would never finish.

After the earl's surly demeanor and distrust, 'twould serve him right if she left him slumped against a rock. And why shouldn't she leave him behind? She owed the rebel nothing. If anything, it was he who owed her thanks for saving his life.

Not that she expected his gratitude.

Linet took in the vast roll of hills ahead of them, terrain that would erode to steep angles of rock and cliff. Could she make it to the Highlands alone? Unlikely, not on foot. Why hadn't she thought to have arranged for horses awaiting them? Then again, the chance to slip two steeds out of Breac Castle's gates without Fulke's knowledge was a near impossibility.

The forest before her posed a daunting challenge, with thick stands of elm, ash, pine, and shrub, wild animals, and rivers to navigate.

Although the English had subdued the Scots and dismissed the possibility of war as but fleeting rumbles of unrest, bands of English troops as well as outraged Scots traveled these lands. To come upon either could result in disaster.

Sweat streamed down the rebel's wan face as he labored with each step.

Guilt rolled through her. Her brother was responsible for Seathan's suffering.

Seathan?

Look at her, one kiss and here she was thinking of him in familiar terms. What next? Would her mind turn to other, more intimate thoughts? She sobered. No, Lord Grey was the last man she would seek out for permanence, or believe capable of giving his love. Warriors like him were drawn by power, by the challenge of battle.

She wanted neither.

One day she would find love, but it would not be from a Scottish rebel intent on war.

Seathan stumbled. "Bedamned," he grunted as he righted himself. Lines of strain dug across his brow as he pushed forward.

"You are keeping a good pace," she lied. She stole a glance behind them. Soon Fulke would order his men to search beyond the castle walls. With the earl's pace but a crawl, Fulke's knights would find them before midday.

The sun peeked above the trees when they finally topped the hill.

She glanced at Seathan. Haggard lines furrowed his face, his breaths hard, ragged gasps. However much they must keep moving, he needed to rest. She started to halt.

He scowled at her, broke free. "Go."

"Are you addled? Without my help, you are as good as dead."

A smile as cold as it was determined touched his mouth. "Dead? I grew up here. Unlike you, this forest is my home."

"And if I leave you here," she said, "your grave."

"Better th-than rotting in Tearlach's cell, or hanging from the bastard's rope."

"In that we agree. However determined—or pigheaded—you are, you would not make it a league before you fell on your arse." She jammed her hands upon her hips. "Which would serve you right."

Green eyes narrowed. "Be gone. I—I need not a weak English lass slowing me down."

Anger ignited inside her. "Weak English lass? I could have left you in the dungeon to die, or abandoned you anytime since."

"Tell me," he said through gritted teeth, "wh-why does my freedom mean so much to you?"

She firmed her lips.

"No answer? I thought not." Seathan waved his hand in dismissal. "You have served your purpose. Leave."

Outrage exploded through her like hot oil poured on fire. "Purpose? You are an arrogant, ungrateful malt-worm. Stay here then and die. I assure you, I will lose not a whit of sleep!"

Linet turned on her heel and headed north. Let the braggart rot in his self-pride. Let him try to make the journey on his own. Yes, he'd make it— about ten paces before he fell on his stubborn, pride-filled face and passed out.

Then Fulke's men would find him.

And kill him.

She glanced back.

Seathan hadn't moved.

The irritating Scot stood atop the knoll with unwavering defiance. Oh, he was trying to look fierce, as if even in his weakened state, single-handed he could take on a contingent of King Edward's men.

She stilled. Sweet Mary, his fierceness was but

deception, proven by his swaying and ashen hue. And she understood.

An intelligent man, he'd realized that at their pathetic pace, it was only a matter of time before Fulke's guards would catch up to them and put her in danger. He'd pushed her away—to save her life.

The lout!

How dare he be noble and attempt to protect her when she was trying to save his sorry hide. Linet stormed back. At her approach, his mouth drew into a formidable grimace. A threatening tactic her brother had tried to use on her as well.

And failed.

Irritated, she poked a finger into his muscled chest. "Your fierce looks will not work. How dare you try to manipulate me!"

Eyes bright with fever bore into her. "As you did to me back in the cell?"

Her finger wavered, then fell. Guilty, but that wasn't the point, neither did she miss that he didn't deny the tactic. Why did he have to go and make this all a mired mess? Her plan was simple. She'd wanted nothing more from him than his escort. Once they arrived in the Highlands, when she walked away from him, there would be no looking back, no remembering him. He meant nothing to her. Never would.

Except now he had to go and be noble.

"I am not a weak-willed maid who will be running off at the first sign of threat."

No, Seathan agreed through the haze of pain storming his mind. On that he agreed. This lass, half English, half Scot, had a backbone many a man would admire. But he couldn't tell her that, or allow her to remain at his side. If he passed out, he couldn't protect her. Alone, he would hide within the woods as he had done many times throughout his life. Rest would help him heal. As for travel, somehow he would make it to his home, Lochshire Castle, to send a messenger to warn Wallace and the other rebels about Dauid.

Seathan shot her a menacing look, one that had left squires trembling in their boots. "I told you to leave."

Lavender eyes flashed with defiance. "You did, but I am staying to help your ungrateful, stubborn hide as your mind is obviously mulled by fever."

Stunned, he stared at this wisp of a woman. The lass was looking out for him? Lured by his status or wealth, women never cared for him without thought of personal gain. She blurred before him.

He focused, barely.

She caught his tunic.

"Wh-What are you doing?"

"I need to check your wounds."

He had to convince her to leave before he collapsed. "I have changed my mi-mind. I will not escort you to the Highlands."

Shock streaked across her face. "But you—"

"Lied." An untruth, but if it would sway her to go, so be it.

Her mouth fell open. She started to shake her head, then stopped. Linet angled her chin. "I do not believe you. You are a man of your word."

"You know naught of me."

"I know you are on the verge of collapse. Instead of thinking only of yourself, you are honorable enough to try to persuade me to leave for my own safety."

He opened his mouth to speak. A dizzying buzz assaulted him. Seathan closed his eyes to ward off the sensation.

Gentle hands caught his shoulders. "Seathan?"

The concern in her voice lured him to admit his tactic. Nay, she must go. He opened his eyes, focused.

A gust of wind, laden with the rich softness of spring, spiraled around her, lifting soft strands of her amber-gold hair in a wayward drift. *Magical.* The unearthly thought whirled in his mind as if he'd drunk too much ale. A heady feeling that numbed the pain strumming his body and made the dangers around them fade.

He inhaled deeply, as if to breathe in her scent would purify his mind, savoring the fragile innocence she wore like a mantle. He'd thought her beautiful in the cell, but with her face embraced within the golden rays, her cheeks rosy against her ivory skin, she seemed angelic. He grimaced. An illusion for sure.

"Seathan?"

The desperation of her voice forced him to focus. "Need to go." Lord Tearlach would be in a rampage until he was recaptured. And Seathan needed to find and warn his brothers of Fulke's search as well as Dauid's treachery.

Emotion overwhelmed him as he thought of the bodies of his knights hacked with merciless glee. John, a man he'd introduced to his wife, whose newborn babe he'd held. And Eoin, a man he'd grown up with, a warrior he'd called friend.

"Do not pass out on me!" Linet demanded.

He glared at her. Naught would stop him from serving justice to Dauid. "A-Aye, lass, we will go." Through grim determination, Seathan started forward. Muscles screamed with his every step. Sweat rolled down him as if a dam had broken. Images of his butchered men drove him on.

Relief poured through Linet as Seathan started forward. His stumbling gait mattered not. When he'd closed his eyes moments before, she'd thought he would keel over.

Time trudged by with aching slowness as they pressed on. With the passing hours, the sun rose to its zenith.

In the distance, the rush of water grew. Birds called out in trees green with buds that would soon unfurl to leaves, sprouts of grass dared to peek through earth ravaged by winter, and the scent of the air, rich with the tang of spring, sifted on the breeze.

The joy she normally found in the rebirth of the land was overshadowed by the threat of danger.

And her doubts that they truly would escape Fulke's wrath.

The earl halted.

She turned toward him. "What is wrong?"

Green eyes torn with indecision watched her.

"Swear on your life what I . . . I am about to show you will st-stay secret."

Her body tensed. Had he found a sanctuary where they might rest? Linet scanned the area. Within a thick stand of ash, boulders lay in a large clump. Except for a sharp drop-off to the right that plunged to a gorge below, nothing that represented an entry existed. So why was he asking for her vow?

Intrigued, she nodded. "I swear it."

He raised his hand, pointed; it trembled. "There."

She frowned. "The trees?"

"Look between the trees. There is a pile of large boulders. A . . . A cave is hidden beyond."

"I see no entry."

"Do you see the moss?"

Linet nodded.

"The mo-moss is woven on a blanket that drapes across the entry."

"Brilliant."

A grim smile touched his lips. "Effective."

It was. The English knights would ride by the rebel hideout.

From behind, a man's yell broke the silence.

Seathan turned toward the sound. "Tearlach's men." He caught her and stumbled forward. "Must get out of sight. Stay on the rocks." He tugged her as he hurried forward.

The steady thrum of hooves increased.

A branch slapped her face; she caught the next one and shoved it away.

He reached toward the moss, tugged the blanket, and moved aside.

Linet hurried in.

Seathan followed. The moss-sewn cover flopped against the entry, smothering them in muted darkness. "Wait." He leaned against the wall, his chest heaving. "Le-Let your vision adjust."

A horse whinnied. The thrum of hooves sounded nearby.

"Over here," a man called out.

"What have you found?" another man asked.

"Footprints," the first man replied.

Linet gasped.

Seathan motioned for her to keep silent, his pulse racing, the wound in his right side sticky with blood. Bedamned. If only there had been time to erase their tracks.

"It looks as though the tracks lead to the rocks," a man said. "Methinks they went into the trees."

"Mayhap," a second man replied. Long seconds dragged past. The clomp of hooves upon rock and leaves echoed from outside.

"I do not see anyone," the first man said, this time his voice closer.

Linet's body trembled against Seathan's. He leaned against the wall for support. Out of reflex, he drew her to him, his other hand clasp around his dagger.

"They must have traveled farther," yet another man stated.

"With the freshness of these tracks," the second man said, "not very much. Wherever they are, they are close. We will break up. Ulric, take two men and ride east. Everyone else, we will circle to the west and meet on the other side."

Hoofbeats sounded, and then slowly faded.

Seathan heaved a sigh.

"They have left," Linet whispered.

"Fo-For now. When they do not find me, they will return and search this area again. Come." Head pounding, he released her. In the muted light, he staggered toward the rear of the cave, focusing on each step.

The dismal surroundings grew brighter as they moved deeper inside. They rounded the corner and the cavern opened to the outside. Sunlight streamed into the darkness like a golden rain to erase the shadows.

A look of awe painted Linet's face. She stepped to the ledge, scanned the gorge sprawled below. "It is beautiful."

"Aye." He stumbled.

She whirled. Worry streaked her face as she hurried back and set his arm over her shoulder to steady him. "You must lie down."

He grimaced. As if he had an option. His legs were beginning to give, and his mind was quickly following. Even now, he fought for coherent thought. With her help, he settled against the layered rock, the sun upon his face.

Linet glanced at his right side, frowned. "Why did you not tell me you were bleeding?"

"Na-Naught but a wee scratch."

"A scratch?" she scoffed. "I have tended to warriors

from enough battles to know the injury is more than that. I need to cleanse the wound. Stay here."

Before he could object, she stood, removed her cape, and withdrew the water pouch she carried. Sunlight streaming behind her framed the slender lines of her body shielded beneath a linen gown.

His rebuke fell away as he took in the smooth curve of her ankle. Her gown concealed neither her slim waist nor generous breasts. Even confused by fever, he couldn't help but admire her supple curves.

Ignorant of her effect on him, after giving him a drink of water, she knelt before him. "I must remove your tunic to see the extent of your injury."

A part of him wanted to refuse. But the warrior in him understood the threat of a wound untreated. This lass, wrapped within her innocence, knew naught of her potent effect.

"I can remove it my-myself." Seathan tugged the tunic over his head, his muscles screaming at the movement.

She grimaced as she leaned closer. Her soft breath skimmed across his inflamed skin, and he gritted his teeth.

Linet looked up.

Stilled.

Green eyes held hers, hot, burning with fever, but also laden with desire. His feral look sparked awareness in her body like flint to steel. Her lips tingled with remembrance of their kiss within the cell, that dangerous moment when she'd forgotten her objective, the reason she'd sought out Lord

Grey. She inhaled, and his scent, that of earthy male and domination, flooded her senses.

She pulled back, but images of him covering her mouth and of her drowning in his taste remained. No, she could not ponder such sensual thoughts. He was a dangerous temptation, one she could never accept. They had little in common except her brother, a man they both despised.

Taking a steadying breath, Linet tore a strip of cloth from her chemise, dampened it, and gently began to cleanse the wound. Honed muscles rippled beneath her touch, skin battered by scars, those of a man seasoned by war. Those of a man who fought for what was his. Those of a man loyal to his country and family.

Unnerved by her attraction toward a man who was dangerous to her on so many levels, she removed the cloth. She wrung the strip of fabric out, redampened it, only to have to touch him again. To be reminded of the man who stirred desires best ignored.

Under her touch, his body tensed and a pained breath hissed from his mouth, but he made no protest.

"The wound is long, but thankfully not deep," she forced out as she fought for calm. "As we travel, I will find herbs to pack against the gash to ensure it does not fester." She again wrung out the cloth, then continued dabbing away the small flecks of dirt outlining the wound. "In time, you should be left with only a scar."

"You are a healer?"

At the softness of his words, she tensed. His simple question fooled her not. He sought clues as to who she was, details she could never give.

"No. I have aided our healer when the necessity arose." She gave him an admonishing look. "You need rest, not meaningless talk." Before he could push for further information, a trait she was learning to expect from him, she stood. "Though it is early, you need to sleep. Besides, with Lord Tearlach's men searching for you, it is too risky to travel."

He eyed her a long moment, then started to get up.

The fool! She caught his shoulders. "If you move about, you will reopen your injury."

Seathan grimaced, shoved her hands away, and pushed to his feet. He gestured toward the far wall. "Th-There are blankets behind the stacked wood. Lift them and you will see other provisions as well."

A grand concession on his part. "Stay there until I retrieve them." With efficient movements, she withdrew the blankets and started to make a pallet, anything to try to keep her mind off Seathan, off a man who made her too aware of herself as a woman.

After all these years, and all the many men she'd met, nobles, knights, warriors from other countries, none had ever inspired but a token of interest. Now, she was attracted to a Scottish rebel who, if he learned of her connection to Fulke, would use her as leverage against her brother. And his trust? No, the pittance she'd earned would be forever lost.

"Linet?"

Seathan knelt beside her, his eyes too sharp, his nearness too potent. "What is wrong?"

The sincerity in his voice unnerved her further. "Nothing, I am but making a pallet."

"You are shaking."

She glanced down to find her hands trembling— from thoughts of him. She swallowed hard. "I am tired."

"Aye, af-after traveling through the night, we both need rest." He lifted the edge of the blanket near him and helped spread it out.

"I told you to wait until I was done."

Seathan scowled. "I am a knight, not a crippled old man."

"You never need anyone, do you?" she asked, annoyance slipping into her voice.

Fevered eyes narrowed. "And what of you? Who do you need?"

"No one," she replied, and immediately regretted allowing her question to become personal. She shook her head. "Lie down and rest."

"You will do so as well." By the ire in her eyes, Seathan expected her to argue. To his surprise, she nodded. Unsure how much longer he could remain on his feet, he lowered himself on the blankets. Every muscle in his body screamed, but they had made it to safety.

The soft weight of worsted wool covered him. "Here is my rolled cape to put beneath your head."

Though her voice was cool, her thoughtfulness touched him. A part of him had expected her to leave, not remain, nor tend to him as one who cared about him. Aye, she cared—that he lived. But she'd freed him from the cell for her own purpose.

Why?

They both had their secrets, he reminded himself as he watched her gracefully move about. How would she react if she learned the rebels were planning an uprising? The bloody English were confident they'd conquered Scotland, a foolish belief. His countrymen were a different breed compared to the thin-blooded Englishmen. Unlike the Sassenach, the Scots would not cease to pursue their goal of freedom, regardless of the odds.

"Here." Linet handed him a cup with water.

Seathan drank slowly, the cool water heaven against his parched throat. He drained the wooden cup then handed it to her; their fingers brushed. Awareness poured through him in a lethal sweep.

"My thanks," he said.

Linet's eyes dilated as if she, too, had felt the heat. She nodded, turned away. "Go to sleep."

The foolish woman. Even in his condition, he could see her weariness. "I—I said you will rest as well."

She stiffened. "I will, eventually. For now I will keep watch."

He shifted, winced at the pain. "Nay. You wi-will lie now or I will drag you down here if necessary."

"I . . ." She again checked his wounds as if they were her only concern, but he saw through her guise.

He shot her a warning look.

With a nervous glance, she slipped between the covers beside him.

Exhausted, satisfied that she'd stay, and ignoring the brush of their bodies, Seathan closed his eyes and succumbed to the inviting bliss of sleep.

Silence.

Long seconds passed.

The slow rise and fall of his chest assured Linet the rebel was asleep. She allowed herself to relax. It was amazing he'd held out this long.

Seathan shifted onto his back. Sunlight caressed the hard planes of his face, and the shadow of a full beard over his square jaw. In rest, his expression softened, hinted at lines carved by laughter. Intriguing. Lord Grey did not strike her as a man who would relax enough to give way to humor.

He mumbled in his sleep.

Drawn, she watched him. Her mouth tingled with remembrance of his lips covering hers. A mere kiss and he'd almost destroyed her. What would it be like if they made love?

Heat stroked her face at her untoward thoughts. She dismissed them. They were but musings. Without his awareness of them, they hurt no one.

Curious, Linet leaned closer, drawn to the man who was as great a mystery as a threat. His warmth curled around her, his inner strength as inherent as his domineering force.

Tiredness washed over her, but a sense of peace as well.

Peace?

Odd when her life at this moment held naught but chaos.

His steady breaths lulled her, as did the safety she felt by his side. She yawned, slid a hand's breath toward him, and for the first time in many days, slipped into an undisturbed sleep.

Seathan opened his eyes, his senses alert. The aches of his body provided an immediate reminder of his escape from the dungeon, and the morning sun streaming into the cave was an indicator that a day had passed. He glanced down at the lass.

Not any lass. Linet.

With his mind clear, he studied her as she slept, noting how her slender body curled against his with innocent trust. Her cheek lay flush upon his chest, her lashes crafting perfect half-moons against her ivory skin, and her long amber-gold hair loosened from its braid now framing her face.

His gaze drifted to the curve of her mouth. Memories ignited of their heated kiss within the cell, of the passion, the unexpected rightness of it that had scorched his soul.

Nay, 'twas only his mind's haze from the torture he'd endured that invited such randy thoughts. Regardless of a woman's passion in bed, well he understood their capacity for treachery. Though an innocent, Linet was still a stranger, a woman with secrets, far from a person he could care for, much less trust.

What had driven her to give him his freedom? The reason involved Tearlach, of that he was sure.

Throat dry, he again took in the inviting lines of her mouth. If he kissed her again, would her taste be different? He lowered his mouth a degree, her soft breaths tumbling over his cheek, her warmth inviting him closer. His body hardened, trembled with anticipation.

Bedamned he would know.

He claimed her mouth. A soft moan escaped her as he guided her, teased her, savored the supple lips that slowly responded.

Thick lashes flew open. Startled lavender eyes cleared, darkened with pleasure. On a shudder, her body softened, molded against his own.

Then she was kissing him back.

Heat.

It burned through him as if a torch thrown. He drowned in the scorching blaze, pressing her back to lay his full length against her soft curves. He had to have her, taste her every inch.

Ignoring the lancing pain of the injury along his side, he cupped her mouth, took the kiss deeper, until she whimpered in his arms and arched against him as does a woman in need.

On a groan, he inched down to taste the silken curve of her jaw, then grazed his teeth along the slender column of her neck, her gasps of pleasure threatening to break his hard-won control.

With every sense steeped in her, he shoved her linen gown away to expose her breasts. God in heaven, they were a wondrous sight.

Linet stilled. Her hand caught his fingers hovering over her breast. "No!"

Seathan met her gaze, the desire in her eyes in direct contrast to her request.

A distant shout echoed nearby.

He turned toward the entry, blinked. God's teeth! He'd been so caught up in the woman, he'd ignored the noise that had obviously pulled him from his slumber.

Seathan withdrew his dagger. His arm ached from the quick movement. He ignored the pain. At least the dizziness of last night had passed.

"What is it?" she asked.

Her wild, sensual look had him gritting his teeth. He placed a finger over her lips, silently groaned at their softness. "There are men outside."

Eyes dark with passion clouded to fear. Linet nodded.

He removed his finger, then shoved to his feet, the blade curled within his hand. "Stay here. They should not find us." With quiet steps, he crept to the entry.

A rustle of clothes sounded as she repaired her gown. Soft footsteps sounded in his wake, then paused. "Can you see them?" she whispered.

"Nay, but they are close." Her scent teased him, as did the memories of her full breasts. Bedamned, what had he been doing kissing her, much less entertaining notions of making love to her?

He peered out an open sliver between the moss cover.

Shadows flickered in the trees.

"They are coming," he whispered.

Sticks cracked, hooves clopped as the men rode into view.

"Lord Tearlach has deployed a large contingent," Seathan said, impressed by the number of knights.

"You are a valuable prisoner."

Nerves rode her voice, which he expected, so why did her reply leave him on edge? He glanced at her; she hesitated, then looked away.

"What?" he whispered, his anger finding a foothold.

"I—"

"We have seen no sign of them since yesterday," a nearby guard stated.

Seathan turned toward the approaching band of men.

"Lord Tearlach is in a rage," said a knight but paces away from their hideout.

"As expected," another knight replied. "Though, I am unsure if his anger is with the Scot or her for aiding in his escape."

A knight nodded. "She is a fool."

Linet gasped behind him.

"Yes," the closest man agreed, "since the viscount's return, he has allowed her far too much rein. A beating would do her good."

The other knight grunted. "Lord Tearlach will find her. When he does, she will regret her treachery. Before this is done, he will bend her to his will."

"Onward," a lead knight called. Soft earth flew from beneath the horses' hooves. The slap of leather and jingle of spurs faded as the knights disappeared into the forest.

Seathan turned. Linet's face had paled. Her nerves now made sense. Anger built as each subtle clue, each fragmented remark of yesterday, fell into place.

Eyes wide, she stepped back as if realizing his fury.

"Aye, Lord Tearlach may want me, but it would seem in this quest, you are the true prize." He stalked toward her. "Bend you to his will? The question, my lady, is why?"

Chapter 4

At Seathan's approach, Linet held her ground. He was furious at learning the men hunted her with equal determination. So much for believing his exhaustion and battered state would save her.

A pace away, he halted. Menace carved harsh lines across his face. "Why do the men want you?" he demanded.

The force of his determination engulfed her, but she refused to look away. "We both have secrets."

Green eyes darkened to a hard edge. "Secrets, aye, but you purposely hid that yours were of a personal nature and involved the Viscount of Tearlach."

Sweet Mary. Did he suspect her blood tie with Fulke? No, she'd said nothing to expose a link to her brother. "The reason for the viscount's anger, his desire to have me back, is my affair."

"Ours." A muscle worked in his jaw. "I have agreed to escort you to the Highlands. A vow I will not break. Until you are delivered, whatever provokes the viscount's anger toward you affects us both." He leaned closer, his face dark. "Do you not think I should know the reason?"

Linet held her ground. "In the dungeon you agreed not to question why I had freed you." At his ominous silence, panic stirred in her soul. Why was she debating with a man who would always view her as his enemy, a dangerous rebel whom she was foolishly beginning to care for? She stepped back. "I need not your help. I can make it to the Highlands alone."

He arched a skeptical brow. "After you risked your life to free me from the dungeon to be your escort, now you decide you will journey across the rugged terrain alone? Tell me, my lady, what has changed?" A cold smile edged his mouth. "Or should I ask, who has swayed your decision?"

With her nerves fraying like spun yarn unraveling, Linet struggled for calm.

At her silence, Lord Grey studied her with predatory intrigue. His nostrils flared. "Is Lord Tearlach your lover?"

"As I told you in the stables, he is a man I despise." The truth. Her brother would manipulate anyone if it meant his own personal gain, including those related by blood.

"Perhaps," Seathan agreed, "but more than dislike lingers between you and the viscount for him to search you out with such furious intent."

She shrugged. "He does not like to be crossed."

Despite the storm of emotions brewing within him, Seathan stepped back. With her beauty and sharp mind, it was easy to see why the viscount would want her. And with the memories of Linet's passionate kiss burning through his mind, easy to understand why Tearlach would order his men to scour the lands for her.

But in this, Tearlach would fail. The bastard would never find her. On that, Seathan gave his solemn vow.

The strength of his possessiveness toward Linet stunned him. He wanted the lass in his bed. What man would not want a woman whose passion rivaled that of a well-paid courtesan? Except, from her innocent reaction to his kisses, he suspected few if any men had ever touched her. An intriguing blend that made him want her all the more.

A whisper inside his mind hinted his feelings for her went deeper. More than those of a night's bedding.

Nay. She meant naught to him. The lass was but a means of freedom. And if he took her to his bed, it would be only for shared pleasure. His previous lover, Iuliana, had used him, etched in his soul the high price of giving a woman his trust, and of the hurt and shame that followed.

Seathan banked his temper, his impatience. Aye, he'd given his word that he'd not press Linet for why she'd released him. But during the time they would spend together, she would lower her guard and he would learn the truth. He was a man who achieved his goals.

A fact Linet would soon learn.

With his moving about, his right side had begun to throb. He sheathed his sword, rolled his shoulders in an effort to loosen the tension thrumming through his body.

"You need to sit," Linet said, her words guarded as she watched him as if assessing his shifting moods.

"Why do you care whether I rest or not since you can make it to the Highlands without me?" He nodded. "Your words, my lady."

"I . . ." She looked away, but not before he caught her shimmer of true concern. "I was raised to do what is right. Unlike Lord Tearlach, whose decisions are based on greed." She turned to face him, her expression fierce with belief. "He is a man who cares not that his self-serving desire devastates the innocent."

Her claim intrigued him. "I am far from innocent."

"True. The viscount's interest in you is purely for the gain of power, to earn King Edward's praise. He has no thought to aid his people or his kingdom."

"It is rare for an Englishwoman to hold such views."

"You forget, I am half Scottish."

"I assure you, your heritage is a fact I well remember." A fact that made him curious to learn more about this complex lass. With her in-depth knowledge of the viscount along with the confidence with which she spoke, any doubts as to her being a lady, a noblewoman high within the ranks of Breac Castle, fell away. For Tearlach to be interested in Linet, her father must have been a powerful lord. Which noble was he?

"Regardless," she continued, "my heritage is not

what guides my life, but the teachings of my father: humbleness, fairness, and respect."

Seathan grunted. "If only Lord Tearlach were guided by the same hand."

At his words, she stilled. "Forgive me. I prattle on about a man who is worthy of naught but scorn while you stand before me shaking. Please, sit."

Seathan glanced down, surprised to find that indeed his body was trembling. Bedamned. No time for delays. It would take a day, mayhap two, before he was strong enough to travel at a solid pace.

He must intercept Alexander and Duncan before Tearlach's men set up an ambush and stumbled across his brothers as the soldiers scoured the viscount's lands for him and Linet.

Weariness flooded him as he strode toward the back of the cave, where weathered rock fell away to expose the vast gorge below.

As he neared the cave's opening, the distant roar of water from the falls grew. He glanced at the pallet where they'd lain. Desire seared him at the memory of waking to find Linet curled against him with innocent trust.

The soft pad of her footsteps within the cave heightened his awareness. He wanted her, aye, but mired in secrets, she was a woman wisdom bade he avoid.

With his mind steeped in emotions he'd rather not feel, instead of returning to lie upon the pallet, he pressed his back to the cool stone wall and slid to sit on the floor. With his forehead resting on his raised knees, for a moment he closed his eyes, appreciating the roar of the water below, the warmth of the sun upon his skin, and the rich scent of the earth and mist-laden air.

He opened his eyes, inhaled deeply, and scanned the gorge. To his right, water surged over the jagged ledge carved by thousands of years of wear. Boulders, some sun bleached, others covered by vines thick with newborn leaves, framed the rush of water, which plunged into an angry pool swirling far below.

Mist rose above the dark churning pool, a mesmerizing shroud of white that transformed glints of sunlight into fragile rainbows. Magical arcs of color as if cast by the fairies.

The fey?

He blew out a rough breath. Aye, he was weary indeed to be thinking such fanciful thoughts. Such musings were typical of his younger brother, Duncan. Never did he allow his imagination to stray to ponderings of no consequence. Or he hadn't since his youth, a time when he'd also believed in true love.

He ignored the impulse to glance at Linet. He'd learned that faithful women didn't exist. Only those who played cruel games, used lovers to invite jealousy, then cast them aside.

"Seathan?"

Linet's soft voice caressed his name. His gaze remained riveted upon the falls. "What?"

The soft scuff of her slippers echoed as she stepped beside him. A breeze fluttering her gown against her slender calves lured him to look.

"With the knights gone," she said, "it is safe for me

to search for plantain. Rest while I am away. I will return before sunset."

He bristled. "You will remain here."

Lavender eyes widened with surprise, then narrowed, a stubborn sign he was becoming all too familiar with. "The herb will speed the healing of your wounds."

"No lass issues me orders."

"But I shall." She paused, arched a slender brow. "It is said plantain also aids in curing the madness of dogs."

Her bravado intrigued him. Who was this woman who feared not her enemy? Irritated that he wanted her, Seathan shoved to his feet, ignoring the burst of dizziness.

He shot her a hard look. "I will accompany you."

She angled her jaw. "Your arrogance amazes me. But I wonder, is it your arrogance or your distrust that I shall not return?"

"Had you wanted to leave, you could have done so numerous times. Yet you stayed, which again raises the question why."

Red swept across her cheeks. "Waste your time wondering about my intent if you will. I, for one, have more important things to do. I must find herbs to help your wounds heal." She paused, shot him a withering glare. "If I was of sane mind, I would leave them to fester to match your charming attitude." Linet turned away.

Seathan caught her arm, whirled her to face him.

Outrage splashed across her cheeks. "Release me."

Instead, he stared at her face, wanting to see her

eyes, to find a truth he could believe in. "Why do you care about me?"

A look of uncertainty flickered in her eyes, her gaze as defiant as shaken. "I . . . I do not know."

The honesty in her voice had him mentally back-tracking, reevaluating. Christ's blade. Did he believe in her innocence? He released her.

"Come." Shoving aside his lingering weakness, Seathan strode toward the cave's exit, his mind wrapped in her, of the vow he'd made. Aye, he'd agreed to guide her to the Highlands, but when would the lass realize he'd omitted to specify the time frame?

With a frustrated sigh, Linet stared at the infuriating man, followed in his wake. The Scot was as unbending as a sword.

"If your wounds become infected, so be it." Linet walked past him, but kept her steps slow. As much as she wished to hurry and leave him behind, the stubborn-headed fool would match her pace and add to his injuries.

In so many ways, his arrogance, determination, and focus on his goals reminded her of her brother, Fulke. But that was where the similarities ended.

Unlike her brother, Seathan was guided by his morals, his concern for his people, and his belief in doing what was right. Though he refused to explain why he accompanied her into the woods, she believed his reason arose from worry for her safety. That he was concerned about her touched her deeply.

Since her parents' deaths, no one had truly

worried about her. Her maids smiled and inquired as to her health, but afraid of her brother, none sought to know her beyond the role of their mistress.

Not that she'd pondered the fact or felt regret. Immersed in her studies, with the day-to-day running of Breac Castle, time to linger, to make small talk as most noblewomen did, seldom occurred. She preferred her busy life, or had until she'd met Seathan.

Lord Grey was a unique man, a leader whose devotion to protecting his people amazed her. Now, however temporary, he'd included her within his safeguard. She should dismiss the sense of comfort his decision inspired, focus on the fact that their time together was but that of weeks. But deep inside, she knew when they reached the Highlands and parted, an emptiness she'd never anticipated would remain.

Sweet Mary, how could a man she'd known for but hours have become so important to her? It made no sense, but then at this moment in her life, little did.

At the mouth of the cave, Linet halted, steadied herself. She must make her decisions based on logic, not the feelings of the heart, a lesson Fulke had taught her too well.

With her mind focused on her task, she peered through a slit in the sewn moss cover. The rumble of water from the nearby gorge filled the silence. Through the break in the trees, a hawk soared high above the treetops.

As she scanned their surroundings, Seathan halted behind her. He did not have to speak, nor did she need to hear the firm tread of his steps to know of his presence. Her body recognized his nearness.

"Do you see anyone?" Caution laced his voice.

Shaken by the sense of completeness his nearness instilled, Linet shook her head. "No." She pulled back the cover and left the cave.

Seathan followed.

The soft, leaf-strewn ground absorbed their steps, the canopy of leaves overhead casting them in shadows.

As they crossed the small field, Linet kept watch for any sign of movement, relieved once they'd again entered the protective shield of the forest.

Seathan glanced over. "You are traveling at a slow pace."

"As if you could move faster?"

"I am far from a green lad ignorant of the demands of war."

Dead leaves stirred by a gust of wind spun past her face. She brushed one away that'd caught within her hair. "A fact you seem intent on reminding me of."

"Who hurt you so that you would challenge a warrior without thought of reprisal?"

His quiet question caught her off guard. Flutters of warmth tumbling through her stilled. She stayed her response. Of course he would want to know, he wanted to learn everything he could about her. More specifically, he sought to discover why she would help free Fulke's valuable prisoner from Breac Castle.

Shaken by the reminder, Linet stepped forward. Tripped.

He caught her, his piercing green eyes riveted on her. "You are upset."

She stared at him for a long moment, too aware of their kiss. He gazed back with the intensity of a warrior, but a man as well. Desire swept through her, leaving her aching with need. If only his inquiry was made purely out of concern. On a long sigh, she pulled free and started walking.

"Linet?"

Did he have to use her name? Did he have to speak with the rich, velvet burr that thrummed through her body in soft waves, sparking memories of his touch?

"Tell me," he urged.

She paused and glanced back at him. A mistake. She silently cursed that she noticed the curve of his sensual mouth, the desire in his eyes, and prayed he didn't see her own need.

"We must find the plantain and seek shelter before the knights return," she said, her voice unsteady.

For a long moment he held her gaze as if weighing an important decision. He nodded. "Look to your left."

She turned. A short distance away, near where the land fell away to the rush of water below, tall leaves clustered together and jutted from the damp earth. Heat touched her face. With her mind lost in thoughts of Seathan, she'd missed the plantain.

Chagrined, she walked over and knelt before the herb. "It is a blessing we found it so close to the cave."

Seathan grunted. "It is common enough."

And so it was.

From the corner of her eye, she observed the Scot. He stood, his gaze alert, scouring the perimeter. Ever the warrior. Only the slight shift of his posture, the paleness of his face, betrayed his weakened condition. Amazing after all he'd endured.

Linet tore free a stalk of the sturdy plant. What had Lord Grey experienced during his life that enabled him to endure so much pain and still persevere?

She picked another hardy leaf. No, mayhap she needed not to know. Already she cared more for Seathan than was wise.

Shaken by the emotions this man made her feel, she immersed herself in her task. The rich, earthy fragrance of the forest scented the cool air as she tore each plantain leaf from its base. The menial job served as a balm to the complexity of her thoughts. After she'd collected enough leaves to make a poultice, she stood.

"Had it been farther along in the season," Seathan said, "we might have found yarrow as well."

Surprised, she glanced up to discover him watching her intently. Had he been observing her the entire time? She willed herself not to blush. "You know much about herbs?"

"After a battle, a healer is rarely on hand to care for the wounded," he replied. "A warrior who neglects learning of the healing herbs could forfeit his life."

"Who taught you where to find herbs and how to properly use them?"

Sadness shadowed his eyes. He hesitated. "My mother."

Her heart softened. "You cared for her very much."

"She was a good woman." Pride resonated in his voice as well as love.

"Where is she now?" she asked, curious about the woman who had raised this formidable man.

"She died giving birth to my youngest brother."

"I am sorry."

He shrugged. "'Tis life's way."

Though he acted indifferent, she'd seen the hurt at his loss. Many years might have passed and perhaps the memories had faded, but his love for his mother had not. A fact she empathized with as well.

Somber, she cradled the plantain in her hands and slowly made her way back toward the cave; Seathan kept pace at her side.

Winter brown grass lay limp around her. "You come from a large family?"

"My past matters not."

Frustration slid through her. "I am not the enemy."

"So you claim."

Could he not allow a moment of peace between them? She shook her head as he made to speak. "It matters not. As you said, your family is not my concern."

"That does not seem to affect my inclination to answer your questions," he muttered, almost to himself. "Soon I will be telling you about the woman who—"

When his words broke off, Linet glanced over. If not for the flicker of emotion in his eyes, she would have missed the importance of his response. Her senses came on alert. Then she understood. He hadn't known countless women at all.

A woman, one woman, had hurt him.

"Who was she?" The sincerity of her question echoed between them.

Seathan rolled his shoulders as if to loosen the stiffness in them. He shielded his eyes and scanned the horizon. "A green lad's delusion."

"And the reason you do not trust women?"

Surprise shuttered his face. For a long moment he studied her, then shrugged. "Aye."

Her pulse raced that he'd admit such a painful truth.

"And what of the reason for your lack of trust toward men?"

"I have known many a fine man."

"A diversion, but not an answer."

Mouth dry, she turned toward him, stopped. "I trusted my father."

"And?"

"Beyond him, it seems when it comes to the opposite sex, you and I share the same view."

Intrigue sparked in his eyes. "It is a safe view." Seathan headed toward the cave.

Linet kept pace at his side. *A safe view.* Interesting comment from a man who lived on the edge—

except with his emotions. Those he safeguarded deep inside.

And what of the woman who'd hurt him? Had he loved her? An ache pierced her chest. Yes, he would have. In the brief time she'd known Seathan, she'd learned he was a man who did nothing by halves. What would it be like to be loved with such intensity by a man who, when he gave his vow, backed it with his life?

The woman who'd hurt him was a fool.

As was she—an even greater one for wondering if Seathan felt anything more toward her than disdain.

Still, memories of Seathan's kiss, the powerful yearnings his touch inspired, poured through her like oil upon a flame. What would making love to him be like? Would he be a gentle lover? Fierce? Would his intensity sweep her into emotions untried? He seemed a man who was thorough, regardless of his task. How could that trait not carry into making love?

Sunlight spilled through the leaves ahead, carving fractured shadows in the patches of snow and earth.

A fleeting smile curved her mouth. How appropriate. The riddled path was so like her life, a battle of darkness and light. And like the sun in the sky moving to day's end, so was her time to reach her mother's clan falling away.

"I have three brothers, two are still alive," Seathan said.

Confused, Linet glanced over. "What?"

"You asked if I came from a large family."

The man would drive a saint to distraction. "That was several moments ago, and you replied that your past mattered not." She frowned. "What made you decide to answer me now?"

"I believed it wisest."

She frowned. "Wisest? That now is the time to share information about your brothers with me? Not when I asked you several moments ago?"

At his silence, realization dawned. "Your sharing of your life is but a ploy," she stated, anger seeping into her words. "You want to see how I will react. Or have me lower my guard so I will share personal information about my family in return, is that not your intent?" She should feel guilty at the question as she, too, used the same tactic. Nonetheless, his offer of false friendship hurt. "I am not a maiden easily won."

"Nay, I would never make that mistake."

"Then, what am I to you?" Linet couldn't believe she'd asked, but she found his answer important. Somewhere along the way, Seathan had come to matter. He was no longer just a means of vengeance against her brother, but a man she wanted in her life.

"An intriguing woman."

"Intriguing? 'Tis better than boring." At her reply, a smile edged his mouth, easing the tension between them. "And what of your father?" she asked, her interest purely personal.

He looked off into the distance. "He died in battle."

Sadly, they had the loss of their fathers in common. "I am sorry."

"Why?"

"Because . . . Because I understand the pain of losing someone you love."

"Did someone's death inspire your decision to free me?"

She blew out a breath. "Why is it you must seek information at every turn? For once, can we not speak without suspicion, or doubts of the other's motive, as people with naught more between them than concern for the other?"

Green eyes watched her unmoved. "We are at war. Letting down one's guard is an invitation to die."

"At war? The rebels' acts are but protests against a battle already lost. This summer past, King Edward seized Scotland. Regardless of your wish, he is your sovereign, your homeland his to rule."

He scowled. "Sovereign? Nay, Longshanks is not my ruler, nor will he ever be Scotland's."

"You argue fact," she said, understanding his outrage. "Nobles throughout Scotland have pledged their fealty to King Edward."

"The Ragman Roll?" Distaste flowed from his tongue. "A worthless document signed by spineless men, or those threatened with their life. Do you believe those badgered into signing were sincere?"

"A fact I had not truly considered. And what of King John?" she asked, moved by the passion of Seathan's reply.

Green eyes darkened with disgust. "King John? No Scot worth his sword acknowledges him as such. From the day he betrayed his homeland and resigned his kingdom to King Edward, he earned his title 'Toom Tabard.'"

Linet frowned. "Toom Tabard?"

"Empty surcoat," he spat. "King of nothing. A true warrior of Scotland would have fought to his death, not whimpered like a frightened dog at the first sign of challenge."

On that she agreed. If faced with the same situation, Seathan would have battled for what he believed in.

She understood why King Edward wanted Lord Grey dead. The Scot's spirit inspired the rebels, like that of William Wallace, the nobleman the earl served. Both were warriors who refused to yield or give up what they believed was right.

Humbled, she drew in a slow breath. After King Edward's resounding defeat of the Scots this summer past, she'd believed the English king would easily smother further rebellion, that the infrequent clashes with the English were little more than pockets of resistance.

After meeting Seathan, she realized King Edward's claim that he'd subdued the Scots was more wishful than fact. To focus his efforts on Flanders, the English king had too quickly dismissed the Scottish rebels' intent to reclaim their kingdom.

"And the reason you freed me?" Seathan asked into the silence.

She looked away. "Never mind."

"Now who is it who evades the question?"

Linet met his gaze, wanting him to see the sincerity in her eyes. "There is life beyond war."

"Mayhap, for those absorbed in nobility's games, those safe within castles filled with knights for protection, stocked with food and weapons to withhold an attack for weeks."

"I am far from a witless woman ignorant of the strife of our times."

"On that I agree. You are far from witless."

She arched a brow. "But I am a woman ignorant of the strife of our times, correct?"

He watched her. "Are you not?"

"Would it matter either way?"

"You again evade my question."

"This is not a game."

"Nay," he said, his voice hard. "I have buried too many friends to ever think that."

She swallowed hard. "As have I," she said, thinking of her father, friends, many who had mattered to her. "It is a waste of time to battle with words. In truth, King Edward's desire for power has affected us all, but we do not have to allow it to guide us."

"Only the innocent, or those protected within castle walls, would believe so, my lady."

So he'd deduced her noble status. She wasn't surprised. Neither would she confirm his claim or lead him to any path that might unveil her link to Fulke. "Mayhap I am but an optimist."

"From the short time that I have known you, your strength is in dealing with facts, not clinging to hopeful beliefs."

"And my weakness?"

"Your empathy."

For an unexplainable reason, his comment left

her on guard. "You care for your people as well. There is no weakness in helping others."

He arched a doubtful brow. "Even your enemy? Even rescuing a condemned Scot from an English dungeon?"

"No, you are not my enemy. You are . . ." Sweet Mary, what was she thinking? She'd almost admitted he was a man she was coming to care for, a man she wanted with each breath. She dropped her gaze. A fact she could never share.

"I am what?" he prodded.

She looked up to find him watching her, his gaze intent, as if he could strip away her shield and read the secrets of her soul.

A distant yell shattered the silence.

Seathan caught her hand. "Hurry. We must reach the cave before the knights arrive."

Face pale, Linet nodded.

"This way," a distant guard yelled.

He started to run by her side, faltered.

"Seathan?"

Chapter 5

Seathan gritted his teeth and hauled Linet toward the steep incline leading to the falls.

Another guard yelled, this time closer.

Bedamned! Plantain flew from her hands as he tugged her with him over the steep ledge of thick grass. The mist of the falls below swirled around them.

Through the billows of fluid white, men riding out of the forest appeared.

"God's teeth," he whispered. "If the knights ride closer, they will see us." Before Linet could reply, he pulled her with him as he shoved back.

Long, mist-fed grass slapped his face. The raging water of the falls below pulsed in a wild mangle as they half slid, half fell down the steep, slippery slope.

An arm's length from the edge, Seathan jammed his foot into the muck, shoved to the left. Pain exploded in his left arm as he slammed into a boulder.

His vision blurred. His head spun as if after a night of too much drink.

But they'd stopped.

Several feet below, the rush of water roared. He dragged in deep breaths, fighting to remain conscious.

"Seathan?"

The worry in her voice had him forcing his eyes open. He saw two of the lass. Slowly, his vision cleared.

Eyes wide with fear, she clung to him. "I . . ."

"Thought we were going over?"

She nodded.

"If we had remained near the top," he said between rough gasps, "Tearlach's men would have seen us."

"I know." Her voice shook.

Protectiveness swamped him. Against the pain, he drew her to him. "We are safe." For now. But how much longer he could not guarantee.

The rumble of hooves had him looking up. Through the mist-coated grass, he glimpsed a knight cantering by, then another as the contingent passed.

What had he been thinking to stand in the open talking to the lass as if 'twas a day of leisure?

Her grip on his arm loosened. "I—I think the men are gone."

"Mayhap, but we will remain here a while to make sure."

"You think they will return."

"They will. Tearlach will not quit until he has us both."

Guilt flashed in her eyes. She nodded, but said no more, a mystery that left him on edge as it had from the first.

Linet glanced toward his side, gasped. "Your wound is bleeding."

Not surprised, he looked down. Blood was slowly staining the garb underneath his arm. He pressed his palm against the wound to staunch the flow. Sticky wetness seeped against his fingers.

"You have torn open the bindings," she said. "They will have to be rebound."

"Aye."

Linet scoured the falls below. She turned back, her face pale.

"We are wedged solidly and will not slip."

She nodded, her look far from assured. "Keep me steady."

Once he'd shifted and clasped her shoulder, she tore the hem of her gown. With his help, she wrapped the cloth around him, secured it, but he didn't miss the awareness in her eyes when she touched him, or the tangle of need woven within.

She tugged the last knot snug. "Take care when you climb up."

He held her gaze a long moment, their earlier intimate conversation haunting him with unsettling warmth. "It will serve its purpose." He shrugged off the odd emotion and focused on his injury. Once they'd reached the safety of the cave, he would tend his wound better. A reopened gash was minor compared to the danger if Tearlach's men discovered them.

Time passed with soul-drugging slowness. His injury pounded as if bashed with a mace, but he focused on the warmth of Linet's body flush against his, the way she settled against him as if she'd given him her full trust.

Her body trembled.

"Steady, lass."

She shot a worried look toward the top. "We must return to the cave."

He heard the fear in her voice, understood her concern with the falls but a short distance below, and with the men scouring the area above.

"We will wait a few moments longer."

She nodded but remained silent.

Against his better sense, his admiration for her grew. Many a pampered lass would be screaming like a stallion gelded.

A wave of fatigue washed over him. Seathan fought past it, then glanced down. Water pounded below them, its rising spray a shimmering mist. Sunlight filtered through the droplets like fairy dust. He grimaced. Twice in as many days he'd thought of the fey. His mind was surely abandoning him.

Enough!

He pushed to his knees, then helped Linet to turn, the angled slope of grass and brambles presenting its own challenge.

"Up you go, lass." He shoved his foot into the soft muck, ignored the pain, and pushed.

Linet's foot slipped at his side. "I cannot find a grip."

"Catch hold of the grass. Pull yourself up."

She shot him a worried glance. "It will mean letting go of you."

He nodded. "I will be right behind you. I will not let you fall."

Her lips curved in a wry smile. "It is not me that I am concerned about."

"I need not the worry of a milk-fed lass." Irritation flashed in her eyes as he'd expected. She made to speak, but he gave her a shove. "On with you."

"Stubborn you are."

He grunted. "I doubt I hold a candle to you."

She muttered something unintelligible. With the flash of anger blazing in her eyes, he suspected the telling would not be flattering. A pang of remorse shot through him. He grimaced. 'Twas a sad day indeed when his mind weakened for a woman whose life was spun in secrets. His thoughts should be on his brothers' safety and his country's freedom.

"Move," he ordered.

With a disapproving frown, Linet grabbed a thatch of long grass above her. She shoved her foot into the soft earth as she pulled. Her arm trembled.

With his right hand, Seathan pressed his palm against her shoulder, pushed.

She moved up an inch.

"Again," he commanded.

This time as she pulled herself, he braced himself against the boulder, wrapped both hands around her waist, and lifted.

Linet caught another hunk of grass closer to the top.

"You are almost there," he urged.

She caught another handful of grass, pulled herself up. Inch by inch, she tugged until at last she disappeared into the wash of green rimming the cliff above.

Blades of grass shifted. Linet's head reappeared, her face flushed from exertion. "Now you."

He gritted his teeth, reached up, and pulled. Pain tore through his side, his injury throbbing as if salt-stung. Sweat broke out on his brow as he reached up and caught a nearby bush. His fingers shook, his body trembled, but he worked himself up farther.

And collapsed.

Limp, he gasped for breath as he lay facedown against the water-slicked grass. He glanced behind him, blew out a deep breath. He'd made it but a hand's width.

"Can you make it?"

The fear in her voice had him looking up. "Aye." He'd suffered far worse than the injuries he'd sustained now. Gritting his teeth, Seathan twisted the long blades within his palm. This time, he wedged his boot against the boulder as he struggled up. Though his arm screamed with agony and his body rebelled, he shoved harder.

Blackness threatened. Mud and grass whipped by as he slid back.

"Seathan!" Linet's voice echoed from far away in his mind.

The edge of a stone dug into his injured shoulder.

He jerked to consciousness, clasped the base of a knotted bramble, looked down. Christ's blade. His boots were hanging off the ledge!

Mud squished as Linet slid down the decline toward him. She laced one hand within his, grabbed the boulder with the other, and held tight.

"I thought I had lost you."

He heard the fear in her voice, the desperation as well. His head buzzed. Aches stormed his body. "I— I told you to stay back."

"And I told you not to leave the cave. 'Twould seem we each have a problem listening to orders." She looked above them, grimaced. "We have to get you up."

In his weakened state, he doubted he would reach the top anytime soon.

"Return to the cave. I will follow once I am able."

"I will not go without you."

From her determined expression, she wasn't going to budge. Fine then. "Where you found the earlier supplies in the cave, there is a hemp rope. Retrieve it."

She nodded. "Do not move."

"As if I have an option?" he asked, his voice pained.

Linet shot him a warning look, turned, and with Seathan's help, started up.

"When you return," Seathan called, "do not climb down."

Frustration poured through Linet as she glanced back. "One would believe you would have learned that I do not follow orders well—especially from you."

Green eyes narrowed.

She ignored him. Anger fueled her as she inched up the steep slope, her body still shaking at the memory of him sliding back, of his losing consciousness as he fell. Until he'd hit the boulder, woken, and caught himself on the bush, she'd thought he was going over.

He would have died.

Damn him, he'd come close. She swallowed hard, her heart still pounding at the thought. Until this moment, though drawn to him and aware that she would miss him once they'd parted company, she'd convinced herself that she would be able to wipe Seathan from her mind.

Now, she realized she'd lied. Once they reached the Highlands and he departed, her heart would never be the same. Not that she loved him. Her feelings ran deep for Seathan because of the man he was, because of his courage and his determination to protect those he cared for. Any woman would feel the same if they came to know him.

She could never allow anything serious to grow between them. She brushed several strands of hair from her face. Besides, he'd clearly stated he wanted no woman in his life.

At the top of the bank, she peered through the blades of thick grass for any sign of her brother's men. Several trees away, a raven sat on a low branch. Otherwise, the forest stood empty.

With one last look toward Seathan, she shoved to

her feet, then ran. Her pulse raced as she wove through the trees, the warmth of the sun upon her face far from erasing the chill within.

Please God, let him hang on.

After a brief but harried search within the cavern, she found the hemp rope. Once she'd scoured her surroundings and found no sign of knights, she bolted to the cliff.

With her heart in her throat, Linet peered over. He still clung near the edge. Thank God. "Seathan," she called above the rush of water.

He glanced up, pain raw upon his face. "Wrap the rope around the trunk of a nearby tree. Then"— he paused, dragging in a deep breath—"drop the length to me, but keep enough to hold your end."

Was he addled? "You cannot climb up alone."

"It will take a bit longer, but I can do it." He closed his eyes, reopened them. "As I come up, pull the excess rope that is wrapped around the tree back, keeping the line taut."

"As simple as that?" she muttered.

"What?"

She shook her head. Linet looked around and found a suitable tree.

Precious time passed. Once he'd secured the rope around himself, she pulled. After several breaks to allow him time to rest, finally, his hand came into view.

Linet sagged with relief.

"Keep the rope taut!"

The man never ceased to amaze her. "If you have energy to be ordering me about, use it to move."

He grunted.

The hemp slackened; Linet pulled to keep it taut. "You are almost there."

With a grunt, Seathan crawled forward, then collapsed against the muck, gasping for breath.

No, she refused to let him pass out, neither did she have the strength to haul him up. "I should have known a man who kisses as mundanely as you would not have the staying power," she called down.

Piercing green eyes flashed open. Scorched her with a wonderful heat. Muscles bunched, pain strained his face, with his eyes locked on hers, he pushed.

Relief punched through her. "A bit more."

He shoved.

His head came to the top, then his upper torso. He collapsed, his lower body still hanging over the edge of the steep incline.

Linet stumbled forward, slid her arm beneath his shoulder, and half dragged him away from the steep slope.

"Put your arm around my shoulder. We must reach the cave before the knights return."

Muscles shuddered beneath her hands as she pulled him, and with sheer determination, he pushed himself to his feet.

Step by excruciating step, they made their way to the hideout. She cursed their slow pace, the smear of blood from his wound stating the cost of his efforts.

Once safe inside the cave, she helped him lean against the wall. "Wait." She hurried to get the blankets, then spread them out nearby. "Lie there."

Through the pain on his face, he grimaced. "You are good at giving orders."

"As you," she returned as she helped him lie down, concerned by his weakening voice. Once she'd made him as comfortable as possible, she stood. "I will be back in a moment."

"Where are you—"

"I am going to fetch the plantain, which I would have long since returned with had you not been so pigheaded." She turned away, furious to find tears in her eyes. He'd almost died. She shouldn't care, should blame his brush with death on his unbending pride, but in the short time since she'd met Seathan, he'd come to mean more to her than was wise. Shaken by the realization, she scanned the woods and hurried away.

The rich wash of sunset streamed into the cave, embracing the stone chamber within its soft glow. Linet shifted to keep her back to the sunlight as she gently wiped the ointment she'd extracted from the plantain over Seathan's wound.

Hewn muscle rippled beneath her touch, at odds with the deep gash in his left side. At least the injury hadn't festered. Thank God for that.

His jaw tightened as she carefully smoothed the gel across his tender skin.

"I am almost done," she said.

He remained quiet.

She hadn't expected a reply. Since her return from retrieving the herb, he'd remained silent. She wanted to believe his reserve was a result of his pain. But she sensed more fed his decision not to speak.

Neither was he ungrateful.

He'd shifted himself on the floor in response to her abrupt demands. If he'd shown her but a hint of contempt, she would have left him to apply the mixture himself. No, something else stewed within his mind.

As she applied the next swathe of ointment, he stiffened. She looked up. Stilled. He was watching her, but within the pain shadowing his green eyes, awareness resided as well.

Heat trembled through her body, spun by her need of him, not as a warrior, but as a man. A forbidden man whom she wanted with her every breath.

As if he sensed her thoughts, his dark brows narrowed with warning.

Realization washed over her. Sweet Mary, he wanted her.

That she could affect this complex man thrilled her, then she grew somber. Seathan was dangerous, a Scottish rebel who viewed her as the enemy. Neither did he know of her blood bond to Fulke. Kneeling here but a hand's breath away, staring at him, wanting him was like playing with fire—a dangerous blaze that might easily leave her life scarred.

Unnerved, Linet broke eye contact. "I need to apply the salve on the cuts across your chest."

Instead of a reply, he started to lift his tunic.

At the trembling of his hands, she helped him remove the neatly sewn garment. Honed muscles, battered by bruises and recent cuts, greeted her.

She silently damned her brother, that Fulke would order a man tortured so. One day his quest for wealth and power would lead to his downfall.

Seathan motioned for her to begin.

"You can talk," she said, her nerves on edge, the silence prodding her awareness of him as if she stood too close to a fire.

He only arched an ominous brow.

Frustrated, she swept her fingers through the silky ointment upon the flattened rock, then carefully smoothed the slippery gel over the first of many cuts. She tried to ignore the ripple of muscle, the warmth of his skin against hers.

And failed.

"We must stay here for at least two days," she said to break the tension, "for you to heal."

"We will rest this night, no more."

The lackwit! "After your blood loss this day, if you try to travel on the morrow, you might die."

"If I remain here and do naught, the cost could be many lives."

If he'd said anything else, she would have argued. Damn him, why did he have to be so noble, put others before himself? Because he was a leader, a warrior whom men would admire. And follow.

Linet nodded. "On the morrow then." But she would ensure they kept their travel slow. As if he'd be able to move faster than a slow walk. But he'd try.

She gently tugged down his tunic after she'd covered the angry gashes, marks that would mend and become lost among the numerous scars littering his body. Unlike the scar he bore on his heart due to the woman who'd hurt him. 'Twould seem that would never heal.

"Rest." Linet stood and walked to the opening. She leaned against the time-worn stone and watched the rush of water pour over the ledge Seathan had clung to but a short while ago. A tremor rippled through her body. Then another.

"Linet?"

At the soft rumble of his voice, she stilled. Exhausted, she didn't want to spar with him further. "Go to sleep."

"Lie with me."

At his delirious command, her heart stumbled. He sought but another body's heat. No, she lied to herself. When he'd watched her before, she'd recognized the raw need burning in his eyes. If she chose, he would give her body its every dream.

Warmth swept through her as she imagined his fingers skimming over her flesh, touching her, savoring her every shiver. "You need rest."

"Look at me."

Foolishly, she turned.

Stilled.

Desire, hot and intense, still darkened his gaze. Sweet Mary, how could any woman turn him away? Yet with the secrets she harbored, how could she accept the temptation he offered?

He lifted his hand.

Her throat went dry. "I . . ."

"Need rest as well," he said into the thickening silence.

Angst, relief, and disappointment swept through

her in quick succession. Lost in her own desires, she'd misread his intent.

Too aware of this Scottish rebel, a warrior who represented everything she'd ever wanted in a man, she closed the distance. With her body aching with need, she stretched out by his side.

He drew her against him.

"You should not be moving," she cautioned, wishing for nothing else than for him to hold her.

A lie.

She wished for so much more.

"Go to sleep," his deep voice rumbled.

She closed her eyes, but with him flush against her, his soft breaths caressing her neck, she doubted she'd find sleep this night.

Seathan shifted on the pallet and pain tore through his body. With a grimace, he shook off the fog of sleep and surveyed his surroundings.

Through the worn stone opening, slivers of dawn greeted him. The rush of water echoed from below. A soft, cool breeze, laced with mist and earth, filled his senses.

The cave.

In his dreams, he'd slept within his own bed, the fire in the hearth roaring hot.

But not alone.

A soft groan caught his attention. He glanced down. Linet lay snug against him, the soft curve of her breast inches away from his fingers, the swell tempting him to touch.

The fragile light of dawn carved soft shadows over her fine-boned face, accented the lush sweep of her lashes and her full lips.

His body hardened. On a muttered curse he closed his eyes, willed himself to calm. But with each breath, he inhaled her tempting scent.

"Seathan?" Her throaty, rough morning murmur had him looking down.

A mistake.

The innocence of her expression stole his every thought, his ability to resist what he wanted most.

On a groan, he leaned down and covered her mouth. The velvet softness of her lips had him deepening the kiss, falling into the sensations she made him feel. As within the cell, he lost himself to her taste, that of woman and need, her passionate response feeding his own.

Linet shifted against him, her eyes watching him with desire.

His body demanding its need, Seathan rolled her over, expecting her to tell him to stop, to play a maiden's game. Instead, like a temptress, her eyes sparkled with longing as she watched him, then deepened to something dark, something dangerous, something desperate.

Slender fingers touched his chest, skimmed down to pause a hand's breath from where he'd hardened to a painful length. "Take me."

And his good intent fractured.

Through sheer will, he held, waited, giving her a chance to withdraw the offer, to deny him what he'd wanted since he'd met her.

The rush of water from the falls below churned within the potent silence.

She'd lost her chance.

In one sure stroke, he tore away her gown, bared her to him for his view. God in heaven, she was everything he'd imagined and more. From the fullness of her lips, to the slender curve of her neck that drew his eyes down to her full breasts.

His body roared with a painful ache. He had to touch her. Injuries bedamned, he had to have her. He reached out, slid his hand along the smooth satin of her throat. Her moan had him reaching lower to cup her soft curves, leaning forward to taste.

"Seathan." She arched against him, her body quivering. "Seathan, wake up!"

At the abrasive urgency in her voice, he paused. The dregs of sleep cleared. He opened his eyes.

Linet stared at him, her eyes wide with shock, but dark with desire as well.

Seathan glanced to where his hand cupped her breast. God's teeth, his making love to her had been a dream!

Chapter 6

"Get off me!" Linet tugged her gown to cover herself, her breasts still tingling from Seathan's touch.

He blinked in confusion, shoved away, and stared at her in disbelief. "God's teeth. I am sorry."

She scrambled back, too aware of him, shamefully, aching to lie beneath him again. "Sorry?"

He blew out a deep breath, shook his head. "It was a dream."

Clutching her gown against her chest, she rose. "It seemed very real to me."

"I told you I am sorry," he said, the grogginess in his voice clearing. "Never would I touch you without your wanting me to."

And she believed him.

The air pulsed thick between them, a force that a bare word would shift into desire.

She shivered, ashamed that after the impropriety of his touch, she wanted to feel his hands upon her again. Trembling, she glanced toward where the sun peeked above the horizon.

"We must leave."

The coolness of his words had her facing him, taking in his pale skin, and his eyes still edged with fever.

"You need to rest at least another day." She paused. "Several would be best."

He shoved to his feet.

"Seathan."

"We will go," he said, his tone even, but his eyes burning with desire that held its own warning.

Shaken by her answering need, she nodded. To remain here, wanting him this much, might lead to a greater risk.

Seathan sucked in a deep breath, shoved aside another limb, and trudged through the dense wash of trees with Linet in his wake. His head spun, his muscles screamed, and the gash in his side ached like a bore goaded. Pain he deserved after waking up with his hand on Linet's breast.

She'd trusted him to keep her safe, a vow he'd given. Yet he'd touched her as if she were a wanton, far from what a lady of her innocence dictated. When he'd released her this morning, she'd pushed back, shaken, and had eyed him with distrust.

Distrust he deserved.

Though she'd insisted they remain within the safety of the cave another day to allow him to further heal, he'd refused. He could not endure another night with her silken body wrapped within his arms, her scent teasing him and inspiring his every fantasy.

Since their departure, she'd remained silent. Had he expected her disposition to improve after his improprieties?

Though she'd nay admit it, he'd seen her desire, which helped bloody naught. That she was a virgin condemned him more. He was a warrior, a man who was always in complete control of his thoughts, of his every move.

Except, 'twould seem, with her.

Even as he damned himself, his body still throbbed with unspent desire. Never had a woman haunted him, much less a lass mired in secrets. The snippets he'd learned about her since she'd helped him escape Breac Castle did not diminish her mystery.

The land curved up, the late afternoon sun pouring over the land. His body protested as he pushed on. At least with the night's rest, his wound had quit bleeding. The tight binding she'd secured around his side would prevent its reopening.

What ties held her to Breac Castle? More important, whom did she seek to evade, the viscount or another powerful lord? And why would she have risked her life to slip into the dungeon to free the viscount's most valuable prisoner? A question that again led his suspicions to the viscount himself.

He'd sensed her innocence. When he'd kissed her, her passion was all that a man dreams of, but her hesitancy was revealing. Unless . . .

Anger flared. Seathan slanted a look at the breath-taking lass who walked at his side. Was she Tearlach's intended, her virginity preserved for their wedding night? That would explain her innocence, her denial that she was his lover, the reason why she would reside within Breac Castle, and why she would have in-depth knowledge of the secret passageways. As a future bride, Tearlach would have disclosed the secret escape routes in case of danger.

As for her dislike of the viscount, perhaps her guardian was responsible for her placement in the viscount's grasp? It made sense. Her guardian could have easily arranged her marriage to the viscount for a political tie, even against her wish. A forced union, more so with a brutal man such as Tearlach, would have given her solid motive to dare to free the viscount's prize prisoner from his cell.

God help her if she had failed in their escape. Outraged, Tearlach would have hauled her into his bed and raped her, marriage be damned. And with his twisted mind, he would have found pleasure in her screams of pain.

Fury roared through Seathan as he thought of the bastard's hands upon her, her silken skin marred by his carnal greed. Trembling, Seathan fought for calm, stunned by the depth of his emotion. Naught had occurred. Linet had freed him, they'd escaped, and the viscount wallowed in the anger of an empty marriage bed.

He scanned the forest ahead, thick with shadows and foliage that might easily hide an ambush by Tear-lach's men. Bedamned. Since he had not arrived to meet Alexander and Duncan at the predetermined place but a league away, by now his brothers would be searching for him. He had to intercept them before Tearlach's men did.

"There is a stream to our left." Linet pointed through the pines to where the gurgle of water echoed. "I need to refill my water pouch."

A wise idea, but from her worried glance, he suspected her motive had more to do with providing him time to rest, which left him humbled.

He nodded. "We will stop."

Weathered pine needles muted their steps as they pushed forward, their rich fragrance combined with that of damp earth and spring. Ahead, water tumbled in a soft rush. A layer of thin ice lay against the shore, giving way to the gentle flow of the stream.

At the mossy edge, Linet knelt.

Seathan joined her. Water rushed between time-softened boulders slick with a veil of moss as they dipped their water pouches into a deep pool near the edge.

"How do you fare?" Seathan asked.

She arched a delicate brow, taking in the sheen of sweat coating his brow. "A question I should be asking you."

He lifted the water pouch, secured the top, and set it on the ground. Leaning over, he took a long drink, the cool flow refreshing against his throat. Seathan splashed water on his face and leaned back. He turned to Linet to find her watching him.

Guilt edged him. "What I did this morning was wrong."

A blush swept up the angle of her cheeks. "It was," she agreed, "but you explained it was a dream."

"Do not excuse me."

She shrugged. "I was but stating a fact."

So she was. Still, that she took his impropriety so calmly while he floundered with the issue left him on the defensive. "Do you always argue so?"

Surprise flared on her face. "Argue? We are but talking."

They were, but his shame demanded her outrage. Frustration gnawed at him. "Throughout our time together, regardless of my words, you fear little."

"You want me to fear you?"

Was the woman addled? He exhaled. "A fool would not. You are secluded with a desperate rebel."

"You will not harm me."

"You seem sure. A dangerous acceptance toward a man you barely know."

Linet secured the top to her water pouch, stood. "And a man who can barely remain standing from his wounds."

He shoved to his feet. The forest swam around him, then cleared. "Who are you that you do not fear me?"

She looked at him for a long moment. Sighed. "The woman who has given us both a chance at life."

A shout echoed from near the top of the hill.

Tearlach's men! Seathan caught her hand, hauled her with him, and bolted for the nearby brambles, his body trembling from the effort.

"Under here." At the outer edge, he dropped, dragging her with him.

Linet scooted against him beneath the leaf-filled limbs.

A flash of a rider near the top of the hill came into view, then another. That hill had been their destination. Thank God they'd paused to refill their water pouches.

Several more men rode past, then disappeared into the trees. The thrum of hooves slowly faded.

Linet turned toward him, her face pale. "They will return."

"Aye, but when they do, we will be long gone."

Worry crowded her face. "How many days before we reach the Highlands?"

"I am unsure." Because their trek northward would come later, a fact she would learn once he reached his castle. He refused to risk her attempting to flee by telling her now. Not that he believed she'd wish to return to Tearlach, but until he knew more about her, he would keep her in his sight.

"Come." He started to inch back.

The crack of a stick to the west had him scrambling back under the shrub, hauling Linet with him.

"I did not hear any horses," she whispered.

"Nor I," he agreed as he scoured the forest in search of hidden men.

"Mayhap the viscount's men have broken into two search parties."

"'Twould appear so." He prayed she was wrong, but no other explanation fit.

After a long moment, the soft snort of a horse betrayed whoever hid in the distance.

"Whoever they are, they have horses," Seathan whispered.

Linet frowned. "If they are Lord Tearlach's men, why would they be hiding?"

"Aye," Seathan agreed. "A question I am wondering as well."

Another stick cracked from behind the distant clump of trees.

"From their actions," Seathan said, "'twould seem they were hiding from Tearlach's men."

"They are rebels?"

"I am not sure. Whoever they are, we will wait here until they have left."

Bushes rustled, this time closer. The bough of a thick fir shifted. A bay appeared, led by a fierce, dark-haired warrior, followed by a blond-haired knight leading a coal-black steed.

"Christ's blade," Seathan hissed.

Worry ripped through Linet. "What is wrong?"

Instead of responding, Seathan rolled from under the bush and stood. His body swayed.

The lackwit! "What are you doing?" Linet hissed as she scrambled out. "You will be seen!" Or worse.

He wove forward.

Sweet Mary! She ran and caught his arm, tugged. "Come back. They will see you!"

Instead, he jerked his arm free, stumbled toward the men.

The fierce man who'd mounted the bay turned. Black hair draped around a face tempered by determination. The scar slashing down his left cheek added to his menacing expression.

No! She bolted for Seathan.

As quick, the second man whirled, his blond hair secured behind his neck, which framed the face of a god.

Seathan stopped. "Alexander, Duncan!"

Heart pounding, she halted at his side. "You know those men?"

With unsteady steps, he continued forward. "Aye, they are . . . my brothers."

Relief swept her and, after it, fear. One man she could escape from if the need arose, but three? What should she do? If she tried to slip away now, surely the men would give chase.

As he continued to move forward, Seathan began to weave.

The fool. She ran and put his left arm over her shoulder, taking some of his weight.

"I need not your help," he said through gritted teeth.

Linet held, sensing his request came from his not wanting to appear weak before his brothers.

Before he could say more, soft hoofbeats echoed in the crisp air as the two men cantered toward them. The largest man, his hair as black as Seathan's, drew to a halt, the menace carved on his face changing to relief.

The warrior with blond hair and a deep cleft in his chin drew up to his side.

The black-haired man jumped to the ground and caught Seathan's shoulders. He studied him in a quick sweep. "God's eyes! Who beat you?" Cobalt eyes lashed toward Linet, darkened. "What happened to him?"

The blond-haired god jumped to the ground, caught Linet's shoulder before she could step back. Fierce green eyes pierced her. "Tell us!"

"The lass helped me escape," Seathan rasped.

"Escape?" At once the blond-haired man's hold on her eased.

The black-haired man looked far from convinced. "From where?"

"I—" Seathan started to sway.

"He needs to sit," Linet interrupted, shooting both brothers a cool glare. "If you have not noticed, he is about to fall over."

The dark-haired man held her gaze a moment longer, then nodded. "Duncan, catch his other shoulder." He and the other brother helped Seathan toward the thicket of trees where they'd hidden a short while before.

Shielded within the alcove of leaves, the blond-haired man turned toward his brother. "I will retrieve the horses." He hurried through the trees toward where they'd left their mounts.

"The gruff one's name is Alexander," Seathan forced out.

"Gruff," the dark-haired brother snorted as he helped Seathan settle against a moss-blanketed stump. "I could not hold a sword to you." His gaze shifted to Linet, grew serious. "You saved my brother. For that I am in your debt."

The blond warrior led the horses into the thick

leaf-strewn limbs which would shield them from view. "How is he?"

Seathan winced as he shifted to a more comfortable stance. "Not dead. And able to speak for myself."

Relief swept Duncan's face, and dimples deepened in his cheeks. "Aye," he shot back with a twinkle in his eyes, "it looks as if you will live. The surly ones always do."

Emotions swamped Linet at the obvious affection the brothers held for each other, their family bond strong. A bond that until her father's death, she, too, believed she'd held with Fulke. A bond her brother had manipulated until he'd gained total control over his inheritance.

Tired, weary of the deception surrounding her life, she focused on Seathan, on a man whom she'd come to admire. "You need to rest."

Grim appreciation shadowed Seathan's face. "Duncan, meet Lady Linet."

An inquisitive blond brow arched with interest. Duncan took her hand, bowed, and kissed behind her knuckles. "My lady, the pleasure is mine."

His Grecian good looks and effortless grace assured her that many a woman had fallen to his easy charm. He seemed an approachable man, a trait not shared by his oldest brother. She glanced toward Seathan. Interest sparked in Lord Grey's eyes as he watched her interaction with his brother. Irritated by his assessment, and the fact that he affected her so when Duncan's magnetic presence and smooth manner had done naught, she withdrew her hand.

"Lord Grey is gravely wounded," she said, her tone cool, "though he would claim otherwise."

Seathan's brothers immediately focused on him.

"He has a deep gash in his left side," Linet continued, "and bruises all over his body."

"Name the bastard," Alexander spat.

Linet flinched at the instant fury. Fulke deserved their wrath and more.

"Lord Tearlach," Seathan replied.

Duncan's eyes narrowed to ice. "I will slay his damnable heart."

"Not before I carve his arse," Alexander stated. He nodded to Seathan. "Tell us everything."

In horrifying detail, Linet absorbed Seathan's account of his friend Dauid's betrayal, of witnessing his men's slaughter, and the torture served to him by her brother. Sickened, she turned away, leaned against a nearby elm, and closed her eyes. 'Twould seem when it came to ensuring that Fulke gained King Edward's praise, her brother spared no one.

She understood the lure of power, of wanting possessions, which caused many a man to make poor decisions. But to hurt others, torture a man until his body was broken, or he died from the cruelty, that she would never understand.

Or accept.

A soft hand touched her shoulder. She turned to find Duncan standing there, his eyes concerned, but like his older brother, watchful.

"I am sorry," he said. "A lady should not have heard such."

"Shielding my ears from brutal truths changes

naught. Seathan suffered much from a noble who sees your brother as no more than a trophy to bestow upon King Edward to earn his praise." At his surprised expression, Linet stilled. She was revealing too much. The last thing she needed was to expose her detailed knowledge of Fulke. "Forgive me, I am upset at the brutality served to your brother."

"Do not apologize. Too often wartime delivers an abundance of grief and pain. Even to those who are victorious." Duncan fisted his hand, then slowly uncurled his fingers. "It is rarer to find those caught in the fray who choose to not only care, but to take risks to right a wrong."

"I but set a man free. Give not my actions valor. 'Tis what most would do."

"Nay, most would not dare act against their lord's wishes and set a valuable prisoner free."

Guilt gnawed at her. Like Seathan, Duncan seemed a man of passion, a man guided by his morals and sharp of wit. 'Twas but his delivery that was more refined.

"I am tired of the killing, of the senseless death." She shook her head. "I wish the fighting were over."

"As do I," Duncan agreed. "But until we chase Longshanks from our soil, we will continue our fight to secure Scotland's freedom, with our every last drop of blood if necessary."

Longshanks—the name given to King Edward because of his extraordinary height. "You will win."

Fierce pride sparked in Duncan's eyes. "Aye, we will."

Of that she had no doubt. After meeting Seathan

and his brothers, men who fought for the people they loved with their very soul, confidence filled her. They would overcome the English king's tyranny and reclaim their country. Unlike King Edward and others like Fulke, men who were driven by greed, the brothers fought for love.

"Duncan," Alexander called.

"A moment," Duncan replied without turning toward his brother, his green eyes too watchful, seeing more than she would like.

"Go tend to your brother," Linet said. "I am fine."

He hesitated a moment longer. "You are sure?"

She nodded. She was fine, but not in the way she'd once believed. Time would heal her wounds while she crafted a new life in the Highlands, but the bond of family she'd once held, of trusting those she loved, was forever lost.

Clear skies framed a vivid display of stars cradled above the treetops, the full moon exposing the forest within its silvery light. A soft breeze thick with the scent of earth and night rustled through the leaves overhead. Seathan stared at the heavenly expanse a moment longer, then shifted, careful to keep pressure off his injury.

"You are awake?" Alexander said, his voice low.

"Aye." Seathan glanced toward Linet opposite him. Wrapped in a blanket provided by his brothers, her head cushioned on a bed of leaves, she lay sleeping, her face caressed by moonlight. He lingered over the curve of her mouth, the soft breaths slipping from her lips to cast a strand of hair about. An ache swept through him. He missed her curled against him, the sense of rightness at having her by his side.

"She is a beauty," Alexander said.

Startled to be caught staring, he turned toward his middle brother and found Alexander evaluating him. "She is," he replied, his words cautious.

Duncan walked over and sat beside Alexander to complete the small circle, their muscled frames shutting out Linet.

Sitting with his back to a stump, Alexander dragged the tip of the stick in his hand through patches of snow around a protruding root. "You care for the lass."

Seathan sat up. "She saved my life."

Alexander looked over, his expression skeptical. "She did."

"You of all people should know of my intent to never become seriously involved with a woman again," Seathan stated. "When I take a wife, my decision will be born of duty, naught more."

"God's teeth, did I say you were involved with the lass, serious or otherwise?" Alexander asked, but Seathan heard his brother's question. After his heartbreak, his family avoided the topic of Iuliana. A foolish mistake during his youth, an affair entered against his father's advice. He'd learned the hard way. In the end, Iuliana's attention toward him was but her vulgar attempt to make her husband jealous.

Nay, after the devastation he'd experienced when

he'd learned of her deception, never again would he allow a woman into his heart.

Seathan studied Linet, irritated by the unfamiliar tug of need. "How could I possibly care for the lass? Besides her name, I know little about her." He eyed one brother, then the other. "Before she would release me from the dungeon, I was forced to agree to her request to escort her to the Highlands, no questions asked."

Alexander blew out a rough breath. "Her refusal to state her reason reeks a foul stench."

"Aye," Seathan agreed, "but against the option of death, her offer was one I could not refuse."

Silence stumbled between them, serenaded by crickets and the rush of the spring-fed wind.

Duncan ground the heel of his boot into the dirt, looked up. "What I cannot figure out is how the lass snuck into the dungeon without being seen."

"She used a secret passage," Seathan explained.

"A secret passage?" Alexander frowned, threw the stick into the night. "I would think but few trusted nobles close to Lord Tearlach would know of the maze of tunnels hidden within Breac Castle."

"My thought as well," Seathan replied. "Nothing else makes sense."

"What is her relation to Lord Tearlach?" Duncan asked.

In brief, Seathan explained his suspicions that she was Lord Tearlach's intended bride.

Alexander muttered a soft curse. "Something is greatly amiss when a noblewoman betrays her betrothed's confidence to release the prisoner he values most."

"It is," Seathan agreed, "but as I said, she may have been forced into the marriage."

Alexander grunted. "You may have given a vow to not question the lass, but I have not."

"Nor I," Duncan added.

"The question is, did she plot against Tearlach out of anger? Or is my release but a scheme Tearlach devised to infiltrate the rebels?" At the flash of anger on his brothers' faces, Seathan nodded. "As much as I wish to believe otherwise, the latter is a possibility we must consider. I assure you, before I deliver her to the Highlands, I will know."

Duncan rubbed his jaw. "The lass will be spitting mad when she learns you will not be taking her to the Highlands posthaste."

"She will be displeased," Seathan agreed blandly.

Alexander snorted. "With the way she issued commands earlier this night to ensure your care, the lass is not one to stand by and be ordered about."

Seathan grimaced. That he knew well. "Aye, another fact that raises further questions as to her true identity. But her upset at the journey to the Highlands being delayed is of less concern to me than finding Dauid."

At the mention of their supposed friend, Alexander hissed his breath through his teeth. "Had someone else told me of Dauid's betrayal, I would have called them a liar."

"If I had not seen him in the torchlight standing

by Lord Tearlach," Seathan said, "I would never have believed it myself."

Duncan shook his head. "His actions make little sense."

"I agree," Seathan replied, the scene of that soul-wrenching night racing through his mind like an ongoing nightmare, "but it neither changes how many of our knights were slaughtered, nor that their mutilated bodies were left for the wolves." A fresh wave of fury tore through him, followed by the weight of responsibility. He exhaled and dropped his hand. "Upon our arrival home and once Linet is secured within a chamber, I will speak with the men's wives."

"You will not go alone," Alexander said.

Duncan nodded.

"As lord of Lochshire Castle," Seathan said, "the responsibility is mine."

Alexander bristled. "The castle and its duties are yours, but Duncan and I have always been here to turn to. 'Tis you who have chosen never to seek either of us for support."

"I need no help," Seathan said, his voice hardening.

"Nay, you think you can do it alone," Duncan charged. "As you always have."

Grief burned in Seathan's gut. "Bedamned! You think the telling will be easy? They were friends, men I have known my entire life."

"Men who were our friends as well," Alexander added, his voice calmer. "But instead of asking for help, for support from the brothers who love you,

you wrap yourself within your title and push Duncan and me away."

A muscle worked in Seathan's jaw. "The men were under my command."

"The men, like you, were betrayed," Alexander shot back. "You may be an earl, but damn you, you are my brother, my flesh and blood. After Iuliana used you to make her husband jealous, Duncan and I mentioned naught. But our silence has not allowed you to heal. Instead, the error of your youth continues to fester inside you and poisons your ability to share your hurt, your sorrows, with your family."

Seathan stiffened. "Alexander—"

"It is true," Duncan interrupted. "The time has come for you to accept that you cannot stand alone. In life or war. The men were our friends as well. We grew up together, trained, watched them wed, and christened their children. We will not step back and allow you bear the full grief and anger, or the telling to those they loved that their husbands, sons, and fathers have been slaughtered."

Humbled by his brothers' support, Seathan swallowed hard. "I had not meant to hurt you," he said unsteadily.

"We know," Duncan said. "But it is time to allow us into your lives as brothers who love and support you, who will stand by your side whenever you need."

"Aye," Alexander agreed.

Nay, he would not share his shame, but he would accept his brothers' offer. Seathan nodded. "Once we return to Lochshire Castle, you will both accompany me to break the news to our people."

Alexander and Duncan nodded.

His brothers understood the cost of his decisions, but not the full weight of the responsibility he bore. Seathan shifted, studied Linet, who lay sound asleep across from him, then looked at the sky so beautiful, so full of peace. The path before him was anything but.

On an exhale, he asked, "What of your meeting with Wallace and Bishop Wishart?"

Excitement sparked in Alexander's eyes. He glanced toward Linet to ensure she was asleep. "Better than planned. 'Twould seem that, fed up with King Edward's tyranny, The Stewart has joined our ranks."

"The Stewart?" Seathan nodded. "After being chosen as one of the Guardians of Scotland upon the death of Margaret, Maid of Norway, I am not surprised by James Stewart's decision, more so with Wallace's family belonging to Stewart's fife. His tactical move makes sense."

"It does," Duncan agreed. "And when King Edward learns of The Stewart's shift in loyalties, he will be furious. But then, that's a state he's been in since the death of his wife."

Seathan nodded, finding it curious such a power-hungry king had found the capacity to love someone other than himself. "But embroiled in war against France, he has little time to focus on the actions of The Stewart. In his mind, he has conquered Scottish soil with little left to do but squelch the last pockets of resistance, a task he's left to Sir Hugh Cressingham and John de Warenne, the Earl of Surrey."

"Warenne," Alexander spat. "The weak-kneed

lackey who sneers down his nose at Scotland. The earl has abandoned his post and ridden to his estate in Yorkshire, leaving Sir Hugh Cressingham with the full brunt to bear."

"Welcome news for the rebels," Seathan said. "So it is Cressingham we must stop. He is a dangerous man who sees Scotland as but a stepping stone to a greater destiny."

"Aye." Duncan rubbed his brow. "His rise from a bastard child to King Edward's trusted minion makes his each achievement all the sweeter."

"The arrogant bastard," Alexander spat. "He gives not a damn for those who suffer because of his lust for power. He may be assigned to keep peace, but in addition to culling the revenues for Longshanks, he stirs up further hatred from the Scots."

On that Seathan agreed. 'Twould be a day to celebrate when Cressingham lay rotting in the earth. "We will strip Cressingham of his power, then sweep across Scotland. King Edward will learn that he has made a grave error in dismissing the Scots."

A hard smile edged Alexander's mouth. "He has."

For the next few minutes, Seathan listened as his brothers outlined their discussion with Wallace, Wishart, and The Stewart, adding his own insight. "I am impressed by the breath of their plans to rid Scotland of England's presence. To shield their actions behind Wallace is brilliant. He is the perfect choice. With his passion, he holds the ability to unite our people."

"King Edward is so caught up in his tangles with

the French and Flemish," Alexander said, "by the time he learns of our plans, it will be too late."

So Seathan hoped. But he would not underestimate a ruler seasoned in war, a man driven by grief.

Regardless, in the end, Scotland would again be free.

"The plans are solid ones," Seathan agreed.

His brothers nodded.

Tiredness washed over Seathan, layered upon the steady ache of his wounds. "It is time to sleep. We travel at first light."

Alexander grumbled, but didn't disagree, and Seathan understood. If the circumstances weren't so dire, his brothers would insist they remain here at least another day to give him time to rest. But with the viscount's men scouring the lands for him and Linet, 'twas not an option.

In the end, it would be Lord Tearlach who paid the price. On that he gave his solemn vow.

Seathan lay down, pulled the blanket over himself and closed his eyes. But with his grief over his men's deaths, and the prospect of having to break the news to those whom the men had loved, he doubted he'd find sleep this night.

Chapter 7

Seated before Seathan upon the large bay, Linet glanced over at his brothers, doubled up upon the black steed. Against the smears of reds and yellows tossed in the evening sky, she caught Alexander watching her, his expression grim. Unsettled by the directness of his stare, she turned and rested her head against Seathan's chest. Seathan's brothers didn't trust her; she wouldn't expect them to.

Since they'd awoken at dawn and broken camp two days past, they'd ridden at a slow but steady pace, stopping only to rest and water their horses. Seathan's determination to travel didn't surprise her, but in his condition, that his brothers allowed him to underlined the danger of being caught by Fulke's men.

She sensed a difference now in his attitude toward her. What had Seathan told his brothers about her? Two nights past, she'd pretended to be asleep to eavesdrop. Instead, exhausted, she'd fallen into a deep slumber.

Now, his brothers' guarded looks kept her on edge. Seathan might be the oldest, a titled noble and a powerful man whom few dared to cross, but 'twould seem his brothers, only knights in a land driven by mighty lords, were a force to be reckoned with as well.

She should find it ironic that a man as powerful as Seathan would have his younger siblings looking out for him, but the strong bond between the brothers, and the fierceness with which they protected him, left her anything but amused. She couldn't help comparing the richness of his life with her own empty future.

Linet shifted against Seathan's muscled chest. With each beat of his heart, emotions she'd rather not feel stirred within, awareness that was destined to go unanswered.

No, that wasn't true. From Seathan's passionate kiss, the intimate way he'd touched her, if she'd allowed him, they would have made love. Warmth coursed through her as she imagined his powerful body claiming hers. She dismissed the stories of fear and pain. With Seathan's passion, his thoughtfulness, she refused to believe he'd be anything but tender.

"You are quiet, but I sense your thoughts are far from calm," Seathan said, the burr of his deep voice sending another shot of awareness through her.

"How can they be?" Linet replied, scrambling for logical thought. "Since our escape, five days have passed, each one raising worries that Lord Tearlach's men will discover us." She paused. "How long before we reach your home?"

"This night."

Surprised, she turned to look at him. A mistake. This close, she saw the way he looked at her, watched as a predator eyed his prey. Though injured, this warrior was far from safe.

Shaken, she turned around. "With you recovering so quickly, we should be able to head for the Highlands within a sennight."

Duncan, riding at their side, coughed, which oddly sounded like laughter.

She shot a covert glance toward his youngest brother, but found him facing forward as if unaware of their discussion, a fact she doubted after having come to know Duncan a bit more these past two days.

At Seathan's silence, she focused on him. "We will be leaving for the Highlands posthaste, will we not?"

"We will depart on our journey when I deem it prudent," he finally replied.

She turned to face him, irritated to find his expression had hardened to a scowl. "Do not try to intimidate me with a fierce look. You promised you would take me to the Highlands."

Only the slightest inflection betrayed his displeasure at her challenge. "And I will."

"When?"

Duncan cleared his throat, and she glanced over to find him watching her with mirth.

As if aware of her embarrassment, Seathan drew

his steed to a halt. "Ride ahead," he ordered his brothers. "We will catch up with you."

Alexander halted his mount beside them, frowning. "It is unwise. Tearlach's men may be about."

"With the viscount's knights thinking Linet and I are on foot, even if they search this route, I doubt they'd believe we would have traveled this far." Seathan nodded. "Go. We are within a league of Lochshire Castle."

Alexander hesitated, then his eyes narrowed. "We will ride beyond the tree line. No more."

Tension hummed between the brothers. That any would challenge Seathan surprised Linet. But the defiant glare Alexander shot his brother assured her that on this, his younger sibling refused to budge.

Seathan's body stiffened behind her. "Wait beyond the tree line then."

Alexander kicked his steed forward. Duncan shot her a wink as the brothers disappeared into the thick stand of pines ahead. The soft clop of hooves faded, then grew quiet.

"Your brothers only want to ensure that you are safe," Linet said.

Seathan turned back to her, his jaw taut. "My brothers' wants are not what I wish to discuss. I have given you my word that you will be taken to the Highlands. I will not break it."

"I did not ask if you had given your word, but when we will be leaving for my mother's home?"

"Upon my return."

"Return?"

Pain flickered in his eyes, then disappeared

as quickly. "There is a matter I need to take care of first."

Her heart softened. "Dauid." The word tumbled from her lips before she could stop it.

"Is not your concern."

"It is," she said, understanding too well the hurt of being betrayed. "You led me to believe there would be no delay in our travel to the Highlands."

"I could not tell the truth and give you the chance to abandon me, to leave me to die."

"From the start you misled me?"

His eyes narrowed. "Dare you accuse me of what you yourself chose to employ?"

"I had my reasons."

"As did I," he said, his voice cold. "I will take you to the Highlands as promised."

"When it suits you, clearly," she added, anger wrapping around her words.

"Aye."

Linet exhaled, striving for calm. Seathan was not to blame for her situation. That honor belonged to Fulke. "How long will you be gone?"

Seathan hesitated, surprised by her quick acceptance, but not fooled. "Until I finish the task." The pulse at the base of her neck pounded. Linet was upset, but on this he would not budge. Until he found Dauid, he'd not rest.

"So," she said, her voice dry, "I sit and wait until your return?"

"You will reside within my home, Lochshire Castle, and be allowed every freedom."

"Including to leave?"

Annoyance flickered through him. "It would be far from safe to travel without a chaperone."

A humorless smile flickered on her mouth. "After traveling with an injured warrior who could barely fend for himself, I will take the risk."

Bedamned. "You will wait for me."

"Dare you order me about?"

"You will not put yourself at risk."

"The decisions I make are my own. Neither you, nor any other, will dictate to me."

"You will not argue with me."

"There is no argument. I am a free woman. Unless"—lavender eyes narrowed—"you have decided to keep me against my will. Then, it would seem that I would be your prisoner." She angled her jaw. "So, tell me, which am I?"

He couldn't help admiring her bravado, that she'd dare challenge him at every turn. Still, it changed nothing. "Do not twist my words."

"Then do not dictate what I can or cannot do."

"God's teeth, you have the sense of a pignut."

Instead of anger, she laughed, a soft, pure sound that had his pulse kicking up.

Her eyes smiling, she looked up at him. "There again, it seems we are even."

He wanted to remain irritated—it would be easier when dealing with the lass—but her sharp wit, and the way she stood up to him when most would back down, drew him to learn more about this intriguing woman.

Seathan nodded slowly. "Mayhap." Her ability to disarm him, and to make him want her, spelled danger. He had too important a task ahead to allow his thoughts to ponder a lass who shielded secrets, a woman who, if he'd guessed correctly, might be betrothed to his enemy.

Silence spilled between them, the breath of wind cleansing the discomfort of moments ago until it shifted into something intimate.

The rich scent of pine, earth, and desire melded into one. An essence so real, so potent, it incited images of her lying naked beneath him, her body arched to meet his.

Her eyes widened. "Do not kiss me," she whispered.

"It would be foolish," he said, even as he caught her chin with his hand and angled her mouth to his. "And a mistake." But it seemed a time for whimsy, to give in to what logic forbade.

On a groan, he claimed her mouth, gentle, probing, wanting to taste her essence, to savor this woman who would stir up a saint.

She stiffened beneath him as if to reject him, but he'd already seen her need, tasted her desire even as her mind fought to refuse. Seathan accepted her silent challenge, enjoyed her strong will. Never had a woman aroused him on so many levels.

He slid his tongue over her lips, teasing, toying with her mouth until her pulse raced beneath his thumb. "Open for me," he whispered.

"No." But her words lacked conviction.

"Open."

For a moment she held firm. Then, on a sigh, she acceded.

Her taste infused him, the slick warmth igniting his body like a torch tossed upon dry tinder. He took the kiss deeper, wanting her full compliance, for her to admit that she wanted him, a truth she sought to deny.

On a shudder, her body softened, then she was kissing him back. Seathan had thought himself ready, but as before, the full impact of her kiss, the heat backed by need, exploded through his mind, and for a moment, all he could do was absorb.

Taking control, Seathan cradled her face within his hands, turning her so he could fully explore her mouth. Christ's blade, her taste was a combination of heaven and sin. The softness of her flesh teasing him to stay, to explore her body until he sated his every need.

With his senses steeped in desire, he nibbled along the curve of her neck, inhaling her scent. His mind spun with erotic fantasies, of the pleasures he could give her. And when she believed she could take no more, begged him to stop, he'd savor showing her there were no boundaries when making love.

Instinct assured him a night of sensual seduction would but whet his appetite. With Linet, he would need a sennight or more to slake his need.

Then, would even that be enough?

"Seathan."

At the rough passion in her voice, his body trembled with anticipation. He kissed the silken length of her neck, his hand skimming where fabric brushed against flesh. "Aye."

"Should . . . we not go?"

"We will."

Her hands shook as she pressed against his chest, shoved. "I do not want this."

He drew back, irritated. "Your kiss tells me otherwise."

Eyes dark with passion, she stared up at him. She drew in a shaky breath. "But that is not the point."

"What is?"

"My freedom," she replied. "Or do I truly have a choice in either?"

Irritation edged through him. "Never have I forced a lass to my bed."

"Yet you pressure me." At his silence, she pressed forward. "I did not want your kiss."

"No?" he asked, taking in her lips swollen from his kisses. "Your body is pressed against me, at odds with your words."

She pulled back. As he began to lean forward, she pushed back harder. "Do not."

The nervousness in her voice stayed his actions. "Why?" he demanded, wanting to hear her say the words they both knew she held back.

She glared at him. "Because, damn you, I want you too much already."

Satisfaction rushed through him. "Who are you angry at?" he asked before she could speak. "Me, for making you admit what you feel, or yourself for feeling it?"

Herself, Linet silently admitted, ashamed she'd taken the turmoil of her feelings out on him. Still, she refused to argue, she'd caused herself enough shame. "We need to go. If you have forgotten, your brothers await us beyond the bank of firs."

"Their choice."

"And leaving is mine."

He watched her for a long moment. "What is between us is far from over."

That she believed. A fact that unnerved her far more than Fulke's threats ever had. This powerful lord had no idea he held his enemy's sister before him. God help her if he found out.

Then a new, unsettling thought came to mind. She'd believed it prudent to keep Seathan ignorant of her blood tie to Fulke. But having come to know Seathan, she'd learned he was a fair man. Should she tell him? Would he believe her? Be furious? No, it was best to remain silent. In but a short while she would be in the Highlands.

The time to tell Seathan the truth had long passed.

At her continued silence, his mouth tightened. Then he kicked his mount forward.

Relief washed over her as if she'd escaped something monumental. She faced forward as he guided his steed toward where his brothers waited. No, she'd far from escaped, but had delayed a moment she feared was inevitable. He wanted her in his bed.

A place where she wished to be as well, but a place she could never choose.

Her heart ached. Never had she imagined that she would be so attracted to a man that she would consider casting aside society's strict rules in search of pleasure. But Seathan had her mind exploring dangerous ground. And if she chose to join him in his bed, would it destroy her when she left? How could it not? Already she cared for him more than was wise. At least she wasn't in love with him.

Lord Grey caught a limb, shoved it aside as they broke through the sweep of firs. In the distance she made out Alexander standing by a tree keeping a lookout while Duncan kicked back against a stump.

Alexander shoved away from the elm with a dark frown. "I see you have decided to join us."

"Mount," Seathan said, his tone equally sharp.

"Tossing orders about after he lags back to kiss the lass," Duncan quipped.

Heat stole up her face. His brothers had seen their kiss. Judging by their expressions, despite Duncan's humor, they still weren't sure what to think about it. Alexander looked particularly grim.

"On with you," Seathan growled.

After Duncan and Alexander mounted, they guided their steeds up a sharp, angled bank.

The trees crowding around the timeworn path forced them to ride single file, which was fine with her. With Alexander and Duncan ahead of them, she didn't have to see their knowing gazes, feel guilt that it wasn't so much the kiss that worried her, but that she didn't want Seathan to stop.

In the rich mix of pine and earth, she caught a whiff of a tangy freshness. Surprised, Linet looked around. "I smell water."

"You would," Seathan said. "My home is surrounded by a loch."

She scoured the thick swathe of trees, but caught no sign of a shoreline.

"Once we reach the crest," he said, "the keep will come into view."

The soft clop of hooves upon the sodden pine broke the silence, the swish of branches as tree limbs brushed against them adding to the sense of expectancy.

If possible, the steep trail grew steeper, angling up toward a sky so blue it was like a path to heaven. Among the trees, wild herbs lay sprinkled about, scenting the air with their bold richness.

A horse snorted.

She glanced ahead. The brothers rode through thick limbs of fir, then Linet lost sight of them. Without warning, the land fell away.

Her breath caught. Before her, a sweep of rolling mountains embraced a large expanse of water, calm beneath the golden, orange-red glow of the setting sun.

Seathan had explained that a loch surrounded his castle, but of all the images she'd crafted, none had prepared her for the majesty of what man and nature had created before her.

On the southern curve of land, cradled within the lake whose smooth surface mirrored the color above, Seathan's home stood as if it was a magical castle inspired by bards. Quarried rock, the shade of a wise man's hair, arched toward the sky with proud defiance, so like the Scots who guarded it within, so like the man who was its lord.

A peninsula jutted from the southern curve of the loch, the only point of entry to his home. In the waning sun, the shoreline shone like a ring of gold cast from a spell.

A shiver rippled through her as reality intruded. However enchanting, the strategic placement, as well as the guards making rounds upon the wall walk, revealed the castle's true intent. This might be Seathan's home, but it was built to be defended against an attack, a fortification designed for war.

And if he chose, her prison.

Seathan halted his steed. "My home, Lochshire Castle." Pride swelled in his voice, that of a man who fought for what he believed, gave everything and more to protect those he loved.

Tears burned her throat. How would it feel to be loved without question? To have a man like Seathan in her life? "It is amazing," she replied, deeply moved. "I never expected to find a castle of such caliber." Nor a man.

"Most do not."

Linet turned, needing to see his face, curious to know more about the man who lived in this magnificent fortress.

"It must have taken years to build." Green eyes held hers, their fierceness sending a shudder straight to her soul.

"Lochshire Castle was built by the Normans and handed down to the oldest son ever since. This is my legacy, a home I will one day pass to my son." He scanned the majestic view before facing her. "No one will ever take Lochshire Castle from me, including your English king."

"My English king?" she asked, irritated by his

reference. "Think you I claim England or its ruler as my own? Or have you forgotten I am half Scottish?"

"When it comes to you, with the secrets you keep, I know not what to believe."

His words hurt. Her belief that he was beginning to trust her fell away.

"I see." She started to turn from him.

Seathan caught her chin. His expression softened. "You do not, but you will."

She jerked from his hold, not wanting his gentleness. Already she cared for him too much. "You may be a powerful lord, but with me, you will find that you do not always get what you wish."

"Wish?" Coldness flickered in his gaze. "I do not believe in anything as fanciful as a wish. You err to compare me with one of the spineless men of your past."

She stiffened. "You know nothing of me."

He arched an intrigued brow.

What had she done? Though he'd not replied, her words but tossed him a gauntlet. She remained silent. To say more would only pique an already dangerous interest.

"Seathan?" Alexander yelled back.

He ignored his brother. For a long moment, he held her gaze. "I see more of your thoughts than you would like." His soft words held a quiet warning. "This is my home, my people. Do not defy me nor make decisions spawned by your emotions. 'Twould be an error, one you would regret." He kicked his steed forward. With care he guided his mount down the steep incline.

The cold certainty of his voice, his single-minded focus, reminded her of Fulke. But though both men were driven, had clear, concise goals, morals guided Seathan's hand.

Nerves wove through her as she scanned the outline of trees and shore surrounding the loch. Where was Fulke now? Had he and his men picked up their trail? Seathan and his brothers had carefully erased the path behind them as they rode, so she doubted they'd left any sign of their travel. Still, she wouldn't underestimate her brother.

Regardless, both men were a threat. Except with Seathan, the threat arose from the need he evoked, a need she'd never expected or wanted, until now. She'd believed once she arrived in the Highlands, she would have no problem watching him ride away. Now, it would be far from simple.

To linger at Lochshire Castle, to learn more about Seathan, to want him more with each passing day, would make their parting difficult. Or was it already too late?

A long ache sifted through her, threatening her composure, assuring her that, indeed, the time to escape the pain of separating had passed.

Damn him for having made her care, for making her want what was forbidden. She refused to stay. Once he left to find Dauid, she would slip out and travel to the Highlands alone. Mayhap somehow she could procure a horse. Her decision made, she focused on the steep path ahead.

A rock tumbled from under his mount's hooves. Seathan frowned. The lass was too quiet, but

Seathan deduced what brewed inside. "Do not think of trying to leave."

"Why would I?"

"Because I have upset you, made you admit you want me. Now, you are still mulling over our kiss, the fact that you want me as well."

"Are you always so arrogant?"

A smile teased his mouth. The lass would always be able to touch him. "More so with you."

"'Twould seem a sour blessing."

"Tell me that after you have come to my bed," he whispered.

Her gasp betrayed her vulnerability, her belief that if he drew her to him, they would indeed become lovers. His body hardened, and his blood pounded hot.

Bedamned. He burned to lay her down, strip her naked, and do what they both desired.

"When you try to leave," he said through a wash of heat, "you will fail."

Anger blazed in her eyes, but she was wise enough not to argue.

He gazed upon his home, which had been hewn from the rock with blood, sweat, and pride. Too many men had given their lives for him to risk Linet's secret jeopardizing the freedom the rebels sought. He was unsure of the exact threat she presented, but instinct screamed that she was more than she appeared. Until he knew the truth, had squelched any threat she offered, she would stay beneath his protection.

Seathan nudged his mount forward and caught

up with his brothers. A sense of rightness as well as pride infused him as he, along with Alexander and Duncan, rode up the causeway to Lochshire Castle.

"Lord Grey arrives!" a knight called in the distance.

Chains rattled, orders were called out, and the thick wooden drawbridge groaned as it was lowered to settle upon the earth.

Home.

Seathan inhaled. A sense of nostalgia filled him as memories of his youth overwhelmed him, of the day he was knighted by his father.

Warmth rippled upon his chest.

A smile curved his mouth as he touched the halved moss agate pendant hanging there, a gift presented after his knighting from his grandmother. A woman who'd long since passed away, but a woman he still loved.

Linet moved in the saddle before him, and the warmth of his memories fell away. He made another vow—she would change nothing. Long before fall, he would know the secrets she held, have delivered her to the Highlands, and she would be gone from his life. He kicked his mount forward.

Hooves thrummed against the weathered wood of the drawbridge as he and his brothers cantered over. The shadows of the gatehouse enveloped them, the cool darkness at odds with the burst of light as they rode into the bailey, his knights crowding within the grassy expanse to greet him.

"My lord," his master-at-arms called. His expression

sobered as he took in Seathan's bedraggled state. "You are wounded?"

"Aye." Alexander dismounted. "Call for the healer. Have her sent to my brother's chamber."

"Aye, Sir Alexander." The master-at-arms turned and hurried back through the crowd.

Linet shifted, and he caught the paleness of her face, and the worry within her gaze. "You will not be harmed."

Her stomach churning with doubts, Linet was far from convinced.

"You saved my life," he said. "For that you will be lauded."

"So you say." On edge, she studied the throng of people, strangers who regarded her with open curiosity, loyal followers who would believe what their lord said. She believed Seathan would not lie. At least she had that.

"Alexander!"

At the woman's lyrical voice, dread swept through Linet.

As if in slow motion, the people gathered within the courtyard fell back, carving a pathway within the crowd.

No one appeared. Relief swept through her.

A glimmer of auburn hair filtered through the crowd.

Linet stilled.

A second passed.

Another.

The blur of a woman came into view.

Grew clear.

Sweet Mary! She didn't need to see the woman's eyes to know their color—gray. Her laughter, her intelligence, and sharp wit—traits Linet had always admired.

She had to get out of here before she was recognized!

"Do you know her?" Seathan asked.

Linet froze. In her panic, she'd forgotten a crucial fact. She sat before Seathan, a warrior who missed nothing.

The auburn-haired woman broke from the crowd. She turned toward Seathan, and a smile burst upon her face. Then, the woman's gaze landed upon Linet. The auburn-haired woman grew still. A frown wove across her brow.

Linet didn't move.

Only prayed that somehow, Lady Nichola Westcott, the Englishwoman she'd met at King Edward's court, wouldn't recognize her.

Chapter 8

Time stood still. Linet braced for the damning moment of recognition, for surprise to widen Lady Nichola's eyes. And for the woman whose brother was King Edward I's Scottish advisor to greet her.

Instead, like a blessing, Nichola continued to stare at her, perplexed.

Duncan stepped to Alexander's side, breaking the woman's line of sight, allowing Linet a brief reprieve. After a quick glance around the bailey, then a frown, Duncan nodded to Alexander. "See to your wife. I will aid Seathan."

Seathan shot his youngest brother a hard look. "I need no aid."

Linet ignored the brothers' interchange. This noblewoman whose brother held a high political office, and ties to King Edward, was Alexander's wife? That would explain the Englishwoman's presence in Scotland, but not how a lady of her stature had come to meet, much less marry, an enemy of England.

In stunned silence, she watched as Alexander strode to Nichola, caught her in his arms, and hauled her flush against him. Before the knights gathered in the bailey, the men standing guard upon the wall walk, he drew her into an intimate and wholly possessive kiss.

Heat swept Linet's cheeks at the bold display, but a part of her envied that a revered warrior would dare show such strong affection before his men. Never could she envision Fulke allowing any woman such importance in his life. But she found nothing weak in Alexander's passion, or his obvious love for his wife. If anything, she lauded his confidence as a man to dare a blatant show of affection.

"Down with you now." Duncan set his hands upon her waist and lifted Linet from her mount.

On the ground, she glanced up toward Seathan and stilled. His face had turned ashen. His eyes, though steady upon her, darkened with pain.

"Seathan!" She caught his hand, her worries about Nichola falling away.

His mouth tightened. Seathan withdrew his hand from her touch, nodded to Duncan without turning toward her. "Take the lass inside," he ordered, his burr rich.

Anger flared. The pig-headed fool. "You need—"

"Nothing." He nodded to Duncan. "Go." Seathan's command severed further argument.

Duncan shot a worried frown toward his brother, then gently clasped her arm. "Come. 'Tis for the best."

Linet hesitated. "He needs help."

As if to prove her claim false, Seathan swung to the ground, his grip tight on his mount, his feet steady upon landing, but she caught the slightest tremor of his body.

"Tell me," she hissed, anger coating her words, "will you appear so powerful if you fall flat on your arse?"

Seathan shot Duncan a hard look.

"Come, lass." Duncan gently drew her away.

Frustrated, she glared one last time at Seathan as his youngest brother led her away. At their approach, people stepped aside to let them pass, but she didn't miss their curious looks.

Nichola? Where was she?

Nerves prickling over her skin, Linet scanned the crowd for the Englishwoman. Relief swept through her as she recognized no one. Thank God, Alexander must have taken her to the keep.

Unable to catch a glimpse of Lord Grey through the crowd, Linet turned her attention to Duncan. "Seathan is barely able to stand on his own," she said in a quiet voice.

"He is," Duncan agreed, "but once in his chamber, he will be well cared for. He will allow it to be no other way." They walked several steps through the throng of people. "Do not judge a man you know little of."

"I may not know him," Linet said, "but I understand too well the actions of power-driven men."

Intrigue sparked in his eyes as he glanced over. "You misread my brother's motive."

"Do I? Does he not wish for everyone to see his strength?"

With a noncommittal sigh, Duncan urged her forward. "Come, my lady. There will be time enough for questions later. And," he said with a smile, "time to get to know better a woman whom my brother finds a challenge."

"I am not—"

"Duncan?"

Nichola! She'd thought Alexander had taken his wife inside!

With a twinkle in his eyes, Duncan drew them to a halt, turned toward Nichola, ignorant of Linet's panic. He lifted the Englishwoman's hand, gave a courtly bow. "Nichola, I have missed the warmth of your smile and the light in your eyes."

The Englishwoman laughed. "You have missed naught but your wife."

Dimples deepened in his face. "Aye, 'tis true." He glanced around, frowned. "Where is she?"

"Out with several women picking herbs," Nichola replied. "She should return before long."

"I will be sure to greet her properly upon her return," Duncan said.

Nichola's lips twitched. "Of that I have no doubt." She turned to Linet. "Excuse my brother-in-law, his desire to charm often outweighs propriety. We have yet to be introduced."

Nichola didn't remember her? Unsure how to respond, Linet chose silence.

Nichola laid her hand upon Linet's forearm. "Forgive me, I did not mean to embarrass you."

"I am sure her lack of response is due to the lass being shy," Duncan replied, his voice dry.

Curiosity flickered on Nichola's face as she cast a speculative look from Duncan to Linet, then removed her hand.

"Lady Linet," Duncan said, "meet my brother, Alexander's wife, Lady Nichola."

"A pleasure to meet you, Lady Nichola," Linet said, praying with all her might that the Englishwoman would not remember her.

Nichola hesitated, frowned. "You look familiar. Have we met before?"

Sweat trickled down Linet's neck. "You are English, are you not?"

A knowing smile touched Nichola's mouth. "You mean, how did I come to wed a Scot and live in a rebel stronghold?"

Heat stroked Linet's cheeks, but the other woman waved her hand in dismissal.

"It is a common enough question." Nichola smiled. "And a story I will tell you once you are settled. That is, if you are interested to hear."

"Yes, please," Linet replied. Not that she planned to be around that long.

"Lady Linet saved Seathan's life," Duncan interjected.

The lightness of moments before fell away. Nichola glanced at Seathan, who slowly made his way toward the keep, then turned to Duncan. "How was he wounded?"

"Wounded nay," Duncan spat. "Tortured."

Nichola's face paled. "By whom?"

Duncan's jaw tightened. "The Viscount of Tearlach."

"May the scoundrel rot in Hades." Nichola paused, met Linet's gaze, her gaze unwavering. "My words are harsh, but I will not ask for forgiveness. Seathan is like a brother to me. If within my power, none will harm him or those I love."

Linet swallowed hard, the woman's warning loud and clear. She would not be foolish enough to incite her anger. The Englishwoman was indeed a good match for Alexander.

"Nor will I," Linet agreed.

Nichola's face softened. "Then it seems we will get along fine." She shook her head, a smile touching her mouth. "Look at me. You have just arrived and here I keep you outside when you are tired and dusty from travel, and with the coolness of this spring day, no doubt cold. Once you are bathed and rested, we will talk more. For now, I thank God for your actions. We owe you much."

Linet shook her head. "Nay, you owe me—"

"Come," Nichola said, trampling her words. "I will take you to a chamber so you may rest." She turned toward the keep.

Duncan lifted a brow, leaned close to Linet's ear. "It seems you have made a friend."

If only that were true. Linet would savor having a confidante, someone to turn to, to reveal her deepest fears. With Fulke as her brother, that would never be Nichola, or anyone within this castle.

"And how is the lad?" Duncan asked as they walked, pride filling his voice.

A sheen of pure joy swept over Nichola. She smiled. "I nursed Hughe but a short while before you arrived. Now, he is fast asleep, and you will not be waking him."

Duncan laid his hand upon his chest. "I am wounded by the charge."

Nichola laughed, smiled at Linet. "If I let him, Duncan would be sweeping the lad from his nap in a trice."

"How could I not, Hughe being my first nephew. He has the devil's black hair like his father, but is blessed with his mother's charming smile and disposition." He winked at Nichola. "Besides, 'tis my right to spoil the babe."

Their easy banter left an ache within Linet's soul. To hold a child of the man you loved. Until this moment she'd not entertained the notion, but Nichola's marriage to a rebel was proof that differences could be set aside, and against overwhelming odds, love could be found.

"Duncan!" a woman's lyrical voice called from behind them as they reached the keep's door.

A bold smile lit his face. He whirled.

Intrigued, Linet turned toward the gatehouse. Inside the stone entry stood a beautiful young woman. Whiskey-colored hair framed a face smudged by dirt. A thick cloak shielded the woman from the early spring chill. Herbs overflowed from a wicker basket on her arm, and her smile glowed with love.

"I will take Lady Linet to her chamber," Nichola told him.

Duncan hesitated.

"'Twould be unseemly for a man not to greet his wife properly upon his return," Nichola teased.

"Aye, it would," Duncan replied. "Rest assured, you will be well cared for. Nichola, make sure she is given a *special* chamber befitting a woman who saved Seathan's life."

Nichola hesitated, frowned. "Special?"

"The chamber within the tower." Duncan gave Nichola a wink. "Off with me now." With an eager expression, Duncan gave a half bow then sprinted to his wife.

Linet's heart ached. To be loved by a man so would be wondrous.

"They are truly in love."

She glanced at Nichola, saw curiosity as the Englishwoman waited for her response. "They are," she replied. It was too easy to become lost in emotions, in wishes that for now were out of her realm.

Easy and dangerous.

Had Nichola truly not remembered meeting her? Was her ignorance an act? No, she'd caught no flicker of deception. For now, thankfully, the woman recalled nothing.

"Come," Nichola said, "you need rest, not idle talk."

But the curious glance the noblewoman shot her suggested she wondered much about Linet's circumstance, including why Seathan had brought her to Scotland.

With a prayer that Nichola's lapse of memory would hold until after she'd left, Linet followed. She entered the keep behind the noblewoman, catching a glimpse of Duncan sweeping his wife in his arms and circling her around. Laughter boomed in his voice as he claimed her mouth in a fierce, loving kiss. Yes, though a rogue, like his brothers, he was a man who deeply loved.

As would Seathan if he ever overcame his distrust and gave a woman his heart.

In silence, she accompanied Nichola up the length of the spiral steps. Even within the vastness of Seathan's castle, Linet felt warmth, a sense that the people here truly cared for each other. But even as the residents bade her welcome, her own deception left her feeling cold.

They ascended to the next level, continued up. After numerous steps, a single chamber came into view, its entry forged with fine craftsmanship and graced with an elegance never expected on such a remote floor.

Linet glanced at Nichola. "An unusual door."

"It is." The Englishwoman smiled. "It was made for an unusual woman. Duncan wanted you to have the best." She drew the door open, but Linet didn't miss the forged brackets impaled within the carved oak panels, or the sturdy length of wood propped against the wall in the corner, ready to secure a prisoner if necessary.

"You will not be locked inside," Nichola said with a smile. "After saving Seathan's life, far from it."

If they knew the truth, her visit within this room would be very different indeed. No, not this room, she would be cast in Seathan's dungeon instead.

"Come, you are surely tired." Nichola entered.

Linet followed in her wake. Though the door hinted at more than normal living quarters, she'd not expected the magnificence before her.

As if a wish granted, sunlight streamed through a single arched window, bathing the room within its iridescent glow. Flickers of dust danced playfully in the swathe of light as if conducted by an unseen hand.

Against the back wall lay a bed sheathed with an elegant, hand-stitched coverlet, its color an unusual blend of yellow and silver. Nearby, a small table sat adorned with an intricately carved bone comb, an ivory-framed mirror, and several fine pieces of jewelry. Upon the far wall hung a finely crafted tapestry bearing a forest scene, woven with images of fairies peeking through the breaks in the leaves.

Overwhelmed with the unexpected beauty, Linet looked up. And her breath caught. Painted upon the ceiling lay a sprinkle of fairies caught in a spritely dance.

Wait, the fairies . . .

She looked toward the tapestry and back up again. Intriguing. At first, she'd believed each of them to be unique. Now, she saw the creator had painted a duplicate of the images woven within the tapestry, except on the ceiling the fairies were revealed to the viewer in full, as if they'd flown from their shield of leaves to play.

"I was enchanted when I first entered the room as well," Nichola said, her voice soft, as if to speak loudly would break a magic spell.

Linet met her gaze. A sense of bizarre belonging infused her, a rightness she'd never anticipated. "The chamber, paintings, everything . . . they are truly wondrous."

"As was the woman who once lived here."

"Who was she?"

The Englishwoman smiled. "The brothers' grandmother. A woman they loved and who loved them very much in return. I never met her, but the stories they tell make me wish I had."

"It is odd," Linet said, unsure whether she should admit her thoughts.

"What?"

"'Tis strange I know, but I feel . . ."

"Welcome?" Nichola finished, curiosity touching her expression.

Stunned to be read so accurately, Linet frowned. "How did you know?"

"When I first entered, I, too, felt the same."

Though lightly spoken, Linet sensed an implication she did not understand. From the other side of the bed, a sparkle of light caught her eye. On the sturdy stand rested a bowl, within sat two halved gems. She gasped.

Nichola touched her arm. "What is it?"

Linet rubbed her brow. "I must be overtired."

She dropped her hand. "Tell me."

"In the bowl, a stone . . ." Linet let her words fall away, unsure of how to explain her urge to walk toward it.

"It is a halved gem, a moss agate," Nichola explained. "It is believed to hold the ability to make warriors powerful and shield them from those who would bring them harm. Seathan wears its mate on a chain around his neck." A smile lingered on her mouth. "A gift his grandmother bestowed to him upon his knighting."

Linet remembered the halved stone around Seathan's neck. "And what is the other halved gemstone?"

"Other gemstone?" Nichola rounded the bed and halted. Her face paled.

Linet moved to her side. "What is wrong?"

"I . . ." She stepped back, a stunned expression on her face. "Nothing."

There was something wrong, but the Englishwoman wouldn't divulge whatever had upset her.

Air brushed across Linet's cheek, and she almost jumped. She turned, expecting to find that a servant had entered. Instead, except for her and Nichola, the room stood empty.

"Lady Linet?" the noblewoman inquired, her voice cautious.

"It is nothing," she said, feeling foolish. She rubbed her arms. "I but felt a breeze."

Silence.

"The window is closed."

Tensing, Linet looked over. Indeed, the window was secured. "What is going on?"

"Worry not. 'Tis a common occurrence within this chamber."

But Linet heard the other woman's unease, again sensed something was amiss.

A warm smile curved Nichola's mouth, but edges

of uncertainty tainted her attempt. "Seathan will explain once he has rested."

Seathan. The reality of why she was at Lochshire Castle hit her. Nerves jangled as she glanced around the amazing room, a chamber filled with love, a room belonging to a woman the brothers loved. Given the minimal time she would remain here, it would be wrong for her to stay in this luxury. She was not the woman they believed her to be. Mayhap she had saved Seathan's life, but righteousness had little to do with her motive.

Guilt had Linet taking a step toward the entry. "Please, a simple chamber is all I require."

"The oddities of the chamber have upset you?"

"No." Linet looked around, torn. "I cannot explain why, but I feel at ease here, more so than in a long while."

"Then there will be no further discussion." Nichola held up her hand before Linet could object. "Please remain. And after saving Seathan's life, it would be our honor." A smile touched her mouth. "Duncan said to give you the tower chamber, a room that is special. I assure you, everything about this room is that."

Words of refusal came to Linet's lips, but a wave of dizziness enveloped her, erasing further objections. She laid her hand upon her forehead. She was so tired. Would it be wrong to remain here? The chamber was indeed beautiful. "My thanks."

Concern darkened Nichola's eyes. "After your hard travel these past few days, you are exhausted."

As Seathan must be. She prayed a healer was treating him now; then he would rest.

Nichola walked to the door. "There is a bowl with water and a cloth on a stand at your side. After you bathe, I will have a servant bring you stew to tide you until we sup."

"No, please," Linet said, suddenly exhausted. "I wish only to rest."

"I will leave you then." Nichola hesitated, frowned. "You are sure we have never met?"

"No." The lie echoed within the silence, feeding Linet's guilt. She truly liked Lady Nichola, and had so upon their first meeting at King Edward's court. But to reveal the truth would yield dire consequences.

The Englishwoman gestured toward the hearth, which was readied with kindling. "You can break your fast in the morning once you awaken. And I will at least send a servant to light the fire."

A chill swept her, and Linet rubbed her arms. "My thanks, a fire would be appreciated."

Nichola paused as if she would say more, then, with a nod, exited the chamber.

The soft clunk of the door closing reverberated through the room. For a brief moment, panic ripped through Linet as if she'd heard the scrape of the wood, the thunk of a barrier falling into place. No. Nichola would not lock her in. 'Twas her own guilt that fueled such a desperate thought.

With a yawn, Linet turned toward the bed, but found her gaze drawn to the bowl. Odd, as she stared at it, the moss agate seemed to glow.

Uneasy, Linet glanced around the chamber but saw nothing else out of the ordinary. Nichola's words that Seathan would explain the uniqueness of this room came to mind. What was there about this chamber that she should know? Was it haunted? A smile flickered upon her mouth. No, it was but her overtired mind conjuring thoughts that she'd otherwise not consider.

As she continued to stare, as if drawn by a force she could not define, she found herself walking closer. With every step, the sense of peace grew stronger, a comfort so deep it touched her soul.

Never one for trivial musings, she wanted to laugh at the foolishness of it all, but however strange, this moment seemed to inspire whimsical thoughts.

At the table's edge, she halted. Framed within a gold-encrusted outer layer, the halved gem's center was a milky white, infused with what appeared to be petrified spirals of moss.

The moss agate.

To its right lay another gemstone. Intrigued, she picked up the unique halved round, the roughness of its exterior similar to the moss agate, but the similarities ended there. Inside, a burst of color extended from a pale green to a deep olive hue within its center. It was as if the gemstone were caught in turmoil.

Why had Nichola paled as she'd viewed the contents of the bowl?

Linet returned the olive-and-pale-green stone. The moss agate was what truly caught her interest.

She lifted the halved gemstone, cradled it within her palm.

A soft pulse of energy seemed to radiate through her; the gem grew warm upon her skin.

Sweet Mary! Linet almost dropped the moss agate as she placed it back in the bowl. What was going on?

The light within the gem began to fade.

She rubbed her arms, and stepped back. She'd felt nothing. No warmth, no tingle had spread through her body. Naught but fatigue guided her thoughts, which a solid dose of rest would cure.

A light knock sounded.

Pulse racing, she whirled, unsure of what to expect. "Enter."

The door opened. A lad around the age of ten summers with a crop of muddy brown hair entered. He gave a brisk bow. "My lady, I am here to light a fire."

She exhaled a shaky sigh. "Please."

He withdrew a flint and knife and hurried to complete his task. In moments, flames stirred to life and slowly engulfed the tinder before catching the larger logs.

The boy stepped back. "Did you need anything else, my lady?"

"No. My thanks."

With a nervous bow, he turned and hurried out.

The crackle of the fire echoed within the chamber, the rich scent of the wood infusing the room. More than ready for sleep, she quickly washed, then stretched out upon the bed, thankful for the comfort, smiling as she realized it was feathers filling the mattress, not straw.

On a sigh, Linet peered at the fairies painted upon the ceiling, her eyes growing heavy. She paused upon the raven-haired fairy in the moss green gown, her silver-tipped wings caught in midflutter as she landed on a lush, purple-tipped thistle. As if a trick of the light, the fairy smiled at her.

Smiled?

Linet tried to sit up, but her limbs, as if weighted by stones, refused to comply.

The tinkle of laughter echoed around her, a soft sound of gentle amusement. Her nose was tickled with the faint scent of lavender.

The soft fragrance soothed her; the quiet laughter in the air was like listening to a child's happy play. Truly at peace for the first time since before her parents' deaths, Linet closed her eyes and fell into sleep's embrace.

Seathan shoved himself to a sitting position, and pain streaked through him at his quick movement. He stared at Nichola in shock. "You did what?"

Alexander immediately stepped beside his wife. "Do nae be upset with Nichola. With the mayhem of your arrival, being told that Lady Linet saved your life, and with Duncan telling her to give Lady Linet the tower chamber, why would she put the lass anywhere else but our grandmother's room?"

Bedamned! "Duncan's meddling caused this mix-up?" His anger shoved up a notch.

Humor glinted in Alexander's gaze. "Aye, but what is your worry? 'Tis you who claims the tower chamber is only a chamber, not a room that holds magic.".

Only a chamber? With both brothers married to women who'd stayed within the tower chamber upon their arrival at the castle, Linet's installment there was no laughing matter.

Nichola shook her head. "I did not mean to cause you upset, but do not blame Duncan alone. Even without his prodding, I would have felt obligated to give her the most luxurious chamber. And with Lady Linet already settled, it would be improper to ask her to move, or to explain."

"Aye," Seathan agreed, but the thought of her staying within his grandmother's chamber left him uneasy.

Nichola glanced from her husband to Seathan, then frowned. "Why do I sense that more than Lady Linet staying in the tower room is at issue?"

Alexander took her hand, blew out a deep breath. "We are unsure of Lady Linet's motivation for freeing Seathan."

Nichola stilled. "You believe she is working in league with Lord Tearlach?"

"I am not sure, but if so, I will find out." Seathan grimaced, the wounds sewed by the healer throbbing. "Whatever her motives, upon awakening, she will be moved to another chamber."

Not that he believed that the room had a spell cast upon it, or that the woman who stayed within was destined to marry the man who brought her to Lochshire Castle. That was but a superstition.

Nichola cleared her throat, slanted a nervous look toward Seathan. "There is one other thing."

"Go on," Seathan said.

"It is about the bowl in the chamber that contains the gems." She reached to touch the other half of Alexander's halved azurite, a gift he'd presented to her when they'd wed.

The hairs on the back of Seathan's neck prickled. "You mean the one gem."

She shook her head. "No." Her fingers trembled. She dropped her hand to her side. "I saw them. There were two."

Chapter 9

"Two?" Seathan and Alexander asked in unison.

Nichola glanced at her husband, then toward Seathan. "I swear, had I not seen them both, I would not have believed it either."

Seathan grimaced. Of the four original gemstones, the only one remaining in the bowl was the other half of his moss agate. His other two brothers were already married. The only other person to have been awarded a halved gemstone was . . .

It could not be! God's teeth, he would see for himself. Seathan swung his legs off the bed and stood. The room spun around him.

Determination tightened Alexander's face as he stepped before him. "You are not fit to be up and moving about."

"Move out of my way."

Alexander didn't budge. "The stones will be there on the morrow."

Nichola stepped beside her husband. "If you go up there now, you will awaken Lady Linet. She is exhausted and needs to rest." Gray eyes pleaded with him. "As do you."

"A few hours are little time to wait," Alexander added when Seathan hesitated, "for all of us."

Bedamned. Alexander and Nichola's reasons for waiting until first light made sense. Besides, if he went to the tower chamber now, he'd look more a fool than lord of the castle.

With a grimace, Seathan settled back upon the bed. He met Nichola's worried eyes. "Describe the second halved gemstone." He would at least have that.

Nichola scraped her teeth across her lower lip, then glanced at her husband.

Christ's blade! "Tell me," Seathan said.

"The gemstone," she said softly, "appears to be Patrik's malachite."

The full impact of her meaning sank in. Seathan shot to his feet. "It cannot be!" The room again blurred, but he focused on Nichola, on the impossibility of her claim. Though adopted, Patrik was family, their love for him as deep as if he were born of their blood.

Alexander caught his arm. "You need to be abed!"

"Lie back down," Nichola urged. "You are going to fall over."

Seathan jerked his arm free. "Not until I know what in bloody hell is going on!"

Alexander shook his head. "I am as upset as you. Upon Patrik's death, the half within the bowl matching the gemstone he once wore around his neck disappeared."

"I know," Nichola replied, rubbing her finger along the side of her gown. "And when we returned from Patrik's gravesite, we all saw the empty space within the bowl where his halved gemstone used to reside. But I swear to you, this stone looks exactly like the same one I saw when you first locked me in your grandmother's chamber."

Seathan clenched his fist. "If Patrik's malachite has reappeared, why now?"

Alexander grimaced. "Mayhap a better question is, was it ever gone?"

Seathan paused. "What do you mean?"

"What if after his death, someone removed it," Alexander explained, "and now has decided, for whatever reason, to return it?"

"That makes no sense." Seathan blew out a frustrated breath. "It is true that the guard sent back with Patrik's body disappeared once he'd finished burying him. But I doubt the guard would reappear to return the stone after all this time. But what other explanation is there?"

Alexander held his gaze. "Our grandmother's magic."

Seathan gave a grunt of dismissal. He had little use for such foolery. "I will check to see if the guard who buried Patrik's body has returned. I do nae think—"

The door opened. Duncan stepped in, Isabel at his side. "'Tis good to see you up and—" He stopped, scanned those within the chamber, and drew his wife nearer. "What is it?"

"Patrik's gemstone," Seathan stated. "Nichola

believes she saw it within the bowl in our grandmother's chamber."

Duncan's face paled. "'Tis not possible."

"Normally, I would agree," Alexander said as he gave his wife's hand a comforting squeeze, "but Nichola saw Patrik's gemstone before it disappeared. I have no doubt she would recognize it if she saw it again."

Isabel frowned. "If so, it is strange that his gemstone appears now."

"Not strange at all when magic is involved," Duncan said, relaxing a degree.

"It could somehow be tied to the disappearance of the guard who buried Patrik," Seathan stated, preferring that logical explanation. But his younger brother's reference to their grandmother, to the notion that she was wielding her influence from the great beyond, settled ill within his mind.

He pushed away the disturbing thoughts, and instead focused on the lad his family had adopted so many years ago, who had died tragically last fall. He ached with the memory, a sadness that only years would ever ease.

What did the reappearance of their adopted brother's halved malachite mean? Was he alive? No, they'd all seen the grave where the guard had buried his body. Still, Seathan couldn't remove the wedge of doubt.

"You think the guard who disappeared after burying Patrik took it," Duncan asked with a look of sheer disbelief, "and now decides it is a fine time to return it?"

"It does sound far-fetched," Seathan agreed.

"So," Alexander broke in with a twinkle in his eye, "our grandmother has added Patrik's malachite to the bowl in her chamber."

Seathan glared at his middle brother. "There is no connection to our grandmother or any binding spell." In his mind, the joke had long since run its course. He walked to the window, a pounding building in the back of his head. He stared into the sky, where night was gradually smothering the last remnants of the day. God's teeth, this new twist wasn't making a dram of sense.

"Until I see the malachite half for myself," Duncan stated from behind him, "I will not believe it is Patrik's."

Seathan turned, waving Nichola away when she gestured for him to sit. "Until Linet awakens and we can inspect the tower chamber, we will have no further answers." His throat grew dry. What if indeed it was Patrik's malachite? He'd believed himself past the worst of his sorrow, but as he thought of his brother, he acknowledged his grief was still very raw.

He blew out a deep breath, caught a glimmer of interest in his younger brother's face.

"Lady Linet is asleep inside our grandmother's room?" Duncan asked with mock surprise.

Seathan scowled at his younger brother.

"I will say," Duncan continued, the humor in his tone easing the somber mood within the chamber, "that I am surprised you placed the lass in our grandmother's chamber"—he winked at Alexander—"with the matching spell and all."

"You donkey's arse," Seathan growled, "'twas your meddling that put Linet there."

"Linet, is it?"

Seathan mentally cursed. He knew better than to play into Duncan's teasing.

"Our brother does seem unusually intrigued with the lass," Alexander prodded. "Methinks mayhap our grandmother has grand plans for the lad."

Seathan scowled at them both. "There is no magic about the chamber." He narrowed his eyes at his youngest brother. "The tale is but a story we made up to worry Alexander when he abducted Nichola."

"It was," Duncan agreed, "but that I should have married Isabel after she resided within the same room seems to me more than a coincidence." At Seathan's silence, Duncan winked at Nichola. "Tell me, did the lass notice Seathan's moss agate in our grandmother's bowl?"

Alexander arched a brow at his wife. "'Tis an answer I find myself curious to know as well."

"You both have the sense of mottled meal," Seathan snapped.

"Nichola?" Alexander asked.

She nodded.

"Whoo, lad, she did!" Duncan chortled.

"It means naught," Seathan said through gritted teeth.

"So that is why you are surly as a mother bear protecting her cubs." Duncan waved his hand with a theatric sweep. "'Twould seem the lad is doomed."

Alexander chuckled. "Aye, 'twill be a priest we will be needing within a sennight."

"Enough!" Seathan stated. "There will be no need for a priest. Instead of discussing such foolery as spells, we should focus on learning the true reason for Lady Linet's appearance at my cell door on the eve before I was to be hanged." At his reminder of his suspicions about her, the smiles of everyone within the chamber fell away.

Somber, Isabel met her husband's gaze. "You told me Lady Linet freed Seathan from Breac Castle."

"She did," Duncan replied, "but we know not her reason or little more about her."

"Do you not trust her?" Isabel asked.

And therein lay the crux of his problem. Seathan glanced out the window, where a floor above Linet lay asleep. "I do not know."

Nichola stood at the chamber window, mesmerized by the moonbeams upon the thin veil of ice remaining along the loch's shore, as if a delicate frame to the mirror of water caught within.

Strong arms wrapped around her from behind and pulled her into a gentle embrace. "I woke to find our bed cold and you gone," Alexander whispered as he nibbled his way along the curve of her chin. "I thought you were nursing our babe, but then I spied you standing amongst the moonbeams." He nuzzled the sensitive column of her throat. "Have I mentioned that I am the luckiest knight within the realm? A fact I will prove once I have you abed."

She gave him a smile, but it fell away as quickly.

Alexander lifted his head, turned her toward him. He frowned as he studied her in the swath of silvery light. "You are troubled."

"I cannot rid Lady Linet from my mind."

"Has she threatened you? By my sword I will—"

"No, it is nothing like that."

"Then what?"

Nichola stared out into the moon-spun sky. "When I first saw Lady Linet within the courtyard, I . . ." She turned to face him. "I thought I knew her."

Alexander tensed. "You did not mention this before."

"Because I am not sure if I do." She exhaled. "With my parents of high noble birth and Griffin's position as King Edward's Advisor to Scottish Affairs, over the years I have met so many people that their faces blur in my mind. But when I saw Lady Linet, she seemed so familiar."

"Did you ask if you had been introduced to her before?"

"Yes. She said no."

At Alexander's thoughtful expression, anxiety rippled through Nichola. "Do you think she was lying?"

"I cannot be sure, but then, we know so little about her." A grimace dug across his brow. "A fact that Lady Linet has used to her advantage. From the first she give Seathan no explanation other than that she wishes to travel to the Highlands."

"This is not making sense," Nichola said. "We know she is English; her speech, clothes, and manner give her away. What other reason would make her so evasive . . ." Her pulse kicked. "Think you that she indeed conspires with Lord Tearlach?"

"I do not know." Alexander slid his fingers along her forearm to capture her hand within his. "Regardless, we must inform Seathan that you believe you have met her."

"Not yet. I may be wrong. Mayhap her appearance merely reminds me of another."

"Nay, I—"

"Before we speak with him," Nichola said, "give me time. Let me see if I can remember her. It would be wrong to cast further doubt upon Lady Linet if indeed she is a stranger to me."

Alexander grunted. "Her own actions have invited that doubt."

"True, but she did free Seathan. We owe her for saving his life."

"Two days," Alexander finally said. "If you remember naught by then, we will tell Seathan."

Relieved, she nodded.

Her husband grunted. "One thing we have learned is that the lass is foolhardy. While Seathan, Duncan, and I were on our return home, I watched her stand up to Seathan without hesitation."

Nichola's mouth dropped open. "It is hard to believe."

A smile kicked up on the side of his mouth. "Aye, a unique sight to be sure."

"And the mark of a strong woman."

"Or a fool."

"Or," Nichola said, "the trait of a woman comfortable dealing with powerful men."

Alexander grimaced as he mulled over that possibility, and she remembered that when she'd first met her husband, she had never imagined she would feel so blessed to be with him. At the memory she smiled, far from intimidated by this fierce warrior, a man who had abducted her a year past, a man whose son now lay asleep in the corner nook.

"What is on your mind?" he grumbled.

"That I am blessed to have you as my husband."

"Aye, you are at that." In a purely possessive move, he swept her into his arms and carried her to a bed still mussed from their earlier lovemaking. "And before our son awakens, a fact I am going to remind you of many times over."

Memories of the places he'd touched, the things he'd done to her this night, had heat sweeping through her.

With a growl, he laid her on their bed.

She smiled, and the fire in his eyes ignited into a ferocious blaze. In a deft move, he ripped the sheer gown from her. Hands on his hips, he scanned her body with uncensored lust. As he claimed her mouth in a powerful kiss, Nichola's thoughts of Lady Linet fled.

Through the carved stone window, the first hints of daylight warmed the cloud-strewn sky, casting majestic hints of purple into a gray-black wash. Seathan ignored the beauty of the sunrise and winced as he shoved himself up the steps to his grandmother's chamber. His brothers' foolish tales of spells and magic were ridiculous.

Still, his curiosity to view the stones within his grandmother's bowl had left him unable to sleep. Was the other gemstone indeed Patrik's?

His heart ached as he thought of Patrik's senseless death. Understanding his adopted brother's hatred of the English could not lessen his grief at losing the man he'd loved.

The fated day replayed in his mind. He and his brothers had searched the nearby woods for Nichola, who was then Alexander's prisoner. At her distant scream, he'd ridden hard, only to come upon Patrik, already dead.

Fresh grief swirled in his throat, the passage of time erased as if the tragedy had occurred but moments before. Patrik had never accepted that Alexander had fallen in love with an Englishwoman. Loyal to his country, to his brothers in spirit, he'd attempted to kill Nichola, to save Alexander from what Patrik believed to be a monumental mistake.

And he'd died in the trying.

Sadness swept through Seathan for a brother lost. Why had he not sensed Patrik's hatred toward Nichola before it was too late? Though none had accused him, as lord of Lochshire Castle, he'd let his family down.

Oddly, after Patrik's death, the half stone gifted to him by Seathan's grandmother had disappeared. Alexander and Duncan believed their grandmother had reclaimed it. Whatever had happened to the malachite, Seathan was sure magic was not involved.

The echo of his boots slapped upon stone, a somber cadence to his unsettling thoughts. Gritting his teeth, he forced himself up the turret, his body reminding him that it needed more time to heal. Seathan pushed on. God's teeth, he would have his answers.

As he climbed the next step, the door to his grandmother's chamber came into view. He halted.

It seemed to glow.

'Twas but the early hour along with his weariness spinning tales in his mind. He rubbed his eyes, looked up.

Shards of sunlight streamed through the darkness to illuminate the entry, but the mythical aura of moments before had vanished. He frowned. The door had not changed. He'd seen an image conjured by exhaustion.

The faint calls of his guards making their rounds and the stirrings of the castle's residents as they began their daily chores echoed within the silence of the turret. The distant clatter of pots and sounds of cleaning from the keep below added to the normality of the new day.

He climbed the last few steps, ready to be done with this deed, then focus on Dauid. Aye, another day, two at most, then he would ride. He would find his people's betrayer, a man whom he'd grown up with, a man whom he'd believed he could trust, and a man who'd betrayed those he'd once vowed to protect.

Anger trembled through Seathan's body. He seized

the emotion; 'twould serve to banish any foolish thoughts of Linet.

He knocked.

Silence.

With a grimace, he tugged the door open, stepped inside, and stopped. Linet lay tangled within the sheets, her long amber-gold hair strewn in a haphazard array to cradle her face in a rumpled sweep. A pale, slender leg peeked from the fine linen. And her breaths tumbled in soft cadence from full, soft lips. His chest squeezed tight. She looked like a fairy who'd drunk a charmed sleeping potion.

He turned toward the bowl.

A shimmer of light flickered from within.

Nay, it was naught but the reflections of the sun's rays. Disgusted with himself for allowing myths to influence him, he strode toward the small table.

Several paces away, stunned, he froze.

Christ's blade, 'twas indeed Patrik's malachite!

Pulse racing, he walked forward, lifted the gemstone, fighting a storm of emotions. How had it returned? He refused to believe his brothers' explanation of magic, focusing on the guard who'd disappeared. If the knight had taken it, why would he bring it back now?

A wisp of cold air swirled around him.

Pinpricks rippled over his skin.

Opening his eyes, he scoured his grandmother's quarters in a slow, methodical sweep. The door stood open as he'd left it. Through the window, sunlight now raced across the sky in a rich blend of hues ranging from purple to gold. But except for him and Linet, the chamber stood empty.

Seathan glanced toward the bed.

Eyes closed, she remained on her side, her even breathing indicating deep sleep.

He studied Patrik's halved gemstone within his palm. It lay cool against his skin, emitting not a sparkle, or a flicker of light. Magic was no more possible than the resurrection of a brother dead. The breeze he'd felt was created by the wind cascading through the castle turret, nothing more.

He returned the stone to the bowl next to the other half of his moss agate. Unsettled, he crossed to the window, where golden rays of sunlight now touched the loch, erasing the fog that had settled upon the surface from the chill of night.

On an exhale, Seathan studied the small plot of land inside the northern walls of Lochshire Castle where Patrik's grave lay.

The sorrow of his burial echoed through Seathan's mind. He, along with Alexander, Duncan, Nichola, and his men had stood before Patrik's grave. With the priest's somber words, Seathan had tossed a handful of dirt upon the fresh mound and shed tears for the senseless loss of a tormented, misguided man whom he'd loved as if they were bound by blood.

However much they wanted to believe Patrik was alive, he and his brothers must accept the truth.

Patrik was dead.

Linet's soft groan, thick with sleep, had him turning toward her.

The coverlet had slid down, exposing the full swells of her breasts. Riveted on her silken skin, on the hint of the darkened tips exposed with each breath, Seathan's body tightened with need.

She wrinkled her nose, sighed, then rolled onto her stomach, cutting off the seductive view. Still, the sunlight outlined her slender body with lust-stirring clarity.

He couldn't look away.

The soft fullness of her mouth slipped open. He imagined covering her lips, sliding down her lush body to savor the taste of her skin, the essence of her womanhood. Desire gathered inside him, fragmenting his hard-won control.

Her brow scrunched. Heavy lids slowly opened, then widened. She tugged the coverlet to her chin as she sat up. "What are you doing here?"

Her sleep-roughened words drove another shot of lust through him like a well-aimed sword. "What do you think?" he demanded, frustrated at Linet for her part in his confusion. Never before had his control wavered.

She wet her lips; he focused on the slick moisture. "You should not be here."

He chose a scowl to shield the feelings she inspired. "You will be moved this day."

Surprise, then panic, flared on her face. "To where?"

"To another chamber." Relief flickered in her gaze, shoving his annoyance up another notch. "You thought I would move you to my private chamber?"

"With you, I am never sure."

"A fact to heed."

She held his gaze. "You do not intimidate me."

"Intimidate you?" A wry smile settled on his mouth. What he wanted to inspire in her was hardly intimidation.

Linet angled her jaw. "It is not funny."

"Nay, far from it." What she made him feel, want, was not at all a laughing matter.

Chapter 10

Heart pounding, Linet focused on Seathan standing but an arm's length away, hands on his hips, his feet spread in a warrior's stance, and his eyes burning hot. She clenched the embroidered bed covering, the delicately sewn coverlet a pathetic shield against this powerful Scot's roving gaze.

Heat swept through her at the memories of his touch, his destroying kiss, and his muscle-carved body pressed against her. God help her if he touched her now.

She angled her chin and focused on the one man she could never have. "'Tis unseemly for you to be within my chamber without a chaperone."

Dry amusement edged through the hunger on his face. "Odd you choose now to worry about impropriety. In the dungeon but days past, you cared not."

"Your arrogance amazes me. Or have you forgotten that had I not freed you from Breac Castle, you would be dead?"

His jaw tightened. "I forget nothing, including the fact that you have avoided explaining why you would risk your life to save mine. Never have we met, neither are we related, and you are English."

"And half Scottish."

"Yes," he drawled, "let us not forget your watered-down heritage as well as your unexplained reason for fleeing Breac Castle."

The arrogant braggart! Eyes narrowed, she tugged the coverlet around her and scrambled to her feet. "You despise the English," she said, her words curt. "For that I blame you not, but to dismiss my Scottish heritage is not only slander against me, but against my Scottish mother as well. Say to me what you will, but the latter I will not tolerate."

His eyes bored through her, eyes that saw too much. They trailed over her, igniting fires of need wherever he looked, evoking memories of her dreams, in which he stood naked before her, then laid her upon his bed and slid into her with exquisite heat.

"I regret you believe that I would slight your mother, Scottish or no," Seathan said at last, his deep burr echoing through the chamber. "That was not my intent. I apologize."

His apology surprised her. Too aware of him, Linet stepped back. "I accept. You may go."

His eyes again narrowed. "You dismiss me from a chamber within my home?"

"Dismiss you?" The arrogant toad! "You crept inside my room while I slept! Or do you intrude upon all of the single women's chambers within your castle?"

Green eyes turned as black as the devil's own. "Collect whatever is yours."

"You will have to wait."

"I—"

She angled her chin. "In case you have overlooked the fact, I am in an indecent state of dress." As soon as she uttered the words, she wished them back. Seathan's hard glare of moments before darkened, a potent reminder he was not only a warrior but a man.

A very virile man.

A man assured of his abilities.

A man confident he would always leave a woman satisfied.

Sweet Mary! "I meant . . . you will depart so I may dress."

He stepped toward her as if a predator stalking its prey. "I will depart?" His gaze moved over her with excruciating, seductive slowness before pausing on her face. "You are quick to command those around you, my lady."

Shivers of awareness slid through her. "Nay twist my words. Any other man would not have dared intrude upon a woman alone in her chamber, much less barge in and issue orders."

"On that you are correct. Any other man in my position would have secured you within the dungeon until he had gained the truth from you as to why you set him free."

"Is it a crime to wish to travel to the Highlands?"

"If indeed that is your destination?"

"Why would I lie?"

"You tell me."

She adjusted the coverlet and held out her wrists. "Fine, then, if you think me so villainous, take me away, secure me until you discover the treachery you believe I conceal."

Seathan closed the distance between them, awareness swirling within the chamber as if a living, breathing thing. "Do not push me."

"Have you not pushed me from the first? Or is it," Linet said, anger rolling over her caution of moments before, "that only you, the exalted Earl of Grey, has the right to order anyone he chooses about, fairness be damned?"

Seathan caught her shoulders. "Fairness?" His voice lowered to a dangerous calm. "An odd word spoken in a realm where King Edward makes the rules, slaughters those who disagree. Had I been as *fair* as your English king, I would have escaped from the cell, locked it, and abandoned you within."

"You needed me to help carry you out."

"Nay, that I allowed you to believe."

She scoffed. "You would never have made it alone. Your injuries were too severe."

"Had the need arisen, I would have crawled to freedom."

"Or died trying."

"Aye."

And he would have. She swallowed hard. "I so tire of men of your ilk, men of arrogance with their thoughts centered on war." She paused. "Perhaps the mistake was mine. Perhaps I never should have set you free."

His hold on her tightened.

"So now will you punish me? Is that how you quell those who dare challenge you? If so, you are no better than the English king. Release me."

"You are afraid." It wasn't a question.

"I fear no man."

"Aye, you do. Your quickened pulse does not lie as charmingly as your lips." He lifted her chin. "You want me. Yet you fear a man who makes you feel, a man who makes you yearn for him in the middle of the night."

Seathan damned himself. Why was he cornering her? This close, with her full lips tempting his and her eyes dark with desire, he couldn't seem to step away.

"You make me feel nothing."

"Another lie. This," he whispered, "is truth." He covered her mouth, hot, hard, demanding a response, tasting the essence of this woman whom he wanted beyond all reason.

Instead of kissing him back, Linet closed her mouth against him.

He almost laughed. After their passionate interlude in the cave, he knew the heat within, the passion she withheld to prove her point. So he skillfully teased her mouth, nibbled along her earlobe, while he lazily seduced her with his fingers, skimming along the silky column of her throat until her body quivered against his.

At her gasp, he deepened the kiss in a hot assault,

using tongue and teeth in his sensual war. He waited for her rebellion, for her to struggle to break free. Instead, she surrendered, totally, completely, the intensity of her response almost driving him to his knees. Neither the kiss within the cave, nor that upon his steed, held a candle to this heat—a blaze that could devastate a man in a trice.

Behind her, the bed came into view, inviting him to lay her upon it, to strip her naked and make love until day changed to night. Then, through the sultry hours beyond, to satisfy her in every way, only to begin again.

Never had a woman evoked such strong desire within him, not even Iuliana, the woman who'd shattered his heart.

Linet's kiss was lush, untutored, and longing. She was an innocent, not his to take. And she never would be. He must keep his focus on Scotland's freedom, on finding Dauid.

Thoughts of the traitor cooled his desire.

Seathan released her. The flush of her face and the stark desire in her eyes urged him to reclaim her mouth. But if he touched her now, with his emotions raw, he'd make the gravest of errors—he'd make love with her. And with her looking at him as if a smitten enchanted fairy, she would allow it.

Enchanted fairy?

The errant thought severed the last of his lust-filled musings. He broke away and glared around the room.

Dust stirred the air in a furious sweep flecked with

glitters of light. The fairies woven within the tapestry hanging upon the wall seemed to smile at him.

Christ's blade! His mind was growing addled. His grandmother had had the second sight, and he'd respected her ability to foresee the future, but it ended there. Magic was but a bard's tale. Naught but his own decisions guided his life.

"What is wrong?" Linet asked, eyes wide, her voice rough with desire.

"Naught." Everything. He could almost feel his body being pushed toward the lass as if unseen hands urged him on while erotic visions of her naked and losing herself in their passion claimed his thoughts. He rubbed the low pounding beneath his brow, irritated with himself for allowing his mind to conjure such nonsense.

Linet glanced toward the sturdy table. Gasped. "The halved gemstone is glowing again."

Again? God's teeth! "'Tis naught but a trick of the light," he growled, ignoring the fact that the hand-crafted bowl lay within the shadows.

"But—"

"I will be back within an hour," he interrupted, determined to rectify this entire damnable situation. "Be ready."

Understanding creased her face. "I know why you want me to leave this chamber." She studied the room in awe. "It is truly luxurious. Peaceful. And belongs to someone you love." With her hand holding the coverlet tight against her body, she began gathering her things, but he didn't miss her trembling. "I will be ready to move upon your return."

"This was my grandmother's chamber."

She turned. "A fact explained by Nichola earlier."

Seathan turned on his heel and strode toward the exit. At the doorway he paused. "On the morrow I depart. I will be gone but a few days. Upon my return, I will take you to the Highlands."

"You are leaving so soon?"

He ignored the shock in her voice and opened the door.

"Wait," she called.

He turned. "A maid will escort you to your new chamber within the hour."

"A maid? You said you would return yourself."

"Be ready," he said, ignoring her question. Seathan strode from the chamber.

The overbearing oaf! Linet ran toward the door, halted. What would she do if she caught him? It was not as if he would listen to her. And if he did, what would she tell him? Regret stole through her. What could she tell him?

The answer was simple—nothing.

Frustrated, she returned to the bed. On shaky knees, Linet sagged upon the delicate coverlet. The memory of his mouth, the touch of his hands upon her, lingered, but she couldn't think about him or what he made her feel.

Seathan was leaving her here alone. Nay, not alone. Nichola was in the castle.

On edge, she stood, rubbed her hands upon the goose bumps prickling her skin. The Englishwoman had not yet recalled where they'd met or her name. Given Nichola's sharp mind, in time, she would. And loyal to Seathan, once she remembered their meeting, Nichola would alert him.

Linet released a shaky breath. For her own safety, before then, she must leave.

She glanced outside the window at the sun-streaked sky. If she hurried, she might slip away before anyone noticed she had left.

Linet dismissed any concern over the maid Seathan was sending. If the woman found the chamber empty, the servant would assume she had descended to break her fast. Hours would pass before anyone discovered her absence. Focused on his plans to depart on the morrow, Seathan would not even know she'd gone.

Her decision made, she hurried to dress. With dawn filling the chamber, she turned one last time to take in the room. She'd spent one night here, merely hours, but for the first time in years, she'd felt welcome, truly rested and safe.

The sparkle of light from the corner caught her attention. The gemstones. The halved moss agate continued to glow. Compelled, she walked over, ran her fingers over the smooth stone. Seathan's stone. An ache built in her throat.

In their short time together, he'd touched her life, had made such a deep impression she doubted she would ever cleanse his presence from her soul.

Against logic, against her every instinct, she cared for him. How could she not? Seathan was a man of compassion, a man of determination, and a man who protected what was his. The people within his castle respected him, his family loved him. Nobles were plentiful throughout the land, but few were men of substance, few were leaders. Lord Grey held the secret many powerful nobles strove for but never found—he was a man who loved deeply.

What would it be like if he loved her? She trembled, shaken by the thought, more so by the emptiness inside her, the desperation to know.

Throughout the time she'd known him, she'd tried to dismiss her feelings for him, assured herself his manner was too hard, too unyielding, and focused on war.

And had failed.

A tear slid down her cheek as the reason burst into her mind. God help her, she had fallen in love with Seathan.

Despite her determination not to, despite his boorish behavior in her bedchamber and her intent not to care, he'd stole past her defenses, entrenched himself where logic had no foothold.

Her heart pounded.

"I am a fool," she whispered into the thick silence. "I thought myself strong, needing no one, and here I love a man who is at odds with all I am trying to achieve."

She rubbed her face, stared out the window to where shards of morning sun swept over the land in a golden caress. An ache tightened in her throat. As if it was any day. A day for hopes. A day in which dreams lived.

Linet withdrew her hand and turned away. No, dreams didn't exist this day, only danger.

With her heart aching, she looked at the bowl one last time. The moss agate still glowed as if beckoning her. Though she might never have Seathan, would it be so wrong to keep a small part of what belonged to him?

Before she convinced herself otherwise, Linet clasped the halved gem. Warmth swirled in her palm and a sense of comfort infused her. With the moss agate stowed in her pocket, she took her cape and slipped from the chamber.

Flames rose in the hearth, the warmth filling the room as Seathan nodded to his brothers. "I have sent runners to several Scottish castles explaining Bishop Wishart's strategy for reclaiming Scotland. With the English king focused on the war against France, working to build an alliance with the Flemish, and ignorant of Bishop Wishart's guidance as well as that of the other Guardians of Scotland, we have the tactical advantage to regain Scotland's freedom."

"Aye," Alexander agreed. "And the heart."

Duncan took a long swig of ale at the war table strewn with unrolled maps, then set down the goblet. "When do you expect to hear word from Bishop Wishart?"

"Another month at most," Seathan replied. "With the English slaughtering all who oppose them, we cannot wait longer."

Alexander grimaced. "With you hobbling about, I still think it unwise that you travel on the morrow."

"Hobbling about?" Seathan asked. "My wounds are well healed and I—"

"You have rested little," Duncan interrupted, his expression hard. "Wait another day, if not two, before you go."

Seathan shoved to his feet, ignoring the tug of healing muscles. "I will wait no longer to find Dauid. Already he has enjoyed his freedom overmuch."

"Fine," Duncan agreed. "Then we will go with you."

"Nay." Seathan took a swig of his ale. "You will remain here for word from Bishop Wishart. Or from any of the other Guardians. We must be ready to fight."

Alexander cocked a brow. "And your leaving will help that?"

Seathan banged down his goblet. "We have a traitor in our midst."

"Aye." Alexander shoved away his ale and stood. "And I still find it difficult to believe Dauid betrayed us."

"As do I," Duncan agreed, standing beside his brother.

Seathan stared at the flames, his friend's treachery tearing at his soul. "Unless I had witnessed his treasonous act, it is the last thing I would have believed as well. 'Twas hard penning the missive to Wallace to warn him against a man we once called friend." He lifted his cup, swirled the golden brew.

"But then, war changes men, twists them into people no longer recognizable."

A knock sounded upon the door.

"Enter," Seathan ordered.

A runner stepped inside. He halted before Seathan and bowed. "My lord, I have come from Bishop Wishart. He sends his blessings and an urgent missive." He passed him a leather-bound writ.

"My thanks." Tension filled the chamber as Seathan untied the cured leather cover, withdrew the tightly wound parchment, then broke the seal. The cured goatskin scraped as he quickly unrolled it and read through the penned words. He stilled. "God's teeth!"

"What is wrong?" Alexander asked.

In stunned disbelief, Seathan looked up. The news threatened the rebels' very foundation. "Wallace has slain the English Sheriff of Lanark!"

Nichola paced along the wall walk in the warmth of the morning sunlight. She glanced toward the tower window of Alexander's grandmother's chamber, the room where Linet had slept this past night, the same chamber she'd resided in upon first coming to Lochshire Castle.

A smile flickered on her mouth. So much had changed since her arrival, since Alexander had abducted her and imprisoned her as *his captive.* The warmth of love filled her. Now she and Alexander had a son.

The shimmering rays glinted off the tower of

rock, the stone laid to build an impregnable defense. A chill swept her, and her smile fell away.

As if a door opened, she remembered standing within an opulent ballroom in King Edward's castle with her brother, Griffin. Of the many people he'd introduced her to, she focused on one.

Lady Linet Dancort.

God in heaven. Her breath caught. Linet was the sister of the Viscount of Tearlach, the noble who had imprisoned Seathan and sentenced him to die!

Except, Linet had set Seathan free.

Why?

A strong hand caught her shoulder; she jumped.

"I meant not to startle you," her husband said as he turned her toward him. Sharp eyes studied her face. "You are upset."

An understatement. She looked about to ensure no one would overhear them.

"Is the news so dire?" he teased.

Nichola lifted her gaze to meet his. Concern filled his eyes, but love as well, a love he'd given her when she'd expected naught but death. That was a year ago. Since then, everything had changed.

Now, he was her husband, a man she could trust, a man she would love forever, a man from whom she would never keep a secret, no matter how hard to reveal.

"Tell me."

His quiet words unsettled her further. "It is about Lady Linet. I know who she is." Then she quietly explained.

Alexander cursed. "Come. We must tell Seathan."

They hurried down the steps, then rushed to where Seathan quietly planned for war.

At their entrance, he turned. Seathan stepped forward. "What is wrong?"

Silence crawled through the chamber.

Nichola glanced once at her husband, then back toward Seathan, and wished she was wrong. "Linet is the Viscount of Tearlach's sister."

Chapter 11

"Lord Tearlach's sister!" Outrage poured through Seathan. Whatever he'd envisioned as Linet's secret paled in comparison to the truth.

From the start she'd lied to him. Everything about her had been an act. Her fear of Tearlach. Her desperation. Her need to escape. She'd been setting him up to betray them.

Nichola shot her husband a nervous glance, then looked at Seathan. "When I first met Lady Linet upon your arrival at Lochshire Castle, I thought her familiar. I asked if we had met, but she assured me she knew me not."

"Aye," Seathan said through gritted teeth, his mind churning with the tales the lass had fed him. "I am sure she did. Whatever her part in the twisted plot devised by her brother, I am sure he planned for me to remain ignorant of their ties."

Alexander's expression darkened. "What do you think is the bastard's intent?"

"To learn rebel plans." Hadn't Seathan suspected

her of deceiving him from the first? The warrior in him had eyed her with distrust, but their passionate interludes had smothered his mind's warnings, his desire obscuring what a blind man could have seen.

Furious, Seathan spun to leave. He almost slammed into Duncan as he entered the room, his face hard with anger.

"A runner has arrived with disturbing news," Duncan stated.

"'Twould seem a day for such," Alexander spat.

Seathan shoved his hands upon his hips. "Tell us."

"The runner states Lord Tearlach has charged Seathan with abducting his sister." Outrage slashed Duncan's face. "Tell me Lady Linet is not the viscount's sister."

"It is true," Seathan replied, hating every word. "I learned the fact but moments ago."

Duncan scowled. "How could you? The runner has barely dismounted from his steed."

"I told him," Nichola replied. "Several years ago, I met Lady Linet at an event at Westminster Palace."

"Why did you not tell us before?" Duncan asked.

Alexander drew his wife against his side. "She told us as soon as she remembered."

Duncan rubbed the back of his neck, focused on Seathan. "There is more. Tearlach has offered a reward for you—alive or dead."

Alexander snorted. "As if the bastard did not want him dead from the first. I'm sure his only regret was not hanging Seathan while he was rotting in his dungeon."

"Which is why," Seathan said, wading through the muddle of thoughts storming his mind, "Tearlach's claim is but a farce."

"A farce?" Duncan asked.

"Aye," Seathan said. "The viscount's search for his sister is well planned. The days he has allowed to pass since Linet and I escaped were to give her time to gain my trust as well as information about rebel activity. Now he allows the lure of coin to aid him in finding her, believing the search will lead to me and to the information she has culled."

Duncan's eyes narrowed. "She is a spy?"

Seathan didn't want to believe it, searched for another explanation, but none came. "With her blood tie to Tearlach and the fact she kept her identity secret, I must believe that. But if she is indeed a spy, why has she not tried to pry rebel information from me?" None of this was making a bit of sense. "Whatever her intent, I will bloody find out." He stalked to the door.

"I am going as well," Duncan said.

Seathan shook his head. "I need not your help."

Alexander walked to stand at his brother's side. "You will have our help anyway. Lady Linet's treachery affects us all."

Seathan wanted to speak with her alone first. But with anger fueling his emotions, mayhap his brothers' presence would offer her a measure of safety.

"So be it." Seathan exited the chamber with his brothers.

"Where is she?" Duncan asked as he strode down the corridor at his side.

"Most likely asleep," Alexander replied, a step away, and with Nichola on his heels.

"Nay, she is awake," Seathan said, fury stroking him with every step. He rounded the corner, then stormed up the tower steps, Linet's betrayal cutting deep.

Sunlight poured through the tower window above like a glistening promise.

Promise? Nay. Linet had lied to him from the start, her every act planned, carried out with deceptive precision.

Except now her treacherous charade was over.

"What are you going to do to her?" Worry trembled through Nichola's voice from several steps back.

"Do?" Seathan continued up the steps, the slap of his boots echoing with solemn promise. "That depends on her." When he asked Linet the truth this time, God help her if she lied.

At the tower chamber, he unlatched the door and shoved. Handcrafted wood slammed against the wall. Seathan glared around the empty room.

Alexander halted at his side. "She is not here."

"I bloody see that!" The chamber's pristine condition left Seathan unsettled. The bed's linen lay taut as if made by a steady hand, the room sparkled as if wiped clean, the air held a slight tang as if scented with newly strewn rushes, and the window stood open, spilling the warmth of the morning sun within. It was as if Linet had not stayed within the chamber last night.

But she had. He'd seen her, touched her, and had

he not thought of Dauid, would have foolishly made love with her.

Bedamned!

Nichola stepped past him. Slowly, she walked around the room, stopped at the window, then turned. "She might be within the great room breaking her fast."

"She might be." Instinct warned Seathan otherwise.

Duncan strode to the bowl containing the halved gemstones and frowned. "Seathan, your moss agate is gone."

Unease cut through Seathan as he stared at the empty space where but hours ago the match to the halved gem he wore around his neck had lain.

"The lass took it," Alexander stated.

"Aye," Duncan agreed.

A twinkle from the ceiling caught his attention.

Seathan glared at the fairies painted above, then toward the woven tapestry where mirrorlike images of the fey hid within the patterns.

Nay, love spells did not exist, his choices carved his future.

Then he remembered his confrontation with Linet this morning. Relief swept over him. "I know where the lass is," Seathan said.

"Where?" his brothers asked in unison.

"I had a servant move her to another chamber." A detail he'd forgotten. Neither did he inform them of his earlier visit, nor how he'd almost made love to her. He needed not a reminder of his insanity, especially since she'd proven herself untrustworthy.

"I still cannot believe it." Duncan's almost dazed

tone stopped Seathan's swift exit. His youngest brother lifted the remaining halved gem within his palm, somber light glistened from its deep olive core. Duncan faced Seathan. "It is as Nichola said, 'tis Patrik's malachite."

His youngest brother's pain echoed in Seathan's chest, in a place even Linet's lies couldn't numb. "The reason for its return must wait. We must find Linet." He turned and strode to the door. She would tell him the truth or by God he'd cast her into his dungeon until she confessed, Tearlach be damned!

Heart pounding, Linet pressed against the stable wall, the rough boards digging into her skin. Daylight erased the shadows she desperately needed to slip from Lochshire Castle. She'd planned on stealing a horse to make good her escape. Now, after several delays and with the sun high above, any attempt to leave would ensure her capture. What was she going to do?

Linet squeezed the halved moss agate within her palm, the soft warmth a soothing balm to her rattled nerves.

A horse whinnied behind her.

Linet started. She needed to remain focused on her escape, not think of Seathan. God help her when he discovered her gone.

She peered toward the tower. The window stood open as if nothing was amiss, as if it were an ordinary day when it was anything but.

Had anyone noticed she'd left her room? If she chose, she could slip back within the tower chamber. A safer choice with daylight upon her. After a short wait, then she could descend to the great hall and pretend to have overslept. No, that wouldn't work. Seathan had ordered a servant to come and help move her to anther room.

A shadow appeared in the tower window.

Linet froze. Seathan! Even in the distance he looked like an enraged god. Sweet Mary, he'd discovered her gone. If Seathan suspected she was trying to escape, the stable was the first place he'd order searched.

She scanned the bailey. With the men engrossed in cleaning their swords across the grassy expanse, Linet tucked her hair beneath her gown, pulled her cloak tight. She kept her head averted and walked at a pace that would not draw their attention. Nervousness rippled through her with every step, but thankfully, she made it to the side of the building nearer the exit.

The echo of hooves sounded. A group of knights cantered in from beneath the gatehouse. Several warriors cleaning their swords glanced toward the men at the entrance before returning to their task. Two guards strode toward the exit, paused, facing the opening and continued to talk.

They blocked any chance of escape!

She scanned the bailey. Sunlight saturated the brilliant blue sky. It would be foolish to try to leave Lochshire Castle now. Her only hope was to hide until this night, and pray that Seathan failed to find her.

On the far side of the bailey, children swung their carved swords in mock games of battle as their mothers washed clothes nearby in wooden tubs. A smith patiently heating a rod of iron within a fire stood waiting until it glowed. In the outer bailey, knights sparred with aggressive determination.

It was all too heartbreakingly familiar. Over the years she'd witnessed similar activities within Breac Castle. Except now, each task was not only a daily routine, but a preparation for war. The knights honing their skills, the smith crafting a weapon to kill, and the children practicing for the reality they would one day face. Heart heavy, Linet slipped into the building before her.

The thick oak door, secured against quarried walls, softly moaned as she pushed it open. She stepped inside, shoved it closed, welcoming the shield of blackness.

No, not blackness.

As her eyes slowly adjusted to the dim interior, candles flickered before her. The unmistakable scent of beeswax tinged with the hint of frankincense and myrrh filled each breath. Curious, she stepped forward, took in the flagstone upon the floor sprinkled with fresh rushes. She'd entered the chapel.

Melancholy touched her. Once she'd believed she'd find hope within sacred walls. After her father's death, Fulke had allowed her to believe that she would be able to choose her path of life. Lies, naught but mistruths concocted to serve his cause. If her brother thought to wed her to the Earl of Fallon to strengthen his royal ties, he could go to Hades.

Guards' voices echoed from outside; grew closer.

Heart pounding, she whirled toward the entry. They were coming in. She had to hide!

Guided by candlelight, she bolted down the aisle, skirting the thick wooden benches. Frantic, she glanced up, found thick beams securing the ceiling above. If only she had a rope to climb, a chest to crawl into, something, anything.

The door was shoved open.

Linet dove beneath a solid wood bench and held her breath.

Footsteps slapped the sacred ground. "A woman entered moments ago?" Seathan's ominous demand echoed throughout the chapel.

Fear tore through her. She pressed herself against the earthen floor, her entire body trembling. *Oh please God, let him not find her!*

"I am not sure, my lord," a guard outside said. "I saw a lass near the chapel. For a moment, I looked away. When I turned back, she was gone."

Fear crowding her every thought, Linet prayed he'd leave. If Seathan came farther inside, bent down, he would see her. Should she stand and give herself away?

Seathan walked past her row, stilled.

Sweat slicked her brow.

"What color was her hair?" Seathan asked.

"I but caught a brief look at her face, my lord, and I cannot say."

But Seathan knew—a luxurious amber-gold, hair that felt like silk a man could touch forever. "Join the others," he ordered, letting his eyes adjust to the dim, candlelit interior. "I will finish searching here."

"Aye, my lord." Quick steps echoed within the chapel as the knight hurried away. The door thudded closed. Silence, thick, harsh, and unforgiving filled the void.

Hands on his hips, Seathan scoured the darkened chamber. Soft candlelight outlined the sturdy pews. Unbidden, the fragrance of frankincense and myrrh drew his memories back to his youth. To the time he'd prayed as they'd laid his father deep within the earth, to the angry words between him and his father before he'd died, and a wrong he could never apologize for, a wrong he would forever regret.

Throat dry, he forced the memories back along with any softness for the woman who deserved his wrath.

"Linet?" His voice boomed into the fragile silence. He scoured the play of flickering light in search of any sign, any shadow exposing her. "I know you are here."

His men's voices echoed from the bailey. He heard Duncan calling to Alexander from farther away.

"You think I do not know you are hiding within the chapel?"

Nothing.

With methodical precision, he took in every curve, each slope of the bench. Though the chapel remained silent, he sensed her presence.

He took another step forward. "You will regret trying to escape."

A rustle of clothing sounded to his left. Then, a darkened image crawled from beneath a pew. He caught the outline of her slender form, a body he'd burned for.

He stepped forward, severing any avenue of escape. "Do not try to run."

Linet stood, faced him, the wash of pale candle-light upon her at odds with the challenge etched on her face. "Run? I came here to pray."

Outrage that she dared lie to him poured through his soul. "Is that what you call hiding beneath the pew?"

At her challenging silence, he stormed over, caught her, and hauled her to him. "I am tired of your lies."

Her eyes widened. "I—"

He leaned to within a hand's width of her face, close enough to smell her woman's scent, near enough to have claimed her mouth. In that moment, he hated her for the way she made him feel. Confused. Aroused. Angry.

"Tell me," he hissed, "when were you going to let me know your brother was the Viscount of Tearlach?"

Chapter 12

He knew! With his hand locking her against his solid frame, Linet stared at Seathan, riveted by his fury, terrified at the outrage in his eyes. Her entire body shook as her mind scraped for words to temper his rage.

Tell him the truth, a voice whispered in her mind.

A hysterical laugh swirled in her throat. As if explaining that she'd freed him to take revenge against her brother would pacify this enraged Scot?

A muscle tightened in Seathan's jaw. "You were not going to tell me."

"Had I told you Fulke was my brother," she said, amazed at how calm her voice sounded, "you never would have accepted my help."

A muscle tightened in his jaw. "Tell me exactly, my lady, how you helped me?"

"I freed you."

"Freed me? Nay, you released me from your brother's cell but always stayed by my side, leaving me far from *free*." He leaned within a hand's breath from her face. "Tell me, did you and your bastard brother raise a toast after you devised this twisted plot?"

She ignored his sarcasm. Under the circumstance, she expected his suspicions. But after all she and Seathan had endured, that he believed her in league with Fulke hurt the most.

Linet shook her head. "There is no plan. As I told you, I despise my brother."

"You are so convincing, but then, any liar worth their coin twists words to convince, spews them with the expertise of a seasoned bard. Tell me," he seethed, "how much were you paid, or rather, what were you promised for your role in this depraved scheme?"

Anger, pure and sharp, pierced her. Before she realized her intent, her hand shot out.

His head jerked; the angry slap upon his cheek echoed between them.

Trembling, she let her hand fall to her side. The slash of red sweeping across his skin made her nauseous. His hold on her tightened. Never before had she reacted with violence, but then, never before had she been in love. "How dare you offer such an insult!"

"And how dare you infiltrate my home, act the innocent to gain information of rebel plans and hideouts in order to pass them back to the English."

Hurt didn't begin to describe the pain of his accusation. "You believe me a spy?" Her words shook with emotion.

"A spy? My lady," he said with cold precision. "Do

you forget that you live in Breac Castle? Or mayhap that your brother, the Viscount of Tearlach, has sworn fealty to King Edward?" Green eyes flashed with fury. "Nay, I believe your memory is clear, as is your intent."

She fought to keep the angry, frustrated tears from her eyes and jerked against his grip. "You may dismiss the fact that I am half Scottish, and the fact I have vowed never to return to Breac Castle, but damn you, you will listen to what I have to say!"

He arched a dismissive brow, irritating her further.

Linet angled her jaw. "I would never betray you, ever. You want the truth, fine. I released you as payback to my brother." When his eyes narrowed, her explanation tumbled out, the memories spilling through her mind with painful clarity.

"Growing up, my father promised me my choice of a husband when I came of age, except he died and Fulke became my guardian. He had been away on campaign serving King Edward, but upon our father's demise, he returned. I owed my brother's detachment during his stay to grief, to the pain of losing our father."

At his silence, she rushed on. "I was inconsolable, but Fulke assured me naught would change, and that in Breac Castle I would always find a home. Grieving, I clung to his words, believing them true, or . . . perhaps"—she shrugged—"I wished them so. Regardless, my brother requested that I oversee the running of our ancestral home. In return, he swore he would honor our father's promise that I would marry the man of my choosing, and on my wedding day, I would receive a generous dowry." The painful memories faded beneath the harsh slap of reality. "And fool that I was, I believed him until the day he betrothed me to the Earl of Fallon, a man known for his abuse, to strengthen his ties."

Seconds passed, each one drowning in deafening silence as Seathan studied her. He gave a slight nod. "A finely woven tale. Indeed, a few bits might hold truth."

Cur! She fought to break from his hold. "Release me."

"Your freedom, you lost with your deceit." He tugged her toward the chapel door.

Fear, cold and vile, cut through her. "What are you going to do with me?"

"Do?" He turned. Candlelight strafed the hard planes of his face, carved shadows of dark intent. "'Tis unwise to give the enemy the advantage of knowledge."

"After everything we have been through," she whispered, "the risks I have taken to save your life, tell me, do I look like the enemy?"

"Yes."

As if a sword had sliced through her heart, her body went numb. If he had wanted to hurt her, he could not have done a finer job. She looked away, not wanting him to see her tears, or to expose any sign of the horrible, heartbreaking truth.

She loved him.

If he learned of her feelings, then he would hold the ultimate weapon.

Seathan caught her shoulder, turned her to face

him, his hard gaze unnerving her further. "Tell me, my lady, how far would you have gone, what would you have sacrificed to have gained the coveted rebel information for the English?"

"I detest you!"

His eyes lowered to her mouth, then flicked to meet hers. Male satisfaction settled on his face. "I think not." He slid his thumb over her lower lip in a slow caress. "If I wanted, I could take you here, now, and you would let me."

She stiffened, furious to feel the heat only he inspired. Ashamed, humiliated that even after he believed her Fulke's pawn, she could want him, Linet closed her eyes. She wished they'd left, that he was now locking her within his dungeon. At least then she would be safe from him.

"Open your eyes."

His rough demand rumbled through her. For a moment she refused, then as if he'd cast a spell over her, with aching slowness, she complied.

Seathan leaned toward her.

"No!"

His mouth covered hers, hard, hungry, demanding her response. "Open for me," he commanded and took the kiss deeper, drawing her flush against him, the hardness of his body making it clear that as much as he despised her, he wanted her as well.

Her mind swam with confusion as warmth coursed through her. She struggled to break free; a war waged and lost.

With a half cry, she accepted him, hating her weakness when it came to Seathan, damning the way he made her feel, wanting his touch and, shamefully, more. And his mouth, Mother Mary, his glorious mouth edged its way across the outline of her jaw as his fingers skimmed over her skin, lingering against the curve of her cape to where sensitized flesh lay beneath. A shudder of need tore through her.

On a half growl, he shoved the cape away. With deft movements he splayed open her gown.

Exposed to him, she felt no shame, but acceptance, as if fate guided her. And she realized, with Seathan, it would always be so.

His eyes dark with need, he cupped the curve of her breast.

Warmth, pure and hot, pierced straight to her core. She held his gaze, wanting to watch him as well. At least on this front, however much he denied it, they were equal. She saw the desire on his face, how his breathing had become quick and shallow, and the flush that had stolen up his neck.

"How is it you affect me so?" he whispered.

His raw, potent words stirred her needs. "I—"

The door behind her slammed open.

Seathan dropped his hand.

Air, cool and blustery, slapped her naked flesh. Mortified by what she'd allowed, had almost given within this sacred place, she dragged up her gown. God forgive her, how could she have forgotten that she stood within a chapel?

As Linet fumbled to repair her gown, Seathan glared toward the entry, his body shuddering with hard-won control.

A burst of sunlight outlined his youngest brother's

furious form along with Linet's bare shoulders. "I see you have found the spy."

Seathan ignored his brother's condemnation, expecting no less, but neither would he tolerate it. "Leave us." It wasn't a request.

Duncan crossed his arms over his chest. "So you can bed the lass on holy ground?"

"Never would I bring such shame to our home." Feeble words when he'd had no intent of stopping. Had Duncan not interrupted . . . Seathan muttered a curse, furious at himself.

Aye, the lass would pay for her guilt, but not here. Neither would he invite her further humiliation.

"Leave us." The calmness of his voice was at odds with the turmoil churning within.

Duncan's mouth tightened. For a long moment, he stood there in challenge. Then he slanted a hard look at Linet, who now covered herself with her cape, before meeting Seathan's gaze. With a curt nod, he turned and left. The chapel door thudded in his wake.

Muted darkness encased them; silence infused the chapel as if a dark omen.

Seathan focused on Linet. Hair mussed, lips swollen from his kisses, she looked like a woman well loved, a woman whom, under any other circumstance, he would finish making love to.

Except, she was the enemy.

Bedamned! Never would she fool him again. The depths of her treachery were astonishing. He drew himself up to his full height. "Before, I thought you an innocent," he said, anger rolling through his words. "But an innocent, however overcome with passion, would not disgrace herself in a house of God." He'd wanted to believe in her innocence, a belief she'd extinguished this day.

Her face grew ashen.

"Neither am I free of guilt."

"As if your admittance changes anything?" she hissed. "You are truly a bastard!"

"Something, my lady, you would do well to remember." Seathan caught her hand, drew her with him as he strode toward the exit.

As before, she fought to break free.

Seathan rounded on her. "The decision of how you leave the chapel is up to you. One word, the slightest sign of a struggle, and I will truss you up and carry you from here like a sack of oats."

"You would not dare!"

He scanned her in a slow sweep, his blood hot. "At this moment, I would dare anything, propriety be damned."

Through her anger, he caught a shimmer of fear. Good, he wanted her afraid. His attraction to Linet was a curse, dangerous, a fact he deemed unforgivable. Without another word, he hauled her from the chapel.

Voices within the great room melded with the clank of platters and the errant bark of a dog. Seathan tried to focus on the stew before him, but even though the tangy scent of onions, venison, and herbs teased his senses, each bite tasted like wind-tossed dust.

Two seats away, Nichola set down her goblet and worried the stem. "I still cannot believe Linet is in league with Fulke." She scanned the knights filling the trencher tables below the dais, then turned back to Seathan. "Even after I recognized her as Lord Tearlach's sister, I don't believe she had a part in planning to infiltrate the Scottish rebels. In the past, during the brief time we spoke, her manner was that of a kindhearted woman."

Seathan shoved aside the nearly full bowl, ignored the uneaten bread nearby, wiped his mouth, and tossed the cloth aside. "Mayhap, but war can change a person." With time behind him and having calmed, he found his confrontation with Linet had only raised more questions. That he found himself agreeing with Nichola left him ill at ease. He shrugged. "One can see why Tearlach would draw her within his cause. Linet holds the ability to convince those around her of her sincerity, regardless the lie given."

Alexander swallowed a long draught of wine, set his goblet on the table with a clatter, and frowned. "The lass is not worth your concern."

"She means naught to me but an enemy caught." And Seathan wished that were the truth. Ever since he'd left her in a guarded chamber, her devastated expression had haunted his mind. Why couldn't he thrust her from his thoughts?

But he knew. The genuine shock and dismay in her eyes refused to leave him. And the acknowledgment that from the start, there had been a part of him that believed in her innocence.

Duncan grunted. "An enemy caught? Is that why you had the lass half stripped when I found you but hours ago?"

Red slashed Isabel's cheeks.

Seathan needed no reminder of his foolery when it came to Linet. He muttered a curse. "Had I felt like dining with a lackwit—"

Two of his guards burst through the entry supporting a battered man. Quiet swept through the great room, broken only by the crackle from the wood-filled hearth.

Seathan's gaze riveted on the man they half carried. "'Tis Bran!" He shoved to his feet, his brothers' chairs scraping as they stood. Emotions stormed him as he strode toward his knight, a warrior he'd last seen fighting for his life when Tearlach's men had ambushed him and his men. He'd believed Bran slaughtered like so many others.

A pace away, he halted. "I thought you dead," Seathan rasped.

A grim smile cut through the warrior's grief-weary face. "Aye, as did Lord Tearlach's men. And the traitor, Dauid." He nodded. "After everyone left, I dragged myself to a shelter by a stream. Over the days, with God's blessing, I recovered enough to travel here."

Hope rolled through Seathan. One of his men had lived; mayhap more had done so as well. "Did anyone . . . anyone else survive?"

Regret paled the knight's face. He swallowed

hard, his silence painting its own grim image of the horror he'd witnessed that night, of the carnage.

"Nay." He shook his head. "I am the only one."

God in heaven. Seathan laid his hand upon the man's shoulder, his body trembling. He looked around the keep at his men. "We all grieve for the lives lost, but their sacrifice will not be in vain." He looked straight into Bran's eyes. "On that I swear before all this day. From their blood shall come Scotland's freedom."

Murmurs of agreement rose throughout the immense chamber. In salute, one by one, the knights filling the great hall stood, swords raised.

Pride filled Seathan at those around him, those who served Scotland, and those who would bring Scotland her freedom.

"My lord," his man said. "There is more. It is about Sir Dauid."

Seathan nodded. "We will discuss this in private." With memories of that fated eve blackening his mind, he strode toward the war chamber.

On either side of Bran, Alexander and Duncan helped him forward. The knights in the great room stepped back as they walked, clearing a somber path.

Determination filled Seathan. More than blood bound his people. For a moment in this war-torn land, he felt hope, belief that not only would the rebels succeed in recovering their country's freedom, but once the battle cries grew silent, Scotland's people would find peace.

The guard opened the door to the war chamber as Seathan neared. He entered, followed by his brothers and the battered knight. The click of the door being secured echoed within the silence.

Seathan faced his man. Flakes of dirt clung to his face, layered atop lines of fatigue, a testimony to Bran's hard travel to reach Lochshire Castle this day.

"Tell me," Seathan stated.

"As I remained hidden near Dauid's hut, recovering," Bran explained, "I saw him return home on several occasions. He looked battered and bruised."

Seathan raised his brows, as did his brothers, surprised Dauid would dare return anywhere he might be recognized. Mayhap confident in his ties to Tearlach, he feared none. If so, he was more a fool than Seathan had believed.

"'Twould seem he believes his obvious fealty to the Viscount of Tearlach will provide him protection," Alexander growled.

Seathan agreed. After Dauid's treachery, he should find no surprise in his former friend's arrogance. Still, the fact gnawed at his gut.

"Was his wife in residence?" Seathan asked.

The knight frowned. "'Twas odd, but never did I see her."

"'Twould seem she holds more intelligence than her speck-brained husband," Alexander spat. "If he ever had any."

Duncan crossed his arms. "Where do you think she is?"

"If Dauid is wise," Seathan replied, "he would have hidden her for her own safety. But then, with recent decisions made, he has proved himself a fool." He focused on the knight. "Did he see you?"

"Nay," Bran replied. "Whenever he was about, I kept hidden."

Seathan nodded. "Dauid was battered and bruised?"

"Aye, my lord, and walked with a limp." Bran shrugged. "An odd one I never could figure out."

"It matters not, there could be many reasons," he replied. "Your stealth and bravery will serve us well." Seathan wanted nothing to alert Dauid that he'd escaped Tearlach's grasp or that he still lived. When the bastard learned the fact, it would be with Seathan's blade against his neck. He turned to his master-at-arms positioned near the door. "Raise a contingent of men. Prepare them to depart."

"Aye, my lord." The master-at-arms hurried out.

He nodded to Bran. "A healer will see to your wounds. Once you have eaten, rest."

"Thank you, my lord, but my wounds are well healed." The knight straightened. "I would ask to accompany you as well. Sir Dauid . . ." He cleared his throat and looked away, but not before Seathan caught the grief in the Scot's eyes.

"Aye," Seathan replied, understanding the man's anger. The knight had lost a brother that day. Dauid's betrayal had left no one within Lochshire Castle unscathed. Dauid had once trained within these walls, supped among the men, celebrated the birth of many a knight's child. Nay, Seathan would not forbid Bran from accompanying him as he traveled to exact revenge. "Gather some food. Then, prepare to ride."

"Thank you, my lord." With a bow, Bran left the chamber, aided by two knights. A guard pulled the door closed after them.

Duncan muttered a curse. "I am surprised Dauid dared return."

Alexander curled his hand around the hilt of the dagger secured at his waist. "Aye, the bastard has the balls of a boar, but I will be stripping him of those as well."

"Dauid is mine," Seathan stated.

His brothers held his gaze, then nodded.

"And when I depart," Seathan said, "I will lead the contingent. Alone."

"What?" Alexander and Duncan boomed in unison.

Eyes blazing, Alexander stepped forward. "By my sword, I shall not wait here as if a maiden fretting for news."

"No," Seathan replied, cutting off Duncan before he could speak. He nodded to his youngest brother. "Isabel has recently given birth. In addition to a wife, you now have twin girls to think of."

"Having daughters or a wife does not castrate me," Duncan replied, glowering.

"Nor does it take away your responsibilities to ensure Lochshire Castle is well guarded," Seathan stated. "Until my return, you will remain here and oversee your family as well as be charged with the protection of our home." He turned to Alexander. "With the mayhem following the slaying of the Sheriff of Lanark, we know not the rebels' next move." He paused. "I have sent a missive to Wallace warning of Dauid's treachery, and I anticipate a runner to arrive with orders as to our next move any day," Seathan said. "Until my return, you will act in my stead."

"And what of Linet?" Alexander demanded.

Linet? How, for even a moment, could he have forgotten her? Was it but this morning when lust had stormed his sanity, when he'd shamefully forgotten his surroundings and had almost taken her in the church?

"I am taking Lady Linet with me," Seathan decided.

"Are you addled?" Alexander boomed, his outrage strangled with disbelief. "With Tearlach's men about, travel will be difficult enough without hauling along a lass who will expose you the first chance that arises."

"Aye," Duncan agreed. "You will need to bind her treacherous mouth the entire journey."

"I have plans for the lass," Seathan said, "which, I assure you, are well worth the inconvenience of her presence." He stared at the flames within the hearth, his fury burning as hot. "Once I have finished with Dauid, 'tis Tearlach who will pay."

"How?" Alexander asked.

A smile tightened Seathan's mouth as he imagined the viscount's surprise. "Linet is now my hostage, a captive I will use as leverage against Tearlach."

Chapter 13

The scrape of leather and the jingle of spurs muted the hoofbeats upon the soft earth, but Linet heard every step, felt the bunch of muscles, the heavy clop as Seathan's steed moved with agile grace through the dense forest.

Seathan's prisoner.

Even now, hours after he'd hauled her from the chapel, his cold words tormented her soul. She'd believed Seathan would cast her within his prison once he learned of her blood tie to Fulke. Instead, he'd placed her under guard within a simply furnished chamber. The minimal pieces within far nicer than those in the dank cell offered to Seathan by her brother.

Remembering the cruel treatment Seathan had suffered at her brother's hands, she sighed, then shifted to a more comfortable position.

"Be still." Seathan's deep burr rumbled in the night.

She tried to ignore his presence, the way her back

molded against his chest. But with each step of his steed, she was rocked yet again against his muscled frame. Even if she wasn't in such close proximity to him that each breath carried the tang of his male scent, she doubted that she would ever forget him.

How could she have allowed Seathan into her heart?

"When will we break for the night?" she asked, refusing to dwell upon dangerous thoughts of him.

"Why do you ask?" Suspicion lingered in his voice.

"You have pushed your men for hours."

He grunted. "They are warriors, men seasoned in arduous travel."

"Even when they are injured?"

Silence.

"Far from enough time has passed for your wounds to have healed."

"If you are cold, I will give you a blanket."

He refused to discuss the topic. So like a warrior, and so like a mule-headed, honorable man who put others' lives above his own. However wrong his distrust of her, he was a man she would always respect.

And sadly, love.

The howl of a wolf echoed in the distance, a hauntingly forlorn sound.

Exhausted by the emotional challenges of this day, she closed her eyes and succumbed to the temptation to lean against Seathan. He tensed, but she wasn't surprised. Since he'd stormed into her chamber stating that she was accompanying him, he'd offered little warmth.

A gentle breeze brushed her face, soft with the

night, rich with the scent of spring. A potent reminder of the passage of time and that, with each new day, the risk of Fulke finding them increased.

How far had her brother expanded his search? He wouldn't quit. Alive, she was collateral to secure a powerful tie. As for Seathan, recapturing him was fueled by her brother's need to strengthen his ties with the English king.

With deft skill, Seathan guided his mount through the dense forest.

Whirls of stubborn snow clung in patches over the ground. Limbs clattered against each other as the warhorse pushed through the tangle of brambles.

However much winter's hand strove to reclaim its hold, with spring upon them, buds would soon appear, then leaves would unfurl upon the barren limbs, proof that life would go on.

And so must she.

Life awaited her, a life without Seathan, a life without his love. To linger on the emptiness before her would serve naught. At the first opportunity, she must escape, travel to safety within her clan in the Highlands. Except now the task presented a greater challenge.

Before, she and Seathan had traveled alone. Now, they rode with a contingent of his men. When they made camp to rest their mounts, guards would be posted, men who knew of her connection to Fulke, men who watched her with distrust. She'd find no aid among them.

Seathan's horse stumbled but caught himself. Off balance, Linet gasped, reaching for the saddle.

Seathan wrapped his arm around Linet's waist, drew her against him. "Steady, lass."

As if she would ever be composed around him. She remained quiet, focused on their journey. With care, he guided his mount through a thicket of snow-covered branches, his touch given not to ensure she was safe, but to prevent her escape.

At the slight pressure of his hand against her cape, she felt a dull pulsing against her side, then warmth.

Seathan's halved gemstone! She'd forgotten she still had the moss agate.

Had he felt it? A foolish question. If so, he would have snatched it from her pocket.

As Linet again shifted before him, for the hundredth time since they'd departed Lochshire Castle, Seathan questioned his sanity in having the lass ride with him. One would think knowing she was his enemy would smother his desire. But his body seemed not to care. He was hard as a rock and aching with the pain of it.

Seathan glanced at his master-at-arms to inform him he would be carrying the lass the remainder of the night, then he stayed the impulse. She was his responsibility, a duty he'd not foist upon his men. Though her actions had set them on this twisted path, he would finish the journey, on his terms.

He scanned the moonlit sky, then the woman sitting before him. Linet's silence fooled him not. He understood well how her mind worked.

"You will fail."

She stiffened. "What?"

"In any attempt to escape." When she remained silent, he motioned to one of his men to pass him a blanket.

A guard handed him the woolen spread. "My lord."

"My thanks." Seathan wrapped the blanket around her.

She tensed—again. "I was not cold."

"Lie back against me." She'd begun shivering shortly after the sun had set. Not that she'd admit it. The lass was stubborn as a mule and twice as ornery. 'Twould serve her right if he abandoned her in the wilds with naught but her wits.

Still, however much she deserved his contempt, he refused to lower himself to such cruelty.

Forcing his hands not to linger, he tucked the blanket around her, then drew her against him, her curves warm and soft. He grimaced. Never could he care for a woman who deceived him, a woman he could not trust. And if she smelled like his every fantasy, invoked erotic images of her naked in his bed, 'twas fatigue that skewed his mind.

Linet shifted. "I—"

He gritted his teeth, prayed for sanity. "Unless you are ready to admit the truth, speak no more lies."

She twisted and glared up at him. "For a well-respected lord, you are quick to condemn."

"Had I not proof of your deceit, I would agree."

Her nose tilted up with disdain. "Proof of deceit? You accept a blood tie to Fulke as proof of treachery?"

"Why should I believe you would refuse to aid your brother?"

She shook her head. "I explained before, Fulke

lied to me, had promised that I would marry the man of my choosing."

"An insignificant lie in a time when women are rarely allowed such a choice."

"To you perhaps, but I was not raised within the normal guidelines of nobility."

That he could attest to. Since they'd met, she'd challenged him on every front. Her lack of fear in facing adversity was admirable. Neither could he deny she was knowledgeable. Qualities he respected, but they changed nothing.

"We are at war."

Though shadows framed her face, anger rolled off her. "War is not a reason for injustice, but an excuse for those who are weak, like my brother, Fulke. For what he has done, I detest him. Never again will he dictate my moves. That I swear to you." Her eyes narrowed. "Nor will you."

"And in the Highlands you will have such a choice?"

"I . . ." Linet stilled, then faced forward. Until this moment, she'd never fully pondered her life with her mother's clan. She'd focused on her escape, on procuring her freedom. She'd assumed she'd be welcomed among them without question. And once settled, that she would be allowed the life of her choosing.

She'd never pondered further.

Now, she understood the folly of her belief. To secure protection from the clan, she must uphold their laws, dictates passed down from the clan chief. And if those decisions included her marriage to procure the well-being of the clan, so be it. What if the man chosen for her to wed was brutal? Or what if after everything, her mother's clan turned her away?

Panic tore through her. She should have sent a missive ahead, explained to her mother's people her circumstances, prepared them for her arrival.

Hand trembling, she reached within her pocket, clasped the halved gemstone until it bit into her palm. She hadn't even thought to carry an heirloom to prove her family tie. Linet swallowed hard. Now, she had nothing but a prayer.

A lone cloud swallowed the moon, casting the forest into a vat of gloom. Darkness clung to limbs illuminated by moonbeams moments before.

"Linet?"

Tears burned her eyes. "Why badger me with questions? Regardless of my replies, you will hold them false."

The hopelessness of her words stunned Seathan. What had drained the strong woman of moments before? He'd only asked about her clan in the Highlands. Then he thought he understood.

"You have no family in the Highlands."

"I owe you no explanation."

"Or," he continued, undeterred by her curt reply, "if indeed your destination is true, they know naught of your existence."

Silence.

"And you are afraid."

"I fear nothing."

But he heard the dread in her voice. He steeled

himself against feeling anything, but against his good sense, his heart softened. She was struggling, had no one to turn to, no one to protect her.

"Once we arrive at your destination," Linet asked, "will you release me?"

Guilt tasted bitter in his mouth. Nay, not guilt. After her lies, she deserved the fate he planned.

"Seathan?"

Lord Grey, his mind echoed. Her address should invite no familiarity. Days of travel remained until they reach the lands where Dauid lived. And once Seathan had dealt with him, days more until the private meeting he would arrange with Tearlach— a meeting he anticipated with great pleasure.

He should be focusing on that, find relief that once he turned her over to her brother, Linet would be out of his life. The last thing he should be doing was pondering the worries of his lust-inspiring, sharp-tongued captive.

"You will let me go, will you not?" Linet demanded.

He guided his mount around a partially snow-covered stump. "We have far from reached our destination."

At his elusive reply, Linet turned, needing to see his face. Shadows greeted her. A sense of doom infused her. Mouth dry, she wet her lips. If there was a God in Heaven, let her be wrong.

She drew a steadying breath, exhaled. "You promised to escort me to the Highlands."

"I did," Seathan agreed. "But that was before I knew you were Tearlach's sister."

Chapter 14

Fear tore through Linet. "Why does my being Fulke's sister matter?"

Silence.

"What?" she asked, her mind racing. "Do you think to use me against Fulke?" A brittle laugh stumbled from her lips. "I detest him."

"My reasons matter not."

They did, but Seathan would not reveal them to her. "And what of my escort to the Highlands?"

Green eyes narrowed. "My word to escort you to the Highlands was given to a woman whom I believed held secrets, but not one who wielded treachery."

The arrogant oaf! "Treachery? And which of my actions spoke of treachery? I fulfilled my word and freed you from your foul cell, aided your escape from Breac Castle, and tended you when you could barely crawl." She paused, fighting to control her temper. "If anyone has misjudged the other, it is I who believed you were a man of honor."

"My decision is not up for debate."

Linet angled her jaw in defiance. "Why? Because you are a man? Or," she barreled on, damn the consequence, "because you are a powerful earl surrounded by a contingent of men who will obey your every wish. Wait, I know," she rolled on, reckless with fury, "it is because I am half English. Yes, a damnable, horrific crime indeed."

The arm around her waist drew her tight against his frame. His mouth paused a wisp from her ear, his action far from that of a lover. "Do nae try me further, unless you wish your mouth and hands bound, and to be carted on the rump of my steed as if a forgotten sack of oats."

He had the brains of a mud-dipped hen! Linet opened her mouth to flay him as he desperately deserved, then stayed her words. However much he deserved a set down, if he bound her, it would end any chance of escape.

She forced herself to relax against him, satisfied as his body hardened against hers. Though he said he despised her, he could not deny he wanted her, a reality that must rub him raw.

In the distance, the soft thrum of hooves echoed through the woods.

Linet searched the moon-swept trees for the rider, the tension from Seathan's body seeping into her own.

Seathan gave a soft whistle, withdrew his sword, and pulled his mount to a halt.

His men followed suit.

Tense seconds passed. The thrum of hoofbeats

increased. As if crafted from magic, cast in the silvery wisps of moonlight, a lone rider, carefully weaving his way through the wash of trees, came into view.

"'Tis Latharn," a knight whispered.

"Aye," Seathan said, relaxing behind her.

Moments later, a stocky knight pulled up before Seathan. "My lord, Tearlach's men are camped beyond the craig."

"Less than a half-day's ride." He paused. "How many?"

"At least fifty, my lord."

"Is the viscount with them?"

Linet heard the muted fury in Seathan's voice, anger he fought to control. The thought of seeing her brother did not please her either. She would rather face a rabid wolf.

"Nay, my lord," Latharn replied. "I saw no sign of Lord Tearlach."

Seathan turned his horse to face his men. "We will ride north until dawn."

"Aye, my lord." His master-at-arms rode through the men, passing along the order.

Seathan shuffled through a pouch. Without warning, he secured a gag over her mouth.

Linet reached up, caught hold of the woven cloth.

He clasped her wrist, drew her arm to her side. "I will not allow you a chance to scream. Try to remove the gag again," he said in a fierce whisper, "and your hands will be bound as well."

Never would she expose Seathan to Fulke, but 'twould seem he hesitated to believe her. Fine, then, let him think he'd won. If he was fool enough to think she would obey him, he deserved to awaken and find her gone.

Frustrated, tired of sparring with a man who would exhaust a saint, she closed her eyes, and fought to ignore the task of wool upon her tongue. She tried to rest, to wipe thoughts of him from her mind, but as Seathan guided his men north, away from any chance of being sighted by her brother or his men, sadness built inside to a steady ache.

She wished it possible to turn back time to when they had arrived at Lochshire Castle. Once she'd ensured Seathan was within the care of his family, she should have left. She'd known Nichola would eventually remember her.

But she had remained, had foolishly allowed her emotions to guide her. However much Lord Grey despised her now, for a moment within the tower, she'd tasted the man, his wants, his desires, needs that had matched her own.

Her heart aching, she focused on the night, on the soft whisper of her breaths as they made a counterpoint to the thrum of hooves around her. But with every inhale, every hoofbeat upon the pine- and leaf-strewn earth, she wanted him more.

Linet pressed her eyes shut, willed sleep to come, mindless hours filled with naught but rest. Even as weariness swept over her, doubts persevered that she would find any reprieve this night.

* * *

Rain, iced with the last taste of winter, battered Seathan's face as he guided his mount through the woods. Thick, low clouds blocked any hint of the sun. A sheen of mist clung to his lashes as the fog before him smeared the weather-torn landscape.

In the murky gloom of morning, he took in the slender woman draped in the blanket before him. Though Linet now dozed, from her restless shifting throughout the night, she'd slept little. When he'd lifted the cloak to check on her, she'd feigned sleep. A man well versed in reading a person's actions, he'd seen through her attempt. Once convinced she'd fallen into a deeper sleep, he'd removed the gag.

If he had not gagged her last night, would she have called for help? A part of him believed she would never expose them. But however much he wanted to have faith in Linet, with his men at his side, he refused to take the risk.

Tiredness swept through him. He wiped his eyes, then studied their surroundings. After pushing his men throughout the night, he needed to find a place to break for camp.

They crested the next knoll. Wrapped within the thick layer of mist, a dense copse of firs spread out before him. Unease crept through him as if an ill-fed wind.

With his pulse racing, he scoured the stand of trees, looking for any sign of men, anything to warn of danger, but he saw naught more than shadows.

He lifted the reins to urge his horse forward, and then lowered his hand. God's teeth, why was he hesitating? Tearlach's men lay hours behind them. The fog and the dense copse of trees would provide excellent cover to shield his men while they rested, a respite they sorely needed. Naught but tiredness spawned the worries in his mind.

Seathan motioned toward the dense firs. "We will break camp ahead."

Tired faces nodded in agreement.

Pride filled him. Though exhausted, his knights persevered without a grumble. Unlike the bloody English, who surrendered when faced with the first adversity, like dogs with their tales between their legs.

A breeze stirred around him, laced with the heavy scent of earth and winter-decayed foliage. He guided his mount down the steep slope, holding Linet secure against his chest. Her face was angelic in sleep, and he found it easy to linger upon the sweep of her lashes, the soft, full curve of her lips.

If her deception had not stood between them, he would have claimed her in his bed, enjoyed making love with her. Irritated by his weakness when it came to her, he turned his focus to the task at hand.

As they neared the stand of trees, he guided his steed into the circle of the sturdy pines.

Needled limbs trembled beneath the flutter of the wind.

Seathan reined in his mount and raised his hand; his men halted. The unease he'd sensed on the knoll returned, this time stronger. He scanned the forest ahead, the wall of trees on either side, listening for any sign of another presence.

Wings flapped. A hawk flew from the thick wave of green, its massive wings spread. The predator's shadow rippled across the ground with steady grace before the majestic bird disappeared from sight.

Seconds passed. Naught more filled the air but the breeze.

Linet shifted before him. With her amber-gold air teased by the wind, she looked like a bedraggled fairy awakening from a spell.

He frowned, irritated by his compassion. After the painful lesson with Iuliana, he was well aware how innocence could be feigned.

"What is wrong?" Linet whispered.

Turning his focus on the forest, he blew out a deep breath. Wrong? That was the problem—he wasn't sure. After the hours of hard travel, he should be ordering his men to break camp. Yet . . .

"My lord," his master-at-arms asked, "are we to dismount here?"

Seathan yielded to his intuition, instinct that had saved him many times in the past. He shook his head. "Turn the men around. We will travel farther north."

"Aye, my lord." The master-at-arms passed out orders. In moments they were retracing their path.

As Seathan guided his steed toward the break in the trees, the overwhelming sense of foreboding increased.

"Why did we not make camp?" Uncertainty crept into Linet's voice, as if she, too, sensed something amiss.

"I—"

Shouts avalanched through the silence, harsh cries tangled with fury. Mail-clad men, hidden behind the dense trees, charged into the opening, swords drawn.

Leather scraped as Seathan withdrew his sword. "To arms!" His shout melded into the first clash of steel. "Hold on," he ordered Linet. He wheeled his steed, charged the nearest aggressor, driving his blade into Tearlach's colors emblazoned upon the man's surcoat.

Shock streaked the knight's face. He staggered back, red staining the sturdy iron rings of mail.

Linet gasped.

Bedamned! He wished to spare her the horrors of battle, but there was no helping it now. "Hang on!" Seathan turned and met the next aggressor's attack with the slash of his blade.

The knight's sword fell, but he ducked then retrieved a dagger.

Before he could throw the knife, Seathan slid his sword across the man's throat.

Lifeblood spurted. The warrior dropped to the ground with a helpless gurgle.

Another warrior charged him.

Sweat streamed down Seathan's face as he pressed through the melee, Linet gripping his arm.

Another knight rushed him from his flank.

Seathan turned, met the swing of the attacker's blade with his own. His hand shook with the impact.

The man swung again, missed.

Linet screamed.

"Steady, lass." How could she not be terrified?

"To the left," she yelled.

He glanced to his other side.

Another warrior was charging toward them.

Seathan shoved his closest attacker back, kicked his mount forward, and drove his sword deep into the man's chest. Yanking his blade free, he whirled his mount, charged, and finished off the other knight struggling to his feet.

Seconds stumbled past as if hours, each one tainted by the screams, the screech of steel, and the stench of death. Around him, blood stained the earth as if a melancholy rain.

As his next attacker fell beneath his blade, Seathan took stock of his men. His knights were pushing Tearlach's men back. From the corner of his eye, he caught several of the bastard's men scrambling for the trees.

"They are retreating," Seathan yelled.

Cheers arose from his men. They fought harder. The sense of victory filled the air.

Seathan battled on, refusing to lower his guard, Linet clinging to him and shaking uncontrollably as he dealt with his next aggressor, then pushed forward.

Tearlach's knights continued to lose ground. At last, with their numbers severely diminished, the viscount's men fled.

"Do not allow them to escape," Seathan ordered. His knights gave chase, disappearing into the forest.

Heart pounding, he dragged in several deep breaths. The thrill of victory faded as he scanned the break within the trees filled moments before with battle. Several of his men lay injured, others were sprawled upon the ground unmoving. Though they'd won, the cost of victory, as with every meeting of the blades, was high.

Linet trembled in his arms.

"'Tis fine, lass, the fighting is over." But not the cost. As always, the loss of his men would haunt him. And now, she, too, would carry images of the carnage.

Those severely injured would be taken back to Lochshire Castle. It would weaken his force, but he refused to allow men who'd fought so bravely to die.

With a soft groan, she slumped against him.

"Linet."

Silence.

Seathan glanced down, stilled. A smear of blood coated her arm. Stunned, he checked his limbs. He did not remember being cut.

Panic lanced him. "Linet?"

A moan fell from her lips.

His heart slammed against his chest. Gently, he turned her, pushed away the blanket.

Her skin was pale as sun-bleached cloth, her eyes dazed as she met his. "I—" She began to violently shake, then her eyes rolled back. She fainted.

God in heaven! "Post guards!" Seathan ordered to several men who had returned. "Everyone else, tend to the wounded." He swung to the ground, looked up, and caught sight of the gash across the opposite

side of her head. Guilt tore through him as he remembered the attacker who'd swung and missed.

Except, he hadn't. Her scream had not been from
fear, but pain. Christ's blade, the lass had taken the
blow meant for him.

He slid his thumb across her cheek. "Linet, look
at me."

Weakly she opened her eyes. "Leave me alone."

Her pain-roughened words struck like an arrow
to the heart. Damn him, 'twas his duty to protect
her. "I am going to lift you down."

"No . . ." She dragged in a ragged breath. "I—"

With his hand supporting her, he dismounted,
then lifted her to the ground.

She cried out.

"Steady, lass."

"My lord?" a knight said as he rushed over.

Seathan nodded to his man. "Bring me water,
quickly."

His knight hurried off.

Bedamned, though his knights chased those who
fled, more of Tearlach's men might be nearby. If the
echoes of battle reached them, the viscount's men
would ride toward them posthaste. Neither could he
dismiss the additional threat if but one of Tearlach's
men reached their lord.

"Linet," he said, his words soft, thick with worry.

She moaned.

Guilt sliced through him.

Solid steps slapped the ground as the guard returned. He handed him the water pouch.

"My thanks." Seathan helped her sit, then knelt before her. "I am going to clean the wound," he explained, unsure whether she could hear him through the pain, but he continued to talk, to soothe her, aware the calming words were as much a balm for him as her. His hand shaking, he poured water onto a clean cloth. With care, he dabbed around the severed skin, the chalky color of her face in stark relief to the angry slash of red.

She moaned, started to turn away.

He gently caught her. "Easy now." The cut was deep. It needed to be sewn and treated with herbs to avoid infection. He'd seen worse injuries, but to men honed for battle. Not delivered to a woman raised in the cradle of nobility.

Sadly used to the coppery stench of blood stinging the air, he scanned the open expanse strewn with the bodies of his enemy as well as sprinkled with his own men. However much he did not want to move her, to remain here was too dangerous. Once his men returned, they would depart.

He clenched his teeth. He should have left her at Lochshire Castle, where she would be safe. No, hurt to discover she was Tearlach's sister, ashamed that after learning of her blood tie he desired her still, he'd sought to repay her treachery and use her as barter, had wanted her punished.

But not like this.

He could not bear to think his anger at himself, his need for vengeance, would cost Linet her life.

She would not die!

He looked at the sky, to where the sun's rays cut through the misery of dense fog like a yellowed knife. As if an omen, the hawk once again flew overhead, its wings stretched wide.

With his heart aching, he lifted the woman who already mattered too much to him in his arms, her every moan like a dagger to his soul. "You will live," he whispered. "Damn you, you will live."

Chapter 15

The next few hours passed as if a curse given. The bodies of Seathan's men were buried, the last of his knights who'd given chase to Tearlach's men had returned, and after dropping the final shovel of mist-dampened earth, they mounted and he led his men northward.

Exhaustion washed through Seathan as he fought to keep the weather-battered trees in focus. Water splashed in thin sheets as he guided his mount through a shallow stream. When he reached the opposite bank, he lowered his gaze to Linet, cradled before him. A soft moan fell from her lips, but she kept her eyes closed.

He studied the cloth he'd secured around her head to keep pressure on her gash, prayed he'd done enough, that she was strong enough to endure the hours of arduous travel ahead. Once they broke for camp this evening, after he'd treated the wound with herbs, he would sew it shut. Until then, time permitted little more. Once Tearlach's men failed to report to their lord, the viscount would scour the area with ruthless intent.

"Seathan?"

At Linet's weak voice, he looked down. With each league traveled, her skin had grown paler.

"Aye?" he whispered, wishing he could offer her more than words. 'Twas his error in judgment that had led them into the ambush. An error that had cost several of his men their lives.

"How . . ." With tortuous slowness, she peered at him through her thick amber lashes, her eyes filled with pain. "How much longer will we ride?"

"Until we are without daylight."

"I—"

"Do not talk."

"Ever the lord," she said dryly.

"Do you ever do as you are told?" he asked, irritated she'd disobey him when she sorely needed rest.

"Do you?"

At her teasing, he wanted to smile. How could he not admire her spirit, be drawn to her strength? But she was his enemy, in league with her brother in God knew what treachery. A fact he must never forget.

And if she is innocent?

The words spun through his mind. Seathan rubbed his eyes and shoved aside the question.

"Rest," he ordered. "No more talking." For a moment he thought she would argue, but thankfully, her exhaustion won and she closed her eyes.

Hours passed. With the sun a burnt ball of orange

struggling to remain in the sky, Seathan scoured the familiar landscape. As designed, the dense line of trees would provide excellent cover, the height, offer a strategic view. No one would escape their sight if they dare approach.

Seathan raised his hand. "Halt."

Exhaustion lined the faces of his men, but the sadness of this day weighed heavy on them as well as the memories of those they'd lost. Like he, they would focus on those who had lived, on the challenges ahead.

With his entire body aching, his injuries throbbing, he dismounted, then lifted Linet into his arms. He strode toward the weather-scuffed flat of stone, a marker used by the rebels.

Many years had passed since he'd visited this hideout, one he'd used in his first meeting with Wallace. He scanned the forest below, thick with shadows carved by the fading light.

Where was their rebel leader now? After he'd slain the Sheriff of Lanark, where had he hidden? A handful of places came to mind, but that Wallace was safe was what mattered the most. With the Bishop of Wishart backing them, as did the other Guardians of Scotland, the rebels would rise again.

And what of Longshanks's reaction to the news of his sheriff's murder? Entrenched in his plans to quell the revolt in Flanders, King Edward would be hard-pressed to break free. Still, the sheriff's murder wouldn't go without reprisal.

A writ to the Earl of Surrey to seize Wallace would no doubt be sent, but unknown to the English king, the earl, despising the Scots, had retired to his estate in England, leaving the treasurer, Hugh Cressingham, in charge. The delay in the missive reaching Surrey would buy them precious time.

He glanced at Linet limp within his arms, ached at the helplessness etched upon her face. With careful steps, he moved beneath a stone ledge carved by time. Beyond was a deep crevice that would shield her from the wind and provide privacy. He wished he could build a fire to ensure her warmth, but with Tearlach's men about, they couldn't take the risk.

"We are here," he whispered as his men settled in outside, and orders for guards to be posted were quietly passed.

A knight walked over and laid another blanket upon a bed of leaves and pine left over from visits before.

"My thanks," Seathan said. Carefully, he set her upon the woven wool.

Linet moaned.

Seathan stroked her hair. "Shhh."

"Seathan?"

"Aye, I am here."

Thick lashes slowly flickered open. "I hurt all over," she whispered. "The most . . . in my head."

He gently untied the cloth around the gash he'd secured earlier. "You have a large cut." That had thankfully stopped bleeding.

She lifted her hand as if to touch it.

He caught her wrist. "Nay, 'tis best if you do not move. Here." He lifted his water pouch to her mouth. "Drink."

"I am not thirsty."

"Do so anyway." With a bit of coaxing, she drank three swallows.

Linet lifted her hand, feebly wiped her mouth. "No more."

He stowed the water pouch. "You must rest. Today . . ." *You almost died*, he silently finished. His throat tightened. "We will remain here for the next couple of days."

Understanding dawned on her face. "Because of me?" She hesitated. "How badly am I injured?"

"You need stitches. After I make you a brew to relax you, I will apply herbs and sew you up." He'd tended many a battle wound: He'd do so now.

A wilted smile edged her mouth. "And I am to trust you?"

"You have no choice."

She didn't argue, alerting him to the severity of her pain. Frustrated, Seathan rose and strode to his mount, haunted by the knowledge that she was hurting—that a woman he believed was a spy was in pain, and he cared.

What if she was innocent? What if the reasons she'd given him for wanting to escape Tearlach were true? That she indeed despised her bastard of a brother?

After witnessing her strength as well as her sharp mind, he could see Linet daring such. The lass had courage many men would admire, strength he lauded as well.

If she'd told him the truth, then he'd wrongly accused her.

He blew out a hard breath, exhausted, confused, and frustrated. With the Scots struggling to reclaim their freedom, his every choice must be made for the good of his people. He could not risk his decisions being guided by his heart.

His heart?

An ache burned in his chest. Seathan shoved open the leather pack, gathered the items needed to sew the stitches. Nay, not his heart. Never again would he allow his feelings to be guided by a woman.

Through the waves of pain, Linet caught Seathan's troubled expression. He was struggling with guilt at her injury.

She reached up, touched the cut along her head, and winced. Having helped treat the wounded in the past, she knew she was lucky to be alive.

Linet studied Seathan as he removed a small packet from the leather satchel hanging on his horse. Fatigue dragged tired lines across his face, yet he never faltered.

He would save her life, yet he wouldn't offer her his trust.

She closed her eyes and turned away, wishing she were leagues from here. The pain throbbing through her body made the moment bearable. At least she could focus on that, let it smother her other emotions. For the pain of her injuries far from matched those delivered by the heart.

The crunch of leather upon stone announced Seathan's arrival.

She kept her eyes closed, not wanting him to see her with her emotions so fragile.

"Are you asleep?"

The concern in his voice was impossible to resist. She opened her eyes. "No."

"Here."

Linet glanced up.

He handed her a different flask.

"What is it?"

"Whiskey."

The numbing haze would soften the pain of the upcoming task. She drank deep, the burn hard and fast.

"Another," he said when she made to hand him back the leather pouch.

After one more drink, he nodded in satisfaction. "We will wait a moment more. When I begin securing the stitches, do not move."

Linet nodded, closed her eyes, savored the slight thickness settling in her mind, and prayed the stitching would be over posthaste. Her thoughts turned to wisps. Then she was floating. Or perhaps it was an illusion inspired by the whiskey, the burn still lingering in her throat.

As if woven by a magical hand, flickers of light swirled above her. Through her hazed mind, she focused on them.

Her lids grew heavy. She let them fall, thankful to drift off. After the coolness of the herbs against her skin, the recurring pinch, then tug of Seathan efficiently closing her wound wove through her dulled mind. Moments later, a cloth was gently wiped across her brow.

"I am finished." A slight shuffle, the soft steps of his leaving.

Thank God the stitches were over. She did not need to have watched to know he had sewn with a fine hand. The herbs he'd applied after would ensure infection didn't set in. Turning her head, she looked out into the night, glanced at where Seathan stood talking to one of his guards.

Another wave of lethargy slowly swept through her. As her lids again drifted shut, a dull pulsing at her side caught her attention.

The halved gemstone.

Hand trembling, she slipped the stone from her pocket. Palm flat, she held it before her.

As if a star drawn from the sky, it twinkled with a soft glitter. A sense of peace infused her, a calmness that she'd felt in the tower chamber of Lochshire Castle.

Unnerved, she shoved it in her pocket. A second passed. Then another. Seathan remained talking with one of the guards, while several other knights stood watch.

Linet closed her eyes, fought to purge all thought from her mind, but as if beckoned, a sense of warmth surrounded her. No, she felt nothing. She was dreaming. And whatever she was thinking, experiencing, it was not caused by the stone.

Warmth grew. A tingling began against her skin below where the stone had lain in her palm.

Hand trembling, she again removed the stone. As

before, it shimmered in her hand. She inhaled deeply, then slowly released her breath. She would not panic.

Linet shot a look toward Seathan; he remained in deep conversation with the guard. She studied the moss agate. Why was the gemstone doing this? What did it mean? And did it have a connection to the other half that Seathan wore around his neck?

As if summoned, Seathan turned.

Sweet Mary!

"You are awake?" His deep voice rumbled as he strode toward her.

She shoved the gemstone out of sight—barely.

Two steps more, then Seathan hunkered down at her side. Concerned eyes scanned her. "How do you fare?"

"Tired." And shaken. But she dared not tell him of the halved stone or its strange effect on her.

"How badly do you hurt?"

"I have fared worse."

He lifted her face with his thumb, studied her with a sage eye. "The little warrior." He shook his head. "I regret what you witnessed this day." His voice grew rough.

"The cause of this day's tragedy is my brother," she whispered. "He is a man capable of great evil, regardless of who must die to achieve his goal."

Seconds passed. He continued to stare at her with unnerving intent.

"I need to sleep." It was the truth, but tired and aching, she doubted she would find any rest this night.

"You do." Without warning, Seathan lay beside her, pulling another blanket to cover them both.

His battle-seasoned frame pressed against her, the heat from his body far from what she needed. "'Tis improper," she whispered, wanting so much more.

"Improper?" He pulled her against him. "And what of our time spent within the cave?"

"Necessary," she replied, even with her body aching, too aware of him. "Now, your men are about."

"Consider them chaperones."

"There is little proper—"

"You are warm?"

With his body pressed against hers, she was burning, but with need. "Yes, except—"

"Then my lying beside you is necessary. Be quiet."

In the moonlight, Seathan took in the ragged stitches upon her brow. They would leave a scar, but that was a small sacrifice compared to her life.

He gently pressed his face against her hair, unable to resist savoring the smell of her, the softness of this woman. She had witnessed more today than most of her sex, yet she'd warned him of the attacking soldier, then had taken a blow meant for him. Most likely, she'd saved his life.

On an exhale, Linet closed her eyes. A wolf howled in the distance, but she remained still.

Seathan drew her against him, assuring himself it was her need for warmth, no other, that guided his actions. He closed his eyes, tried to sleep. After the last two days, he should have succumbed with ease. But he found himself listening to her even breaths, feeling her steady pulse against his skin.

Each beat was a testament that she lived, another chance given.

And what if she had died?

No, he refused to entertain such thoughts. She was here, alive, safe. He drew her closer, the feel of her against him like a balm to his soul.

Unable to sleep, he stared at the canopy of stars. Who would have believed the changes so little time had wrought? When he'd departed his home, he'd savored meeting Lord Tearlach. And with Linet his prisoner, to watch her brother's fury, aware he had no recourse but to obey Seathan's commands if he wanted his sister alive.

But after she'd almost died this day, he found himself reluctant to hand her over to her brother.

Why should he hesitate? The lass had placed herself in danger when she'd walked into his cell. The decision was hers. But if her reasons for revenge against her brother were true . . .

A sword's wrath. Why was he still debating this? She could never matter in his life. And he held no proof of her claim except for her word.

Should that be enough?

On a long inhale, her sweet essence weaving into his every breath, he closed his eyes and gave way to sleep. The answers would come in time. Before he confronted Tearlach, he must deal with Dauid.

Seathan stared at the moon against the western sky as it slowly sank beyond the horizon. Another night past.

He scanned the forest below. In the dark of night, black fingers of branches melded into each other.

Two days had passed since they'd arrived at the rebel hideout. Linet had continued to heal, and any doubt of her recovery had fled. As to her being in league with Tearlach, with each discussion, he found himself believing more in her innocence.

Seathan rubbed the back of his neck and hated that, for the first time in his life, a woman left him unsure.

"Seathan?"

At Linet's soft voice, he rolled over, found her face but a whisper from his own. His body immediately hardened.

Her mouth parted as if to speak.

"Are you well?" he asked, the absurdity of his question not lost to him. After the first night, she'd been able to stand; by the second, he'd allowed her to walk with him. But if he said naught when she watched him with such desire, it would allow his temptation to grow. And 'twas dangerous for him to touch her now. He already wanted her too much.

"You are not sleeping?" she asked.

Nay, his entire body was damnably awake. "It will soon be morning."

"Are we leaving today?"

"On the morrow." Silence stretched between them. He should get up, leave her. With his body hard, it was far from safe to remain lying next to her, pretending she needed his body's warmth. He could have given her another blanket and slept nearby.

Except then, he couldn't touch her.

A soft pressure made him start. Seathan reached over, caught her, caught her hand upon his chest. His heart jumped.

The moment shifted, became dangerous.

"Do not," he warned.

"What?" she asked, her voice thick with desire. "Touch you, tell you that you haunt my every thought?"

Damn her, did she know what she was doing to him? "Go to sleep." He should be awarded sainthood for those words.

"Seathan?"

He glanced around, frustrated to find the rocks he'd made their bed behind now offered a wall of intimate seclusion. His men lay asleep some distance away. "What do you wish?"

"To know . . . To know if you want me."

Chapter 16

The silence of the night echoed between them. Even after asking Seathan if he wanted her, Linet was stunned by her own audacity.

She should be embarrassed, lower her head in shame at her wanton words. Except, for the last two nights she'd lain beside Seathan, embraced by his muscled body, listening to his every breath, and with each one, wanting him more.

The injury upon her head was healing, but with each passing day, her needs grew to an unbearable ache. Needs that had little to do with her injury and everything to do with Seathan.

Beneath the moonlight, piercing green eyes darkened to vibrant black, eyes of a predator, those of a man who without a word had staked his claim.

She shivered, but felt naught but heat.

And desire.

He leaned a degree closer, his body tense against hers. Frustration flashed on his face; he shoved away.

Panic slid through her, tangled with hurt. "You do not want me?"

"Do not ask."

The strain in his voice bolstered her courage. She moved beside him and pressed her hand against his muscled chest.

"Do not," he said, his burr rough.

But he stayed not her hand, allowed her freedom to roam, as if giving her the ultimate choice. Her breath trembled from her lips as she lifted away his tunic. Battle-hewn muscles glistened beneath the moonlight, the hard planes rippling down to where black, coarse hair disappeared beneath his trews. Throat dry, she glanced up to find him watching her.

"I am but a man," he said through clenched teeth. "Do not touch me unless you want me to touch you . . . everywhere."

Another wave of heat washed through her. How could she want anything else? It seemed as if her entire life had spiraled to this moment.

Damn tomorrow or the days ahead. Life guaranteed naught. But here, now, it offered her this moment, a memory however wrong, she would take. If her future was to be without him, then for this one night she would have him, would savor the memories of joining with the man she loved.

"Make love with me."

Still, he hesitated, his expression torn.

Linet skimmed her fingers across the muscles of his chest, savoring the taut skin, the quiver of flesh beneath.

Seathan caught her hand.

She angled her head as if a dare; her heart pounding. "Will you stop me?"

"No." With a fierce growl, he hauled her to him, claimed her mouth, hot and hard.

Heat stormed her at his sensual assault, a burn so hot, she doubted she could feel more. Impossibly, he cupped her face, slanted his mouth, and took the kiss deeper.

Waves of need stormed her. Her body shuddered, craved, ached to feel his touch, his mouth everywhere.

"This is wrong," he whispered as he kissed the curve of her jaw, cupped her face, then covered her mouth again.

She arched her body against his, telling him with actions that it was right and so much more. "I need all of you," she whispered.

He pressed his brow against her, his entire body trembling. "You are too weak."

Moved, she laid her palm against his cheek. "My weakness is from wanting you."

With a predatory hiss, he laid her against the blanket, pressed the entire length of his body against hers. Leaning on his elbows, he stared at her, his breathing hard, stark desire carved on his face.

"Before I touch you," Seathan said, his voice somber, "there is something I must tell you."

Fear slid through her. She tensed. "What?" she asked, not wanting anything to extinguish the magic of this moment.

His fierce gaze held hers. "I need you to know that I believe you, believe you freed me to exact vengeance on your brother."

Emotions stormed her. "You believe me?" she asked, stunned by his admission. "Why?"

He stroked her cheek with a sweep of his thumb. "Never have I met anyone like you, a woman who would dare to go against convention, a woman ready to barter with the enemy to right a wrong, a woman who chooses the right path however difficult." He paused. "Ever since you appeared before my cell offering to free me, I have suspected you."

She nodded, still stunned. "How could you not? I was a stranger."

"But against everything," he continued, "against my doubts, my suspicions, the challenges offered during our journey, you persevered. When you saw Nichola, it took immense courage to maintain your calm, but you did. Your actions, decisions, are the sames ones I would have made." He pressed a soft kiss upon her mouth. "Forgive me, Linet."

Happiness swept through her. Tears of joy shimmered in her eyes. "I do." Questions tumbled through her mind like an avalanche unbound, but she set them aside. Tomorrow would offer time to talk, to ask more questions. For this moment she would savor this gift, this one night. She pressed her lips against his. "Make love to me, Seathan. I need you so much."

Seathan stared at Linet, drawn by the sheen of moonlight against her amber-gold hair, the way her eyes shimmered with sincerity and desire. Why had he told her of his change of heart? In the end, she would live in the Highlands with her mother's clan while his life was here.

"I want to see you." He cared not that his voice trembled, or that his emotions were wrapped around his words.

She reached up to loosen a tie.

"No, let me."

"But I . . ."

The gift of being her first lover came with responsibility, a charge he would savor. He again leaned forward to cover her mouth, tasting her every moan, her each shiver of awareness. Her body began to shift beneath his, a restlessness she'd yet to understand, but he would teach her the meaning and so much more.

"Are you not going to touch me?"

Her voice, rich with desire, evoked his own. "I will," he whispered. "But this time, your first time, is for you."

Her eyes widened. "You know I am a virgin?"

"Aye," he replied, painfully aware of the fact.

"How?"

God in heaven, the lass would be the death of him yet. "I will tell you—later."

A blush stole up her face. "I am sorry; I am doing this badly."

"As we have done nothing, I beg to differ." He focused on her, the fullness of her mouth, the discoveries he'd find this night.

The intensity of Seathan's gaze pierced her, the blatant desire of which she'd only dreamed. He reached out. With aching slowness he loosened the ties of her gown. At times his finger would graze her skin, but with her garment falling open, he touched her no more. Frustrated, Linet reached up to help him.

"Do not."

"Is making love supposed to take this long?"

A satisfied smile grazed his mouth. "When it is done right." Then he lowered his mouth over hers, her body exposed to his, the hard planes of his chest pressing against the softness of her own. She arched against him, wanting more, to be done with whatever caused the overwhelming ache deep within. Floundering, she reached up, wrapped her arms around his neck, and pulled him flush against her. His hardness wedged against her woman's place, the sensation a frustrating bliss.

"Easy, lass."

The deep timber of his burr stroked her needs. She pulled her mouth away, her breaths shallow. "I want, need—"

He pressed his finger gently upon her lips. "I know exactly what you need." Dark eyes held hers. "Trust me. Give yourself over to me completely."

This was making not a bit of sense. "Am I not almost naked?"

Seathan groaned. He pressed his lips to the column of her neck. "Trust me." His words reverberated against her skin, inciting new responses.

Caught in a turmoil of sensations, her body raging for his touch, she nodded.

He pushed away the last remnants of her gown,

leaving her surrounded by naught but the night. Appreciation settled on his face. "I am going to touch you," he said as his mouth slid along the silky column of her throat, pausing to taste, to tease as he wove his way down. "All over, watch you as you fall over the edge."

Heat pulsed deep to her core, a steady ache that raised its own demands. "And," she gasped, "what do I do?"

"Enjoy."

"What of your enjoyment?"

He laid his brow against her shoulder, his body tense. "I assure you, before this night is over," he said on a ragged breath, "I will find mine as well."

"But you are touching me and I am just lying here."

He gave a pained smile. "I will let you touch me, but not now, not . . . never mind."

"Lovemaking is very confusing."

"Only if you make it. Linet?"

"Yes?"

"Just feel."

His fingers swirled along her collarbone, along the slope of her breasts, teasing the edge, and for the life of her, even if she'd wanted, she couldn't speak.

For long seconds he toyed with the curve of her breast, first one, then sliding to attend to the other. Her body tingled, heated, and it was all she could do not to whimper. Never before had she experienced so much, felt so alive. It was as if her skin had become sensitized to his every touch, each of his movements igniting deeper awareness.

Eyes glittering with desire, he lowered his head, touched her nipple with his tongue.

She gasped.

He watched her, held her gaze as he licked her with long, slow swirls until his mouth closed over the hard nub.

A spasm tore through her. "Seathan!"

His finger caught her other nipple, rolled it with his thumb as he continued to suckle.

Sheer pleasure swept through her. When she thought she couldn't feel anymore, he pressed his hardness against her.

On a gasp, Linet arched against him.

"You taste wonderful."

Heat flushed her cheeks at his outrageous words, but a part of her savored them.

"Now," he said with a positively wicked look, "I shall see if you taste as good everywhere." Seathan slowly slid down her body, tasting, touching her, savoring her as he traveled with maddening slowness to her most private place.

She should stop him. Never should she allow him this intimacy, but when he hovered above her downy curls, looked at her with such raw desire, she wanted nothing more.

"Tell me you want me," he said, his breath soft upon her most private place.

"I . . ." She shuddered. "I want you."

"That you want me to taste you."

Heat rolled over her.

"Tell me."

Mouth dry, her body caught in a glorious heat, she nodded. "I—I want you to taste me."

With his eyes fixed on her, he swept his tongue across her swollen folds, slow, steady, savoring, giving her no quarter.

Sensation built, swirled inside her in a mind-numbing haze.

With a needy moan, Linet arched, and Seathan caught her, settled into a more comfortable position, his eyes never leaving hers. He wanted to watch her as she felt every sensation, as she was initiated into womanhood, and when she fell over the edge. Never had he been with a woman who was so open, so sensitive to his every touch. Already he could feel her body coiled tight, see her entrance glistening, ready for his entry.

Her taste excited him, a sleek, heady aroma of woman and need. His body hardened further, urging him to drive deep within her. He held back. When he found his release, it would be with her joining in the erotic bliss. But not her first time. This special moment he would watch, enjoy her initiation into passion.

So he took his time, savored her whimpers, how she shifted beneath him as he licked the soft, sleek folds, toyed with her hard nub, then slowly suckled, only to begin again. When her movements became frantic, he slid his finger deep inside her tight sheath. She was wet, wonderfully so.

"Seathan!"

He loved watching her eyes glaze, how her body trembled with emotion, then began to shake. "Let go," he urged, then suckled her mercilessly as he stroked her.

Her body's tremors grew and she arched, then began to twist.

He held tight, pushed on. With a long moan, she found her release, and he savored this special moment, the fact he was her first, and the pleasure pulsing through her.

As her body shuddered beneath him, he moved up and lay beside her. Gently, he drew her against him, kissed her brow. "You are amazing."

A breathless laugh fell from her lips. "I think I am the one who should say that to you."

He smiled, for the first time in his life, truly content. Not wanting to ponder the disturbing thought further, he nipped at her neck; she groaned. "And did you find enjoyment in my touch?"

A sated smile settled across her lips. "You know I did." Her brows wedged into a frown. "Is it not unseemly to speak of our intimacy?"

Long used to women seasoned in bed, he found her embarrassment charming. "Shall I tell you that you taste of honey, that I love your woman's nectar upon my tongue?"

She buried her head within the curve of his neck. Touched by her shyness, Seathan caught her face within his hands, needing her to see him, and to know he spoke the truth. "There is no shame in what we do, in what I say. These are the words of your lover. Of that, never be ashamed."

"No one has ever . . ."

"As you are a maiden, if any man had, I would be forced to find and kill him." He realized he meant it.

She gave a shaky laugh. "I am no maiden now."

"In many ways you are," Seathan said, suddenly somber. "I have but made love to you with my mouth. Your innocence is still intact."

"Oh." She worried her lip.

He stilled, his body screaming in protest. "Do you wish me to touch you no further?" If she said yes, as much as he wanted her, he'd honor her request.

Her expression grew serious. "Nay, I want you, more so than I would have ever believed."

"Though I have prepared you, our joining will hurt, but only at first."

"I still want you."

He wasn't sure whether he should be humbled or charmed. The woman kept him off balance as no other lass had ever. "Come here." He wanted her willing, her innocence given without question.

She reached down.

Seathan caught her hand.

Surprise registered on her face. "I was but going to touch you."

The pleasure of her caressing his maleness drove a shot of heady lust through his already raging body. "It would not be good."

She frowned.

"Now is not the time to explain." An understatement.

"But you took me in your mouth," Linet said. "Do you not want me to taste you as well?"

Her innocent question loosed an avalanche of

erotic images, of her naked, kneeling before him, of her tasting him, sating her own desires as well as his. The vivid scenes stormed his mind, threatening to break his hard-won control.

"If once we are done, you wish to explore my body, then you may." And he would die with her innocent touch, but he'd go a happy man.

"That seems fair."

He chuckled, a half-pained sound.

"That is funny?"

Seathan shook his head. "Nay, far from it."

"Then—"

"No more talk."

The heat in Seathan's eyes erased any doubt of his intent. He rolled her over, his body caging her beneath. Awareness shivered through her, her body still quivering from her previous release.

"Do not be afraid," he whispered.

And she wasn't. She'd given herself to him body, heart, and soul, though he would never know that. His kiss was hard and deep, but Linet savored it, matched his intensity. With her body sensitized, on fire wherever they touched, she wanted him to experience the same—with her.

He nibbled on her ear.

"Seathan?"

"Aye," he said between nips.

"Are you sure I cannot taste you now?"

A growl rumbled from his throat. He rolled, pulling her to sit on top of him.

The oddness of her position, with him lying naked beneath her, set off a myriad of emotions.

"What are you doing?" she asked as she wondered what to do next.

"My lady, 'twould seem you wish to be in control, so that I give you."

She frowned. "How am I in control?"

A pained smile creased his mouth. "I assure you, you are."

"But you are stronger, a warrior who could easily take me if you chose."

He released a long, rough sigh. "We are making love. The power I give you is of choice. I will not touch you unless you ask, taste you unless you beg."

"Beg?"

Mischief twinkled in his eyes. "Beg."

Memories of his mouth on her most private place sent another wash of heat through her. Yes, she would beg. "And what else?" Her voice wavered.

"Anything but taste me."

She frowned. "You said I was in charge."

"Not of that."

"I was not aware there were rules."

"Do you always talk this much?"

"When I am nervous."

He caught her hands, placed them upon his chest. "Except for tasting me, I give you full control."

Anticipation rippled through her. "Truly?"

Seathan nodded.

Her every fantasy whirled through her, the whispers of women she'd overheard spawning new, decadent thoughts. Did she dare to do that?

"Linet?"

"Yes?" Nervousness made her voice waver.

"You can begin anytime."

He was laughing at her! Fine then. With her knees straddling his wonderfully male body, she leaned down and kissed the strong column of his neck.

He groaned but didn't touch her.

A smile curved her lips, and her doubts fell away. As she touched him, tasted him, she let her hands roam his hard planes, slide through the luxurious matt of hair rippling across his chest. Curiosity had her inching down.

She flicked the tip of her tongue upon his nipple.

Seathan sucked in his breath.

"You like that?"

"Aye."

He sounded in pain. Still, he said it pleased him. Linet lowered her mouth, suckled, remembering too well the sensations of his mouth upon her. Enjoying her newfound freedom, she mimicked his action and caught his other nipple between her thumb and forefinger; he groaned louder. Thrilled this pleased him, that he enjoyed her touch, she applied herself, his musky taste wondrous. The thick hardness of him pressed against her woman's place was exciting in itself.

Her body hummed, his hard length fueling the ache deep within. Wanting more, she pressed herself against him. She slowly rocked, savoring the intimate bond.

Without warning, Seathan caught her, flipped her on her back, and poised himself at her entrance, looking more the warrior than her lover.

"What are you doing?" she asked breathlessly.

"Reclaiming sanity." He nudged her with his hard tip.

Her folds, slick from his lovemaking, tingled with pleasure as he slipped within. Her body throbbed. She arched against him.

He pushed deeper—halted.

Linet frowned up at him.

Concern edged his brow. "When I take you, it will hurt."

The care, the seriousness of his tone, made her love him all the more. "I know, but I want you." *Always,* she finished in her mind.

Seathan pulled back. With his eyes fixed on her, he drove deep.

Pain lanced through her, and she cried out.

He drew her against him. "I am sorry. If I could, I would spare you the pain, but it is over. Now, you will feel naught but pleasure."

He wouldn't understand that her tears were for the sanctity of this moment, not for the loss of her virginity.

"Make love to me, Seathan."

He kissed her, stroked her until she forgot the pain, teased her until her body again throbbed with need. Only after she arched against him did he move, slow, deep strokes that had her body trembling, spinning out of control. At her groan, he increased the pace. A wave of emotion hit her, harder than before, tossing her up, his next stroke taking her higher. Her body stiffened.

"Let go," he urged, driving faster, if possible, deeper.

And she gave him her all.

Shimmering lights exploded in her mind, bursts of red, purple, and white. The warmth of his seed spilling into her as he found his release tossed her on a higher plane and left her floating in a pool of ultimate bliss.

With her body shaking with pleasure, he drew her against him, pressed kisses upon her jaw, along the line of her chin. "And to think, we have only begun." With slow movements, he began to roam down her body, kissing her, teasing her in her most sensitive places.

Linet gave a sated smile. "I will die if you continue."

"Aye, most likely." He winked at her. "I have been known to cause a casualty or two." Then he applied himself, erasing any coherent thought.

Happily, Linet closed her eyes and soared.

Chapter 17

Feet braced, hands on hips, Seathan stood upon the ridge, the slash of hills and roll of trees captured within dawn's purple-gray light. Pockets of stubborn snow clung within crevices, nooks that with a warm day would melt.

He should savor the beauty of the sunrise, look forward to soon having Dauid in his grasp. Instead his thoughts remained on Linet. He rubbed his brow and turned toward where she slept.

They'd made love most of the night, and he had little regret. Yet he'd taken her virginity, a choice that held its own consequences.

Damn him, well he understood the rules they lived by. She was not a commoner. She was a noble-woman, and now, thanks to their impulsiveness, no longer a maiden. However wrong his actions last night, if again given the choice, he would make love with her.

Which said damnable little for his character.

That Linet had sought his bed mattered not. She

was an innocent; her lack of knowledge when it came to desire skewed her full understanding of her actions. He was an earl, wielded immense responsibly daily, had taken many lovers over the years and well knew the pull of desire and the responsibility of decisions made. Though she'd uttered the words, in the end 'twas his decision to accept. Now, it would be his decision what to do next.

Should he escort her to the Highlands to live with her mother's clan? Rationally, a wise choice. After Wallace's slaying the Sheriff of Lanark and with the next rebel attack on the English planned in but a few months, he needed to focus on their strategy, not on a woman who made his blood hot, a woman who'd learned quickly and excelled in the intimacies of lovemaking or a woman who shattered his willpower and dragged unpredictability into his life.

A thought hit him, an idea so foreign he'd never allowed it to flourish until this moment. What if Linet carried his child? What if after their night of lovemaking, his heir grew within her womb?

They'd spent but one night together. The chance of her being with child was slight. The image of her round with his son seized his mind, conjured images of her holding their babe with a look so pure, so loving, his heart ached.

He stared at her. Was it possible he wanted her to have his child? A ludicrous thought, a foolish notion to even ponder. Each had their own path, hers in the Highlands and his focused on war. Except, the image of her nursing their babe wove through his mind, the glow upon her face, the way she'd lift her eyes to look at him with love.

Throat tight, he stared over the forest-swept land, brittle beneath the tip of the ascending sun. The glaze of fog sifted through the treetops as if a spell.

"Seathan?"

At the whisper of Linet's sleep-thickened voice, he willed away his dangerous musings, thoughts that presented yet another reason why he should keep his distance.

He strode over. The slowness of her movements as she pushed herself up to sit had him kneeling before her. "You are hurting?" He never should have touched her after the first time. She'd been a virgin, unused to the demands of love play, however gentle.

A sexy smile softened her mouth. "Not at all."

Her throaty words wrapped around him with lust-instilling accuracy. She reached out to him, and he found himself taking her hand, against common sense, against all of the reasons he'd just compiled as to why he should leave her alone.

"I still need you."

His blood pounded hot as he gazed upon her. The first rays of sunlight spilled over her amber-gold hair, framing her creamy skin in a shimmering wash, illuminating eyes wide and vulnerable. The contradiction of this sultry female and the stubborn woman who always challenged him, aroused his passions to a dangerous level, and left him wanting her, aching to possess her with his every breath.

"You must be sore." What was he doing lingering?

Each moment he stayed weakened his willpower further.

She knelt before him, and the blanket tumbled away, exposing her supple body to his view, the fullness of her breasts but a whisper away. The curve of her hips lured his gaze to her woman's place.

Linet leaned forward to slide her body against his. "I feel naught but desire for you."

He shuddered. She was magnificent. The reasons to leave her untouched clouded, smothered by her taste still lingering on his lips, her woman's scent filling his every breath.

He willed himself to maintain control. "We have but a few hours to rest."

She scanned the waning darkness. "We will leave this day?" Her voice trembled, a reminder of all that stood between them.

"On the morrow." Though he believed her reasons for freeing him, he'd not reveal that his guards had sighted her brother and his men to the west. In another day, Tearlach would have traveled far enough away and they could safely begin their journey to catch Dauid.

Her eyes clouded as if in deep thought, then cleared. Full lips curved upward in blatant invitation. "So we still have a few hours . . . to rest?"

God in heaven, he wasn't a saint.

Seathan caught Linet's jaw, lifted her face to meet his, and a shiver of anticipation ripped through her.

"Just what is it my lady wishes?"

The sensual purr of his voice ignited memories of their lovemaking, of the erotic acts he'd performed upon her, intimacies she'd never had any idea existed. But now she knew.

And wanted more.

Memories to treasure once he'd left her.

She willed away the painful thoughts of their parting. They had another day, time she would make count.

As she had fantasized, Seathan lowered her to the blanket. Slowly, his body covered her, inch by amazing inch. As the thick tip of him caressed her most intimate place, she arched to meet him, but he caught her hands, pressed her back, and slowly licked the inner skin of her palm while his eyes never left hers.

She shivered at the rush of desire.

"Never hurry the taking."

"You are tormenting me," she whispered, her body already wet for him, aching for him to touch her everywhere.

Male satisfaction shimmered on his face. "'Tis a pleasing way to suffer."

She laughed, a rough, wanting sound, amazed at the layers that made up this man, his ability to care, his thoughtfulness on every level, and his painstaking attention to every detail. The latter she especially appreciated.

With a wicked look in his eyes, he stroked her, skimmed his fingers over her sensitized flesh until she moaned with his every touch. Instead of filling her, he used his tongue and mouth, driving her insane. Finally, with her body on fire, when she thought she'd die from pleasure, he rose, sank deep inside her, then stilled.

Her body clenched around him. She gasped. "Seathan—"

"Steady, lass." He nibbled the soft skin of her neck, teased her with his tongue. "The more you rush, the slower I'll decide how best to proceed in seducing every inch of you."

Her body trembled with anticipation. "You are a braggart."

He gave a husky laugh, bent, and suckled her breast. Through thick black lashes, he watched her. "Your moans throughout the night said different."

Heat stroked her cheeks. "You are shameless."

"Aye." He withdrew, and then drove deep. Seathan covered her lips, taking, demanding, making love to her with his tongue as his body followed suit. He offered no quarter, his slow pace increasing with each entry until his quick thrusts had her panting, her body quaking. When she thought she couldn't take more, he pressed the palm of his hand against her sensitized flesh and rubbed.

She shattered.

Waves of light exploded before her, magnificent bursts of white, orange, and yellow, then an explosion of green as she felt the warmth of his release.

Sated, her body quivering from passion and still joined to his in the most intimate way, she lay there not wanting to move as emotions churned within her. The storm of feelings was unlike any she'd ever weathered. Her hopes and dreams combined into a passionate wash. This moment with Seathan was

perfect, amazing, everything she'd ever prayed for
and more. It was as if nothing else existed but him,
perfection in his every breath.

With him wedged deep inside her, she stared past
his naked outline into the night. The last few stars
shimmered in the sky as if a magical dust. Warmth
swept through her. She'd thought herself in love
with Seathan before, but those feelings paled compared to the emotions churning inside.

Drowsy, happy beyond belief, she inhaled his wonderful male scent, closed her eyes, and stroked her
fingers across his chest. "I love you."

Seathan stiffened.

Sweet Mary, she'd not meant to say the words
aloud. Her eyes flew open. His face shuttered to an
emotionless mask, he began to pull away; panic infused her.

"Stay." And she prayed he would.

"I cannot." He withdrew and began to dress.

Frantic, her body warm from her release, at odds
with the icy restraint of his actions, she reached over
and touched his arm.

Seathan stilled, watched her.

"I . . ." Did baring her soul to him mean nothing?
She hadn't meant to tell him she loved him, but she
had. Linet struggled for composure, but how could
she regain her poise when the person she loved was
pushing her away?

He stood, his body rigid, the face of her lover of
moments before now hard, distant, like the warrior she'd first met. No, not like the dangerous
man caged within Fulke's cell. Too much had hap-

pened between them. Even though Seathan now believed her innocent of conspiring with her brother, he obviously didn't fully trust her or plan to keep her close.

"Seathan—"

He stood. "Do not say more."

She shoved to her feet, raising her hand for him to stay back when he started toward her. Her heart shattered, splintered into fragments. What had she expected? Never had he indicated that he wanted more than having her in his bed. The hurt was hers to bear, pain she'd invited by allowing her emotions to rule her decisions.

His eyes scoured her nakedness with a lover's awareness, then he turned away.

Embarrassment swept through her. Furious that he could cheapen the beauty of the hours they'd spent together, she stepped before him, lifted her chin with defiance. "I said naught more than I feel."

He remained silent.

She waited, willed him to speak, to give her some indication of what thoughts ran through his mind. After a long moment, his hard expression softened.

Aching, Linet stepped closer. "I care not that you are an earl, nor for your wealth. 'Tis you that is important. But I want naught more than you would give me freely."

His mouth tightened into a hard grimace.

Her composure broke. "Damn you, Seathan, we made love. I ask naught except for you to speak to me, to tell me what you are thinking. Do not push me away. We must talk about this."

"What we did was wrong."

She shook her head. "No. Never in my life have I felt anything more right. Tell me, did you not feel the bond when we joined, the touching of our souls? It was special, magical, as if it was meant to be."

"We felt naught but lust."

Linet started to say more, then paused. Odd. Through his bluster, she caught the hint of apprehension. Mayhap his pushing her away had to do with the woman he'd spoken of before, the one who had hurt him? It made sense. Not that in his state he would agree or admit such. But she had to try to make him understand.

"It was special to me," she said.

His face softened further. "You were a virgin. The first time is always special."

"Memorable perhaps, but not special. I have spoken with other women of the gentry"—she pushed on when he made to speak—"women who warned me of what to expect on my wedding night. The brutality, the pain. They advised me to smile as if the act brought me pleasure. With you, I never had to pretend. It was real."

"For you."

"And you felt naught?" she challenged, daring him to deny the pleasure he'd found.

He glanced at the rising sun, strain harsh on his face. "My feelings for you have no bearing on the battles ahead of me."

"I do not understand."

"Because you are not a warrior," he said quietly, "with a warrior's worries for those he leaves behind."

Tears glittered in her eyes at what he didn't say, wouldn't say, and she loved him all the more. "You are trying to spare me hurt?"

He stared at her long and hard. "With all that stands between you and me, nothing more can exist between us. I will not lie to you, nor pretend otherwise."

She ignored his dismissal. "When we made love, you felt it as well, the magic in our joining?"

He tensed at her words, but didn't deny them. "The magic we gave to each other. Physically. Nothing more."

She remembered the gemstone hanging beneath his tunic, and how earlier, the matching half she carried had warmed. "But you felt it," she insisted.

"Linet."

She stepped to a hand's breath before him, determined to prove what he refused to admit, that more existed between them than a heated romp. She loved him. Whatever happened, she would love him until the end. She may have been innocent, but she recognized love. If he was fool enough to insist that what they shared was merely physical, by God, she'd show him otherwise.

After last night, aware of what he enjoyed, she knelt before him.

He scowled at her. "What are you doing?"

"Finding my pleasure." Before he could stop her, she took him in her hands, claimed him with her mouth.

"A sword's wrath."

She thrilled that she excited him, that within her

mouth, he hardened to slick steel. She closed her eyes, savored the salty male taste of him.

A low rumble sounded in his throat; his body shook.

Without warning, he caught her, hauled her to him, his face raw with passion. He backed her against the ledge, and with the moss-slicked rock cool against her, poised himself at her slick entry, then drove deep. She gasped as he impaled her over and again, his every thrust taking her higher. As she touched the stars, Seathan spilled his seed into her fertile warmth.

Seathan laid his head against her neck, his breathing hard. "Scotland is torn by war. I can offer you no promises."

Linet's hand caressed his cheek as hope bloomed. It wasn't a declaration of love, but it was enough. "I ask for none."

As if a silent bond had been forged, he carried her back to their pallet. His gaze intense, he slowly made love to her until they were both exhausted. Then, while he held her against him, she fell into a sated sleep.

Seathan guided his steed up the next brae, Linet cradled in the saddle before him. Two days had passed since their discussion had turned erotic and set the tone for further intimacy. Though he'd admitted nothing more to her, when they'd made love, intense emotion beyond what he'd ever experienced had poured through him.

Warmth tingled against his chest.

He grimaced, ignored the pendant pulsing against his skin as he'd done for the past two days, and searched the horizon.

Magic didn't inspire his emotions. What he felt was the passion of a man who'd joined with a virgin, a woman who dared give fully of herself when making love. Linet's enthusiasm to explore, taste, touch him during lovemaking was any man's dream. How many times had he wished for the confines of his chamber, to remove the risk of being interrupted? He longed for days with her in his bed, to show her how much more there was when it came to making love.

It would be all too easy to acknowledge her words of love as truth. Yet he didn't dare. Accepting them would require evaluating his own feelings toward her, emotions that already ran too deep.

He glanced at the sun high in the sky. Hours of travel remained before they halted, hours before he could find privacy and plunder her silken depths. And he would sate himself with her, until the time came to part.

A reality approaching too fast.

Fortunately they'd avoided her brother and his men, but after dealing with Dauid, he and Tearlach would meet. Except now he would leave Linet safely hidden. If Tearlach survived their confrontation, never would he find her. 'Twas ironic. Before, he had savored the upcoming clash of blades, anticipated driving his sword deep into the bastard's heart. Now, caring for Linet had complicated everything.

However much Linet claimed that she despised her brother, blood ties ran deep. How would she feel after the viscount fell beneath his blade? What if she never forgave him?

"Once I am through with Dauid," Seathan said, his words revealing none of the turmoil churning inside, "I will escort you to your mother's clan in the Highlands."

The echo of hooves broke the silence between them, an empty, lonely sound.

For a long moment she remained silent. "I am no longer your prisoner?"

"No."

"My thanks."

Though she worked to keep her reply free of emotion, he heard the hurt.

"I am sure your mother's clan will accept you," he offered, remembering her earlier fears.

"It is not your worry, is it?"

Irritation flared. "Aye, it is. You are within my protection."

"A temporary condition," she returned, her words cool. "I belong to no one. When shall we arrive at our destination?"

Irritation sliced through him at her cool response, but perhaps it was better not to talk of their future, or lack of it.

"We shall make camp shortly," he replied.

The wind, rich with the scent of rain, kicked up. The field of brown grass, dotted with winter-dried heather, waved beneath the gust.

Seathan glanced skyward, took in the cloud-filled

sky churning in angry gray swirls. In the distance, he caught the lash of rain falling to the ground. He'd wanted to travel farther this day, to reach Dauid's home. However, it would serve little purpose to push on this late in the day. Tomorrow, and facing Dauid, would come soon enough.

After several quick orders, his men made camp within a thick copse of trees, the sturdy branches providing solid cover.

Hours later, with the patter of droplets tapping upon the evergreen branches overhead, the air rich and clean with the scent of rain, Seathan laid out his bedroll. He turned, and Linet stood nearby, watching him. Soon they would part. It would be simpler if he kept his distance, severed ties already too deep. And if he did, he'd be more of a bastard than he was now.

He reached out; she took his hand. With his mind steeped in emotions he'd rather not feel, he drew Linet to the ground and made love to her.

Chapter 18

Seathan peered through the rain-drenched shrubs and gave a reassuring squeeze to Linet's shoulder as she sat by his side. He scoured the darkened sky, the thick gray banks of clouds so low it was as if he could touch them.

A storm was coming.

Across the open field stood a battered hut, smoke swirling from the chimney. A home where he'd spent many a night visiting Dauid and his wife. A home where he'd always felt welcome. A home that now housed a traitor.

Anger urged him to storm the hut, yet prudence stayed his hand until the men he'd sent to ensure Tearlach's knights weren't hidden nearby returned.

Was Dauid living within his home as if nothing were amiss? Did he believe Seathan dead and feel safe? Had Dauid sworn an oath of fealty to Tearlach in return for protection? Nothing else made sense.

Seathan again scanned the surrounding forest. Winter-browned leaves fluttered past. A raven flew overhead. In the distance, a roebuck grazed. The animal raised his head, his tail twitched, and he bounded off.

Faint footsteps hurrying through the brush sounded.

One of the knights crouched atop a nearby knoll turned. "My lord, Sir Richard returns."

A moment later, his knight slipped into view. He halted before Seathan. "My lord, I circled Sir Dauid's home. I saw naught but aged tracks."

Seathan nodded, faced the battered hut. And prayed his former friend was fool enough to reside within. He nodded to Linet. "You will remain here under guard."

"God's speed."

Her face reflected the sobriety of the situation, a gentleness, an understanding that had him wishing for another night to find solace in her arms, to forget the battle, to feel the emotions she inspired. Those were but fanciful musings, thoughts for a man free to dream of a future devoid of strife.

A muscle worked in his jaw as he turned to the hut. Whatever treachery Dauid was about, Seathan would learn. Then, the man he had once called his friend would die.

After selecting several knights to remain and protect her, Seathan waved his men forward.

With slow precision he crept across the field, his knights spread out around him. The scent of wet earth filled his nostrils. The cold, sodden ground absorbed any sound, and the winter-ravaged grass was high enough to shield their bent forms.

A thump of wood sounded.

Seathan waved his men down. He peered through the brown blades, the mist of his breath vanishing before him in a trice.

As if beckoned, Dauid stepped from his home. Grief savaged his former friend's face, the sadness upon it as if drawn by years.

'Twould seem his betrayal haunted him. Seathan clenched the hilt of his sword. As if he gave a damn for Dauid's remorse. Never could those slaughtered be resurrected. Their bodies were naught but soul-less flesh and bone rotting deep within the earth.

As if sensing their presence, Dauid halted. He looked around, frowned. Fading bruises marred his face. A deep gash lay above his left eye, the skin surrounding the cut a cesspit of yellows and grays.

Satisfaction stung Seathan. Whatever the reason for the beating, it far from served the bastard his penance owed.

Dauid shaded his eyes from the sun, scanned the field one last time. Dropping his hand, he limped with a pained expression toward the woodpile.

After the traitor began stacking wood into his arms, Seathan waved his men forward. Grass and dirt softened by rain absorbed their steps. Gusts of wind smothered any other sound.

Several paces away, Seathan stood, motioned for his men to wait. He walked forward, halted several paces away.

With the last piece of firewood filling his arms, Dauid wiped his brow with his shoulder, turned toward his home.

And froze.

Recognition flooded Dauid's eyes a second before fear. Knuckles white upon the wood, he shook his head. "Ho-How?"

"How?" Seathan stalked to within a pace of him. "How did I live? How did I survive Tearlach's butchery?"

Dauid started to speak, then closed his mouth. His throat muscles worked as he swallowed hard.

"Think you your silence will sway me on the matter of your betrayal?" Seathan demanded. "Damn you, tell me!"

Shame clouded Dauid's eyes. He glanced at the knights a short distance away, and then lifted his misery-laden gaze to Seathan. Finally, he shook his head. "I am sorry."

"You are sorry?" Fury congealed so deep in Seathan's mind, it bordered on darkness. Steel scraped leather as he unsheathed his sword. "Aye, you will be."

Dauid stumbled back, the wood scattering upon the ground. He reached for his own weapon. "Seathan, wait!"

Seathan charged, swung.

Steel scraped as their blades met. Dauid's sword tumbled from his hand. "Christ!" he gasped, and rolled.

Seathan's blade sank into the ground a finger's width away. On a curse, he freed his sword. Memories of his men's suffering as they lay dying on the battlefield that night burned in his mind. Nay, Dauid did not deserve a death served by steel.

Too quick.

Too impersonal.

Seathan sheathed his blade, shoved his fist into his friend's face. Grim satisfaction infused him as blood spurted from Dauid's mouth. His mind a furious haze, he swung again, each blow, each crunch of bone, meager payment for the lives lost.

Chest heaving, he raised his hand to again slam his fist into Dauid's face, then paused. Dauid lay there watching him as blood slid down his jaw, not turning away, not once raising a hand to deflect the next blow.

Furious, Seathan caught his shoulders, jerked him to his feet. "Fight me, or by God I will beat you to death as your traitorous heart deserves!"

"Kill me then," Dauid rasped.

"And end your pain? Give you a quick death when the men you betrayed suffered?" Seathan shoved him hard.

Dauid stumbled, straightened, favoring his left arm.

Seathan raised his fist. Blank eyes stared at him, the emptiness within as if Seathan stared into the face of someone already dead. "Why will you not defend yourself!"

Dauid's lower lip trembled. "I sw-swear to you, I wanted to betray no one."

Seathan removed his dagger and shoved the blade against Dauid's throat. A line of red drizzled down his neck. "My knights died, were butchered because of you."

Tears filmed his eyes. "Think you I do not know that? Think you that I did not grieve with each life lost? They were men I'd fought beside, my friends as well."

Seathan pressed the razor-sharp steel harder against Dauid's throat. "Grieving? Is that what you call standing beside Tearlach as you watched the slaugher of Scots whom you had sworn to protect?"

"You—" Dauid struggled to breathe. "You do not understand."

"Nay, that is where you are wrong. I understand completely. You forget, that night I saw you standing beside Tearlach as they dragged me away." He angled the blade over the hearty pulse at Dauid's neck for the lethal slash. "You betrayed your people, were responsible for their senseless slaughter. If there is any confusion, it is yours. You should have ensured I was dead."

"Wait!" Dauid gurgled out.

"For more pathetic excuses?"

"For Brighde!"

Confused, Seathan hesitated.

"Kill me," Dauid forced out, "I deserve to die. But pl-please save her."

"What does your wife have to do with your treasonous acts?"

"Tearlach abducted her," he whispered.

He grunted. "Why should I believe you?"

Dauid stared at him, his bruised and swollen eyes silently pleading. "Af-After what I have done, you should not. Yet you must."

This was not making an ounce of sense. Storm clouds brewed overhead, his men waited nearby for his next order, yet he hesitated, found himself wanting to believe Dauid, a man who'd been his friend all his life.

"Tell me," Seathan demanded.

"Tearlach . . ." Dauid closed his eyes, blinked them open with effort. "He tortured me, used his dagger in cr-creative ways. When I refused to tell him where you hid, he broke my left arm. Still, I said nothing." He swallowed hard. "Furious, he took Brighde to use as his whore. If I did not tell him where you hid, he swore once he was done with her, he would give her to his men for their use, to torture her for th-their pleasure. And . . . And when she was naught but a pile of tears and worn goods, he would kill her."

Seathan eyed him with skepticism.

Tears flowed down his former friend's face, mingled with the trail of blood. "I swear to you, I knew not that you would st-still be near my home, that so many of your knights would be in accompaniment, and that"—his throat worked, then he swallowed hard—"that so many men I loved, men who were brothers to me, would die. I believed if you were nearby, you would be alerted to Tearlach's presence and escape. I swear to you, had I known of the consequences, I would have allowed my wife as well as myself to die."

"You stood alongside Tearlach."

"Drugged," he whispered. "After I fought him before, he ensured I would stand at his side without a fight. Numb with pain, my mind hazed by herbs and unable to move, I watched in horror as his men attacked yours."

Reeling from the confession, Seathan relaxed his grip on his blade. "Why did you not come to Lochshire Castle, explain, ask for my help?"

Dauid closed his eyes, then forced them open, the grief within immense. "I thought you dead. How could I think your brothers would believe such a tale, a claim that sounded as if cr-crafted by a bard, much less offer help?" He paused. "A claim I hardly expect you to believe now."

Did he believe him? Logic bade he dismiss Dauid's claim as a lie, but truth rang within his words, a tale too extreme to be anything but real. Still, Seathan hesitated.

"Kill me," Dauid whispered. "It is a fate too easy when I have brought death to many a fine man."

The dagger trembled in Seathan's hand. "On that we agree."

"You hate me, how can you not? But please, when you are through with me, find a way to save Brighde's life."

A part of Seathan ached to believe Dauid told the truth. The other urged him to kill the traitor, leave his body for the wolves.

"Where is your wife?"

"Within Tearlach's home, Breac Castle."

Seathan's breath came out in a hiss. The entire time he was beaten, tortured night after merciless night, Brighde had been locked in a chamber above, raped, for that bastard's pleasure?

His entire body trembled with fury as Seathan sheathed his dagger and stood. He stared at Dauid, who remained still, as if not daring to move, not begging for his own life, but for that of his wife.

If Linet faced a similar fate, how would he feel?

For the men murdered, Seathan wanted to hate Dauid, to kill him. But Dauid had made the decision of a man fighting to save the woman he loved, a warrior who'd revealed a rebel hideout, believing no harm would come. If he'd stood in Dauid's position and had believed his men would have escaped harm, would he not have done the same, then warned the rebels once free?

"We will find Brighde," Seathan promised, "over the dead body of every bloody Englishman if need be."

Shock flickered in Dauid's eyes. "We?" He scanned the knights who surrounded them. "Nay, I deserve no forgiveness. What I ask is for my wife alone."

"And force me to solve the problem you created? Nay, Dauid, I think not."

Wary, Dauid turned to him, hope dawning within his battered expression. A bloodstained tear dripped, wobbled down his cheek. "I am shamed, unworthy to ride at your side."

Raw emotion stormed Seathan as he recalled every minute they'd spent together over the years, every time they'd laughed or confided in each other.

"The shame is mine for ever doubting you." Seathan extended his hand toward Dauid. "I always help a friend."

Dauid stared at his hand, lifted his gaze. "I can never repay you."

"Come." Seathan caught his right hand. "'Tis time to make the bastard pay."

Through the bruises and swelling skin, a grim smile curved Dauid's face. "Aye, 'tis long past time."

"But"—Seathan secured his blade—"Tearlach is mine."

Dauid nodded. "Fair enough."

Relieved, Seathan carefully supported Dauid's right shoulder. He turned to face his men, Dauid leaning against his side. "Dauid has not betrayed us. 'Tis Tearlach who deserves our fury. I will explain later at camp."

Dauid limped at his side as they headed toward the shield of trees where the remainder of his men hid. Now, they had to figure out how to rescue Brighde.

Mud clung to his boots as he walked, the wind cold and sharp.

Breac Castle. 'Twas the last place he wished to see, the memories of his time spent within ripe with horror. He scanned the cloud-churned sky. An icy slap of rain pelted his skin, then another.

At the line of trees, Seathan spotted Linet. In the mayhem, he'd forgotten about her riding with him. They needed to leave immediately to rescue Dauid's wife, but she couldn't come with them, neither did time permit him to escort her to the Highlands. Where could he hide her?

Lochshire Castle.

He needed to send a runner to inform his brothers of their change in plans and his need for their help. He would add several more men as guards and send her with them.

Thunder rumbled in the distance.

"Seems we are in for another storm," a knight at Linet's side said.

She nodded, focused on the small contingent of men as they neared. Relief swept through her as Seathan walked closer, supporting his friend.

What had happened to change Seathan's mind about killing Dauid? Not that his friend looked in any condition to fight back. A deep gash lay across his left eye. Bruises lay scattered across his face in angry hues of yellow and red. He favored his left leg, and leaned against Seathan to avoid pressure upon his foot when they walked.

Several moments later, they stepped beneath the canopy of branches.

When Seathan's gaze met hers, coldness swept through Linet. She'd seen that look before. Whatever had happened in the field, somehow it involved her, or more specifically, her brother.

He stepped past her, supporting Dauid, no warmth in his face. "Come." Seathan looked toward his men. "To your posts." He continued to walk deeper into the trees.

Her unease grew as she accompanied them. She slid a sideways glance at his friend, who studied her with undisguised interest. Why wouldn't he? Few lords traveled with a woman in tow. Much less a lady who he would learn was the sister of their enemy!

Beneath a large oak, Seathan halted, gesturing for her to sit.

On shaky limbs, Linet complied, choosing the trunk of a fallen tree.

He carefully lowered his friend upon the weathered bark several paces away, then stood. "Linet, may I introduce you to my friend, Sir Dauid."

His friend? "My pleasure."

"Dauid," Seathan continued, "Lady Linet."

He nodded, glanced at her curiously. "My lady."

"Sister to Lord Tearlach," Seathan added.

Fury sliced through the half-swollen eyes. Dauid tried to stand, but his left leg buckled beneath him. Clinging to the stump, he glared at Seathan, then his look ebbed to caution. "Why is she here?"

"To use in barter with her brother."

"To barter!" Linet gasped.

Seathan knelt, clasped her hand within his palm. "That was before—"

"Before?" Dauid asked.

"Before I learned her innocent of her brother's foul deeds—as are you."

Dauid remained silent, his face drawn in thought.

"I am no longer to be bartered?" she asked, unsure, confused, needing to hear him say the words. Her heart shuddered with anticipation.

Tenderness softened his face, and he gave her hand a gentle squeeze. "Nay, as I said, you are free."

"And my travel to the Highlands?"

Seathan hesitated. "Upon my return."

"Return? Where are you going? I do not understand."

"Aye, on that I agree," Dauid said. "You have

Tearlach's sister and are not using her against the bastard."

"Nay," Seathan replied, his eyes never leaving hers. "I owe her my life. She freed me from the viscount's dungeon. 'Tis a long story, one I will relate to you later. Suffice it to say, she has shown more courage than any woman I have ever met."

Dauid swallowed hard. "Forgive me, my lady. I knew not that you had saved Seathan's life. For that I cannot thank you enough." His paused, shook his head, grief in his eyes. "God's teeth, Seathan, I—I thought you were dead." Long moments passed as he struggled for composure. "Had I known that the viscount imprisoned you—"

"And tortured him," Linet added, her own anger finding its mark. "You claim to be Seathan's friend, but because of you, he almost died. What kind of man are you? What kind of man betrays a friend?"

Dauid's throat worked. "A man who does not deserve the forgiveness Seathan offers."

"On that I agree." She narrowed her eyes. "How—"

"Enough," Seathan stated.

She glared at Dauid, who returned her hard stare without flinching. Little love was lost between them, on that she was fine.

"Your brother is ruthless in who he uses for his gain," Seathan stated. "Like you, Dauid was but a pawn, his life torn apart on Tearlach's whim. At first light, two of my men will accompany you back to Lochshire Castle. When I return, I will escort you to the Highlands."

"And you?" she asked.

"Dauid, my men, and I will ride to Breac Castle."

Surprised, Linet took in the battered man, noticed old scars atop fresh bruises that Seathan had delivered this day. Why would Seathan allow this man to ride with him while he shuttled her to safety?

"He is unfit to travel," she said.

Dauid's eyes hardened. "I will ride."

His passionate vow shook her. "Why?"

"I must rescue my wife, Brighde."

"You wife is in Breac Castle?" she whispered.

"Aye. Your brother has made her his whore."

Sweet Mary! Speechless, she struggled with the knowledge of yet another horrific wrong her brother had committed. "Had I known of his treachery, I would have . . ." Done what? Sadly, little. She shook her head. "I am sorry."

Dauid watched her with a critical eye. Moments passed, his expression eased. "As am I, but we will save her.

"Aye," Seathan echoed. "Even if we have to tear down every bloody stone in the castle."

A tear slid down Dauid's cheek, but pride, fierce and deep, shone in his eyes as well.

The strength of their friendship left Linet both humbled and saddened. She wished she and Seathan shared the same bond. Their physical connection was beyond doubt, affirmed by their days of intimacy. But how did he feel about her?

As if she had to wonder? His answer of moments ago made his feelings clear. Once he'd freed Dauid's wife, he would escort Linet to the Highlands and out of his life.

Hurt robbed her of breath, carved an ache so painful it tore through her soul. The friendship and trust she yearned for were not gifts he offered her.

Nor ever would.

Working past the pain, the hurt of his rejection of her heart, she focused on their goal of freeing Brighde. She might never win Seathan's love, but she'd not stand by when she could help to right her brother's wrongs.

Linet shoved to her feet. "I am going with you."

Seathan's face darkened. "*Absolutely not!* You will travel to Lochshire Castle, where you will be safe."

"Safe?" Somber, Linet shook her head. "As long as my brother lives, is any one of us truly safe?"

He strode forward, caught her shoulders. "Linet—"

"My brother is the cause of this. Had Fulke not abducted Brighde, threatened Dauid until he was forced into a horrific decision, you would not have been imprisoned, nor your knights killed." She angled her chin and struggled beneath his touch. "My brother has harmed so many, and it must end. I may have been ignorant of his actions, but now I know. I refuse to stand by when I can help repair his wrongs."

Seathan brushed away a tear she'd not realized she'd shed. "You are still recovering."

She scoffed. "Dauid can hardly walk, yet he rides with you on the morrow."

"His wife—"

She tried to break free; he held her close. Anger ignited, grew blazing hot. "I have knowledge of the layout of Breac Castle, experience in moving through the maze of secret tunnels." At his darkening expression, she shook her head. "Do not think to forbid me. My stake in this is as great as either of yours. Besides, if you leave me, I will follow on my own."

Seathan glared at her, furious she dared defy him, wanting her safe. Damn her, if they were alone, he'd strip her naked and make love to her. Never had a woman made him furious and want her at the same time.

A soft chuckle at his side had him glaring at his friend.

"Had I not witnessed it with my own eyes," Dauid said, "I would not have believed it possible."

"What?" Seathan growled.

"'Twould seem," Dauid said, far from deterred by his friend's surly attitude, "that you have met your match."

Seathan eyed Linet, wanting her, feeling more confused and torn than ever in his life. "Blast it, come with us then. It is your life to risk."

Sadness etched through the determination on her face. "Yes, it is. Mine and no one else's." She turned and walked away.

Seathan forced himself to hold still. Not to race after her and demand that she return to the safety of Lochshire Castle. He blew out a rough breath and prayed that letting her accompany him was not the worst mistake of his life.

Chapter 19

Night crept around them like a morbid omen. On edge, Linet peered through the thick branches of a fir. Sheer rock jutted from the roll of land scraping toward the sky. Atop the magnificent outcropping loomed Breac Castle.

A castle where she'd grown up.

A castle that had held her dreams.

A castle that now held naught but danger.

Three days past, Seathan had sent his knights to deliver a writ to his brothers. The men would have reached Lochshire Castle. With a contingent of men riding at their sides, Alexander and Duncan should be en route.

"Linet?"

At the concern in Seathan's voice, she turned. In the fading light, green eyes studied her, his gaze too intense, seeing more than she wished to reveal.

"It is not too late for you to leave," he said.

And be safe, she silently finished. He would say no more. Except for ordering his men to tie her up and haul her back to Lochshire Castle, he'd exhausted every angle to convince her not to accompany them.

With each reason, she'd refused.

"Linet—"

"I am going." On stopping Fulke, she and Seathan were equally determined. Her brother had hurt too many people. If it took her until her dying breath, she would end his brutality.

The sun sank beneath the horizon, smothering light that would expose them to Fulke's guards. She prayed they'd find Brighde alive.

"Over there." Seathan pointed out to his men the rain-washed trail that he and Linet had used to escape.

Time-worn rock angled down the steep grade before them as if nothing had changed. But it had. She could hardly fathom how much she'd transformed since her escape with Seathan barely more than a fortnight past.

And in that wisp of time, somehow love had offered her both enrichment and ruin.

Pushing aside a thick limb, Dauid studied the steep slope littered with loose rock. "It will take the entire night for everyone to reach the top. The rain will make the climb more treacherous."

"Aye, but the storm provides necessary cover." Seathan studied his friend, his injuries still a consideration. But he understood Dauid's determination, one he would have shared if Linet had languished within the bastard's grasp. "You are sure you can make it?"

Dauid nodded, his jaw set. "Aye."

Seathan glanced at Linet. "Are you ready?"

She arched her brow. "Are you?"

Seathan bit back a scowl.

"There is no winning with women," Dauid advised.

Uncomfortable at his friend's easy acceptance of Seathan's relationship with Linet, of his implied belief that more existed between them than a bed shared, Seathan stood. As much as he enjoyed her company, was intrigued by her wit, he did not delude himself. With the demands of war upon him, he could never allow more between them than a physical connection.

A bond soon severed.

Seathan waved his men forward.

Rocks clattered and scraped as the men ascended. The climb was slow, tedious, and at times the slide of rain-slicked stone forced Seathan to detour before continuing up. He blinked against the steady downpour and pushed on.

Hours later, the muted light of dawn slipped into the dismal morn. They had to reach the tunnel before any guards saw them.

Sweat streaked Seathan's face, his muscles screamed, and the slash of rain that had battered them throughout the night fell harder. As he climbed upon the next shelf of rock, the mouth of the tunnel loomed within the pitiful light.

They'd made it!

"The tunnel," Linet said, gasping for breath.

Seathan turned, his own breathing labored. As much as he'd wished her to stay behind, pride swept him at her determination. Throughout the climb, she'd not complained, but strain lined her face and weariness darkened her eyes.

He wished they could stop, to allow her to rest, but with Fulke's guards on alert above and the skies growing light, to linger could be fatal.

At the top, Seathan climbed over the edge of the cliff. "Come." He caught Linet's hands, pulled her up, and drew her inside the entry. For a moment, she rested against him, and he wrapped his arms around her, savored the feel of her body against his as he waited for Dauid and his men to reach the top.

As if sensing his worries, Linet met his gaze. "We will save Brighde."

"Aye," Seathan replied, though it was not Dauid's wife who was foremost in his thoughts.

As the last of his men reached the tunnel's entrance, Linet stepped from his arms. "Thank you, Seathan, for trusting me." She turned, waved to the men, and then started forward.

Without question, Seathan followed her through the dark maze, his belief in her very different from his doubt during their journey out. The contrast gnawed at him, a sharp reminder that less than a moon had passed, not enough time for her to have earned his trust.

Yet it was as if he'd known Linet for years, long enough to want her in his arms each day, and long enough to want her for a . . . Bedamned. He shoved the dangerous thoughts aside, focused on the tunnel around him.

Without the luxury of a torch, blackness engulfed

them, a vat of darkness so unending it was as if they'd tumbled to Hades. "Use the wall to guide you," Seathan passed to the men behind him, thankful for the darkness that shielded his emotions when he thought of Linet, emotions he struggled to understand.

In silence, his men followed behind him.

After several moments, Linet paused. "Here."

Blackness clung to his eyes. "We have not reached the end of the tunnel."

"I know," Linet agreed. "We have too many men to cut across the bailey to reach the stables. We must use a passage that circles the entire castle. Before, I doubted you strong enough to travel the greater distance." The sound of clothing rustled at his side. "There should be a torch hidden nearby. Feel along the wall for an indent concealing a flint and a torch."

Seathan ran his hands over the cold stone. "Why is there not a torch at the entry?"

"My father reasoned the absence of light would hinder any possible intruders from attacking."

"Smart man."

"He was indeed." Pride filled her voice.

With the torch lit and Linet by his side, he started down the unfamiliar tunnel. She guided them through the maze with an expert hand.

As they rounded the next corner, a foul stench slammed against Seathan, igniting horrific memories of chains, spikes, and his screams. His body trembled against the brutal memories, the horrors he'd suffered beneath Tearlach.

"Seathan," Linet whispered.

A gentle hand lay upon his arm, drawing him back to sanity. He stared at Linet's face caressed by the torchlight. Worry filled her gaze. As did love.

A love she'd admitted.

A love he dared not believe was real.

But he wanted to, ached with the possibility.

His dreams crumbled beneath the stench. "The dungeon," Seathan said, his voice flat.

Linet's fingers gently squeezed him in silent understanding as he grappled with his demons.

"The way is blocked," Dauid said from behind them.

Seathan lifted the torch higher. A large flat stone sealed their path, its weight beyond what he and his men could move.

"There is a door to the right," Linet said.

Dauid stepped into the flickering cone of light, his face tired, drawn, but etched with hope.

Seathan believed they'd find Brighde, and prayed she was still sane after the horrific abuse she must have endured. He ached for his friend. He wouldn't . . . couldn't think of how he'd feel if—

Giving himself a mental shake, Seathan pressed his ear against the stone.

Tension hung in the air as potent as the foul stench of the dead and dying beyond.

"I hear nothing." He smothered the torch, then shoved.

The door edged open.

Sword drawn, he waited, ready in case a guard shouted an alert.

Silence.

Seathan peered out. Seeing no one, he relaxed and turned to his master-at-arms. "Pass the word back to take it slow." Muffled orders sifted behind him as he stepped into the chamber that had spawned his nightmares.

A shudder rippled through him, then another. He dragged a deep breath, steadied himself as he looked around. Torches shoved in sconces illuminated the dank prison and the filth of dying men locked within their cells beyond. Groans and pain-filled cries evoked horrific memories of how he'd suffered while locked within.

Seathan stepped forward, grateful for Linet's hand on his arm, a potent reminder that indeed, beyond evil, goodness did exist.

As his men filed into the dungeon, he broke them into groups to search the cells and release everyone imprisoned, or to aid those incapable of fighting into the tunnel.

Steps echoed. The rusty creak of a cell sounded, followed by cries of relief.

In the center of the dungeon, Seathan stared up the stone steps descending from the keep. Jaw tight, he turned to where his men completed a final sweep of each cell.

Linet walked to him, her eyes wide with concern. "She is not here."

He drew her to him, his frustration matching her own. "Tearlach must have secured her elsewhere."

"Within his bedchamber as he vowed," Dauid rasped.

Seathan eyed him hard, understanding his friend's pain. He nodded. "We will find her." Her condition another matter.

"I will go," Linet stated.

"No." Everything inside Seathan protested her intent. She mattered too much to take such a risk.

"I must. Alone I have a chance to slip past the guards and search the upper floors." Linet took in the men helping the injured into the tunnel. "If we all go, the odds are we will be seen and challenged."

Dauid blew out a harsh breath. "She is right."

Aye, Seathan silently agreed, not that he liked it. But if Tearlach was alerted to their presence, he would kill Brighde.

Linet held Seathan's gaze, seeing his frustration, his realization that her going unaccompanied was the only chance they had to find Brighde—if she still lived.

"It is the only way," she whispered. From the fierce look in his eyes, she thought he'd again refuse.

Emotion flickered on Seathan's face: worry, grief, and need. "Come back to me," he growled, then hauled her to him in a hard kiss. Then he broke away.

And she saw it in his eyes, the passion, the trust, and more, the feelings he'd never admit. An ache grew in her heart. By letting her go, he'd acknowledged her importance in the mission and, subconsciously, in his life. Yet she doubted he realized that he loved her.

"We will wait within the tunnel until you return," Seathan said. "Hurry."

At the top step within the dungeon, she glanced down. The last of Seathan's men filed into the tunnel, but he stood by the stone entry and watched her as if her leaving broke his heart. She pressed a kiss to her hand, held it out to him, then slipped through the door.

Heart racing, she hurried along the passage. Lowered voices had her pressing against the cold stone wall. She peered ahead.

Beyond the alcove, with their backs toward her, two guards discussed a woman the other had bedded.

She glanced at the turret beyond, hoping the servant's garb she'd taken from a chamber outside the dungeon wouldn't draw attention. She'd donned it and knotted her hair before smearing her face with ash to disguise herself.

Fear trickled through her as Linet walked down the hallway as if she had not a care in the world.

"Halt," a guard ordered.

She stopped.

"Where are you going?" he asked.

"To pick up the soiled laundry." She kept her voice low and her eyes downcast.

The man gave a dismissive grunt. "Be on with you."

She hurried down the corridor. Thankfully, the men resumed their talk about the woman.

At the entry to the stairs, she made her way up. At the top floor, she began her search, room after room, turning up empty.

Tired, her spirits eroding, she approached the next room—her chamber. A wisp of melancholy wove through her. The books her father had ordered copied for her sat cradled within the hand-carved shelves, the ivory comb her mother had given her the night before her death lay on a small table, and next to them, a carved dagger, a figure Fulke had made when he was but seven summers.

Everything looked the same, untouched, as if time had stood still when more than a fortnight had passed. It was as if she could lie down, close her eyes, and the life-altering events of the days before would disappear.

Except everything had changed. She'd learned of her brother's evil, and had found Seathan's love.

She exhaled. *Brighde.* She must find her.

Linet slipped into her parents' chamber, now usurped by Fulke. Memories washed over her, of laughing with her parents at night, of her father telling tales of dragons and knights and a lonely princess saved from a horrible wizard.

Except that the nasty villain had turned out to be her brother. She thrust the dark thought away.

With quick, efficient movements, she searched the chamber, pushed aside the extravagant bed hangings of intricately woven silk.

Tears burned her eyes. Brighde wasn't here. Where was she? With her brother's twisted ways, perhaps he'd already sent her elsewhere, or she was dead.

Frustrated, Linet turned to the door. She dreaded breaking the news to Dauid, witnessing a man who'd lost so much devastated further.

A slight scratch fractured the stillness.

Linet turned. Listened. Faraway voices of servants murmured from down the hall. The laughter of a man echoed through a window from the outside bailey. Her shoulders sagged in defeat. She'd heard nothing.

Linet reached for the door.

A faint noise sounded, this time from the back of the chamber.

Heart pounding, she whirled, caught sight of a large, full-length painting. She'd forgotten her father's private chamber beyond her parents' bedroom. He'd used it to keep household records, draft letters, and work on other estate details.

Linet ran to the door. Her fingers trembled as she slid aside the painting, unlocked, then opened the hidden door.

A woman stared back at her, her face battered, her clothes hanging in disarray, her eyes strangled with fear.

"Brighde?" she asked softly.

The woman trembled.

Linet's chest squeezed tight. Only God knew what this poor woman had endured. "I have come with Seathan and Dauid to save you."

A glimmer of hope flickered in her eyes. "Da-Dauid is here?"

"Yes."

The joy on her face faded to shame. Fat tears formed on her lids, then rolled down her cheeks. "Go. Let him believe I am dead."

Linet resisted the urge to reach out and touch

her, unsure whether she'd cringe from physical contact, but she needed to make Brighde understand. "Your husband loves you."

The woman looked away. "I am tainted, soiled, disgraced."

Fury tore through her. "Rape is the disgrace of the assailant, the act of a coward."

Brighde's quiet sobs echoed within the chamber. "What does it matter, the deed is done."

"Dauid loves you."

She shook her head. "He loves the woman I was. One who would smile and welcome him into his bed. He knows not what has been done to me, the men whose desires I have endured, the lustful acts they committed."

Linet shuddered inwardly, aching for her. "Do you love your husband?"

She sniffed. "A-Aye," she whispered, "but it is too late."

"No. Listen to me. If not for yourself, then for his safety, you must come with me. He loves you very much and will not leave without you."

Brighde lifted her eyes. Hope lingered.

"Quickly," Linet urged. "We have little time."

"I think not."

At Fulke's voice, panic ripped through her. Linet whirled.

Eyes the color of sun-burnt clay glared at her, the soft angle of his cheeks an awkward frame to the fury carved beneath. Muscles bunched as he crossed his arms. "Why, it seems I have an intruder." His gaze crawled over her with malice. "By the looks of your filthy gown, your skin smeared from cleaning the hearth, a serving wench. My men enjoy a woman, especially one who has not learned her place."

Fear threatened to erode Linet's bravado. "You disgust me."

Dark brows narrowed. "You released the Scottish rebel."

"I left Breac Castle alone."

Hatred, pure and simple, flashed on his maliciously handsome face. He stepped forward; his hand shot out.

Pain seared her. She stumbled back.

"Liar!" he spat.

She raised her hand to where her face throbbed. "I am telling the truth."

He scoffed. "It is no coincidence that Lord Grey disappeared from my dungeon, nor that the dungeon guard was found unconscious after you escaped." He leaned closer. "When the guard woke, he told us that his tongue was thick and his brain foggy. He mentioned a servant wench had surprised him with wine. It takes not a wise man to deduct who delivered it."

She took a step back, her body trembling.

Fulke caught her shoulders with his hands. His fingers dug into her tender skin. "I should give you to my men for their use. Pity, 'twould soil goods that I need for other purposes." His smile ominous, he shoved her away. "Then again, there are ways to cause pain without leaving marks, ways to make a man believe his new bride is pure."

"I shall never wed the Earl of Fallon."

Satisfaction oozed on his face. "Terms have already been discussed, the documents signed."

"You bastard!"

"Now that you have returned, his carriage will be sent for on the morrow."

She angled her chin. "The earl will refuse to marry me. He expects to bed a virgin—which I am not."

"I care not who you spread your legs for," Fulke drawled. "I will send a missive this night that en route from your latest travels, the Scottish rebels robbed your carriage and raped you." He gave a cold smile. "Nothing has changed. The earl will accept you, whore or not."

She thought of Seathan, of the love they'd made, his infinite tenderness. "I was not raped. I gave myself to him, to the man I love."

A terrifying calm entered Fulke's eyes, a void so dark she wished for his fury. At least that would indicate he had feelings, unlike the creature before her.

"I will find the rebel," her brother stated. "Then, I will kill him and display his head on a pike, a warning for all who dare touch what is mine."

"You do not own me."

He caught Linet's hair, twisted hard. "That, my dear sister, is where you are right. You were bought and paid for by the Earl of Fallon." He shoved her into Brighde.

Linet's head pounded as she fought to focus, as Dauid's wife steadied her.

Fulke glared at Brighde. "Tie her up."

Brighde's hands trembled as she reached out for the rope Fulke held. "I am sorry, my lady." Unsteady hands quickly wrapped the woven cord around her wrists.

Her brother nodded. "Like your wrists, your shrewish tongue will soon be tamed." Fulke paused. "I hear the earl prefers a whip."

"I refuse to go."

Fulke laughed, a cold, brittle sound. "When I am through with you, you will beg to leave here." He walked over to her, grasped her jaw. "I do not make threats." He shoved her away.

Linet landed hard against the stone floor. Pain sliced through her skull. The room spun, her head pounded as if impaled by a mace.

"Clean her up," Fulke ordered. "She looks like the whore she is, fit only for rutting with the Scot. A gown will be brought in for her to wear." His gaze narrowed on Linet. "Then we will talk. It can be within my chamber or in the dungeon with you naked and spread upon the rack."

"No!"

He ignored her plea. "Now that I know you are no longer a maiden, I will not hesitate to turn you over to the inventive desires of my men. And I have new, creative machines that will bend the stoutest of men—or women—to my will. You will marry, that I swear to you on your life. The condition you are in when you say your vows is of your choosing." Fulke turned, strode from the chamber. The door slammed in his wake.

Through the haze of pain, Linet focused on his words. The dungeon! Where Seathan and his men waited.

God in heaven, what was she going to do now?

Chapter 20

The bells tolled.

Seathan stared up the steps. Too much time had passed. *A sword's wrath, where was she?* "Linet should have returned by now."

"Mayhap her caution slows her down," Dauid said, "more so if she has Brighde alongside. They would not want to take unnecessary risks."

His friend's reasoning made sense, but he heard the worry, the fear that echoed his own concerns. Seathan glanced at the two bodies slumped within the passageway. "When these guards do not return from their rounds, others will come searching for them."

Dauid nodded grimly. "Time is running out."

Unease rippled through Seathan as he again glanced up the steps. Something was amiss, he felt it, sensed it as surely as his next breath.

"Do you think she has found Brighde?" Dauid asked.

Seathan exhaled. "I pray so."

Long moments passed. Sunlight illuminated,

then slowly began streaming through the narrowed windows.

Bedamned, he'd wait no longer. Seathan clasped his hand on the hilt of his sword. "I am going to find them. Remain with my men in the tunnel."

Dauid shook his head, his face grim. "I am going with you. 'Tis my actions that have led to the danger we face, and my wife that Lady Linet seeks to find."

"Your leg will slow us down. Alone, I have a better chance of slipping through the castle unseen."

"We have a solid number of knights," Dauid said. "We could confront Tearlach's men."

"Aye," Seathan replied. "But if Linet has found Brighde, an attack might hinder their escape, or worse, expose them. Until Alexander and Duncan arrive with reinforcements, we are grossly outnumbered."

Dauid muttered a curse. "I do not like the feel of this." He gave an abrupt nod. "Go then. If you have not returned when the bells again toll, by God we are coming for you."

Seathan nodded.

His friend drew him into a fierce hug. "God's speed."

On a prayer, Seathan hurried up the torch-lit steps. At the top, he turned. The last of his men were filing into the tunnel. With his sword readied, he edged open the door.

The rich aroma of bread filled the air as well as the scents of sage, rosemary, and other herbs the cooks used in their daily preparation of food. In the distance echoed the murmured voices of women and children and an occasional man.

He waited, listened for any sign of Tearlach or any of his knights.

Nothing.

Seathan shoved the door wider. Instead of opening to the great room as was common, the entry led to a corridor that branched off into several hallways. This unique feature underscored the massive size of the castle as well as its original Scottish owner's meticulous planning and wealth.

A pity such magnificence now belonged to a cruel noble obsessed with his own power.

He hurried along the corridor, the torches burning in their sconces melding with the sunlight trickling through the carved windows.

At the entry to the great room, he peered inside. Dogs lay sprawled in distant corners while servants cleaned trencher tables and children swept the floors with hand-bound straw.

The knights had already broken their fast. Most likely, they were practicing with their swords in the bailey.

He slipped past the entry. A short distance away, he paused before the two sets of steps leading up. Sparse walls adorned one entry, the other boasted paintings of prestigious nobles, each portrait illuminated by a candle within a sconce. He started up the painting-lined turret.

The soft pad of footsteps echoed from above.

Seathan glanced back. Christ's blade. Not enough time to return to the floor below.

A shadow rippled along the curved wall of stone in the stairwell. The soft pad of slippers scraped above him. A woman approached. He sheathed his sword and withdrew his dagger, hid it behind him.

A servant rounded the curve, her arms filled with an empty jug. With a frown, she halted.

"I am seeking Lord Tearlach," he said with the authority of someone welcome within the castle.

She hesitated. "My regrets, my lord, I know not where Lord Tearlach is. I was sent to fetch the empty water jugs. If you wish, I will find him."

"Nay, it is a task I can easily do."

"You are a Scot." A blush crept up her face. "My apologies, my lord. My words are not said unkindly. It is just that as of late, more Scottish nobles than English enter Breac Castle."

Aye, those who were weak-kneed and have sold their honor for their safety instead of standing their ground against King Edward. "Go," Seathan said. "I will find Lord Tearlach myself."

"Yes, my lord." The woman half curtsied. With the jug held tight in her hands, she hurried by.

'Twas a sad day when during a time of war, a Scot within an English-held fortress was a common sight. Neither was he surprised by the woman's lack of concern at his presence. With the English king all but dismissing Scotland's rebels as a threat, to the residents within Breac Castle, war between their countries no longer existed.

A belief they would come to regret.

Once the servant disappeared, Seathan sheathed his dagger, drew his sword, and headed up the turret.

As he reached the second floor, he took in the limestone floors inlaid with granite, the hand-woven tapestries lining the walls, as well as the simple yet elegant sconces crafted with fey-inspired images.

Linet's scream echoed from the end of the corridor.

Seathan bolted toward the entry.

"Go to Hades!" she yelled.

He flattened himself against the wall.

The door to the chamber was open. Tearlach stood halfway across the room, feet spread in an aggressive stance. Below him Linet lay on the floor, her hands and feet bound, slashes of red streaking across her face.

The bastard had beaten her! Fury ignited. From his limited angle, Seathan saw no one else within the chamber. Where was Dauid's wife? He'd find her after he'd killed Tearlach. The viscount would never touch anyone again.

Sword raised, Seathan strode inside. "Tearlach!"

The viscount whirled. Satisfaction crawled across his face. He flicked a glance toward Linet. "I see your lover has arrived to save you. Touching."

The door behind Seathan slammed shut.

He whirled.

Five guards stood against the wall, their swords drawn.

God's teeth!

"A guard spotted you and your men near the entry to the tunnel at first light," Tearlach said. "I was curious as to your actions, so I allowed you entry."

"My men," Seathan hissed. At Tearlach's scowl, he

understood. With the complexity of the maze, they hadn't yet been discovered.

"I will find them. The tunnels are being searched as we speak." Satisfaction smeared his face. "Once I found Linet, I knew how you had learned about the secret entry. Now, you will regret that you dared return—the cost will be your life."

"No!" Linet yelled.

Disdain darkened Tearlach's gaze. "Just think, dear sister, you will watch your lover die, something to ponder as the Earl of Fallon takes you in your marriage bed."

With a roar, Seathan charged the viscount. Satisfaction swept him as his sword severed flesh.

Tearlach screamed, stumbled back. "Seize him!"

Steps echoed behind him.

Seathan whirled, met the first knight's blade.

Steel scraped.

With the skill honed by countless battles, he angled his sword, drove deep, shoved the attacker away, then spun to deflect the next assailant's charge.

The man swung.

Blades met; shuddered against the force.

Seathan withdrew his dagger, shoved its razor-edged tip into the man's chest.

Eyes wide with pain, he collapsed.

Pain streaked across Seathan's left shoulder. He cursed, rounded to meet the third attacker. Before he could swing, a knight slammed hard against his side.

The warrior before him dove for his feet and tugged.

Air rushed past him.

"Seathan!" Linet screamed.

Seathan slammed against the floor. Pain ripped through his skull. He kicked free, started to roll away. A knight caught his hand. Another warrior secured his other shoulder. A third man held his blade to Seathan's throat.

"Do not kill him!" Linet begged.

Tearlach glared at his sister, his hand pressed against the deep cut in his shoulder; blood dripped through his fingers. "Silence!"

Frantic, she met Seathan's gaze. She couldn't allow Fulke to kill him. "Please, I will do anything if you spare his life."

Seathan struggled against his captors. "Agree to nothing!"

Tears burned her eyes. Seathan didn't understand. He'd trusted her and now he would die. No, there was still a chance. She refused to look at him. If she did, she'd fall apart.

Decision made, she met her brother's gaze. If it saved Seathan's life, it'd be worth the cost. "If you spare him, I will marry the Earl of Fallon."

"No!" Seathan roared.

Fulke laughed, a cold, ugly sound as he held a piece of cloth to his wound to staunch the flow. "My dear, the time for choices is long past. Whatever was once yours now belongs to me." He arched a brow. "As for Lord Grey, his life is forfeit."

She twisted on the floor. "You bastard! Have you no conscience? No respect for our parents or their wishes?"

"None whatsoever. You were a fool to believe I ever did." Her brother gestured toward the guards. "Take the Scot to the dungeon."

The guards lifted Seathan to his feet, the blade flush against his neck. As the two knights hauled him toward the door, he pretended to comply, limping to give the illusion he was too weak to fight.

A step.

Two.

The guards' grips slightly relaxed.

He dropped, used his entire weight to jerk free of the knights' hold.

"Get him!" Tearlach yelled.

Seathan rolled, grabbed his blade, and with quick thrusts, dispatched one of the three remaining men. Sword readied, he faced the other two knights.

A boom echoed from outside.

"We are under attack," a guard yelled from outside. "To arms!"

Tearlach glared out the window.

Another boom echoed within the castle. Rocks exploded, then landed with a hard clatter.

"'Tis the rebels," another man shouted. "They have a catapult!"

Relief stormed Seathan. Alexander, Duncan, and their men had arrived!

Fury burned Tearlach's face. He cast the cloth aside. Blood stained his right arm. "Help the men below. I will take care of Lord Grey."

Swords raised, his knights rushed toward the stairs.

Shouts echoed from below. The distant clash of blades rang out.

He strode toward the viscount while the sounds of battle raged outside. "No one will save you now," Seathan spat, his fury for the torture Tearlach had delivered, for his brutality to Dauid's wife, and his abuse of Linet melding to this one moment.

"You think not?" Fulke reached toward Linet.

Seathan dove for Tearlach. Primal satisfaction surged through Seathan as he slammed his fist into the viscount's face, felt the crunch of bone. "Never will you touch her again!"

On a screech of pain, Tearlach caught him, rolled, slammed his fist into Seathan's face.

His vision blurred.

Linet screamed.

Tearlach delivered another blow, his fist ramming Seathan mercilessly. "This time," he seethed, "I will watch you die, will savor the last drip of blood draining from your worthless body. Then, before her intended mounts her, I"—he dragged in another breath—"I will give Linet to my men for their pleasure." He raised his fist, swung again.

Through the wash of pain, Seathan caught the viscount's hand inches from his face.

Tearlach's hand trembled.

Seathan held. "Neither you, nor any other man, will ever touch her again." He shoved.

The viscount fell back, scrambled to his feet.

Seathan lifted his blade, the shouts of battle below rising to a fierce din. Aiming his sword at Tearlach, he charged.

The viscount angled his blade, deflected his blow.

Steel screamed within the chamber as if a curse.

Pain seared Seathan's shoulder. His blood stained the woven silk carpet, an irony of red against the muted blues and creams. He wove, fighting off the dizziness and a weakening arm. Time seemed to still as he fought, each swing stealing much-needed strength.

Victory glittered in Tearlach's eyes as he held his ground against Seathan's next attack. Pushing free of Seathan's blade, the viscount swung hard.

Seathan caught the blow, barely. He shoved.

The viscount stumbled back, but both men had lost their swords.

"He has a dagger!" Linet yelled.

Sunlight glinted off the blade in Tearlach's hand.

In a deft move, Seathan withdrew his own dagger. With war-honed precision, he threw.

The viscount gasped. He glanced to where blood, rich and thick, surged from the blade deep within his chest. His dagger clattered to the floor. Eyes wide with disbelief, he collapsed into a heap.

Dragging in deep breaths, Seathan walked to stand before him. "Rot in Hades where you belong."

The viscount stared at him, hatred melding with fury. He opened his mouth as if to speak. His body trembled, then stilled, and his eyes stared into nothing.

Another boom echoed from below. A Scottish battle cry echoed. Men screamed.

"Seathan!"

He hurried to Linet, knelt, untied her, and helped her stand. He drew her into his arms and held her tight. "Thank God you are safe." Would he ever forget the sight of her tied and beaten?

A sob escaped her. "I thought . . ."

Seathan stroked his thumb across a bruise upon her face, his hand trembling. "We are both safe."

She glanced over to where Tearlach lay dead, and then lowered her head.

"He gave me no choice," he quietly said.

Linet rested her cheek against the curve of his neck. "I know."

Emotions welled inside him, the feeling immense. There was so much he wanted to say, to tell her.

The echo of battle below rose.

He sucked in a steadying breath. "I must join my men."

She lifted her head, understanding in her eyes. "I know."

He cupped her face within his hands, pressed a gentle kiss upon her mouth. "I will return, on that I swear." And he would, if he had to crawl. He started to turn.

"Wait." Linet hurried over to a door he'd not noticed before. She pulled the heavy wood open.

Brighde stumbled out, her eyes wide as they fell upon Seathan. "Dauid?"

The sight of the battered, bruised woman filled him with fresh rage, but he focused on the fact that she lived. "Is hiding in the dungeon with my men."

Relief swept the woman's face. Then she stared with shock and relief at Tearlach sprawled upon the floor.

"He will harm you no more," Seathan said.

Another Scottish war cry echoed from below.

Seathan turned to Linet. The feelings she inspired burst within his heart. There was so much he wanted to tell her.

And no time.

"Stay here until I return," he ordered.

Defiance appeared through the bruises darkening upon her face. She reached down, lifted her brother's sword.

Seathan's eyes narrowed. "You will not fight."

She swallowed hard. "It was my brother who brought devastation to many."

"Fulke is dead." He gently removed the blade from her hands, set it upon the bed. "The responsibility of Breac Castle is mine."

Shock widened her eyes. "Breac Castle is *my* home."

"Nay, Breac Castle belongs to Scotland. I reclaim what is rightfully ours."

The cacophany of blades echoed below, this time closer.

Bedamned. "We will talk when I return. Stay here!" Seathan turned and bolted toward the battle below.

Chapter 21

Emotion swamped Linet as she stood on the wall walk and stared through the crenellations at the setting sun. The orange-red glow embraced the land, a soft silk of color blanketing the roll of hills and endless forest beyond. Her home was safe. She curled her hand upon the weathered stone.

No, this majestic fortress was no longer her home.

After the rebels had defeated her brother's knights, as Seathan had promised before he'd bolted from Fulke's chamber, he'd reclaimed it for the Scottish cause. His seizing this formidable stronghold for the rebels made sense, and after the weapons were secured, he'd stood in the middle of the bailey and accepted fealty from her brothers' men.

But a part of her grieved for a home lost.

The wave of linen had her looking down. Warmth filled her at the sight of Dauid and his wife below, how he held her in the shadows.

Linet turned away from their private moment, thankful they'd been given a second chance. Before the knights within the castle, Seathan had surprised Dauid by appointing him master-at-arms of Breac Castle. He and his wife would remain here, never again to be apart.

Theirs was a happy ending, a fate that would elude her. But she had plans and would make her own path, the life before her one within the Highlands.

"I thought I would find you here."

At Seathan's deep burr, she turned. An ache built in her heart as she stared at the powerful Scottish lord, a man who commanded many, a man as admired as feared, but to her, the man who'd taught her to love. Surrounded by the green of the forest and the flow of streams, this powerful Scot had won her heart. But he still shielded his love from her, and with his emotional scars, he forever would.

"I have always enjoyed standing upon the wall walk and looking over the land," she said, her voice calm, giving no hint of the turbulent emotions brewing inside.

He caught her waist and drew her to him. "'Tis almost as beautiful as you."

Within the safety of his arms, her heart ached. She wanted the one thing he would never give. She knew that now, had known it since she'd watched him walk toward her after the battle. Since then, he'd not spoken of their future, only plans to strengthen Breac Castle's defenses.

His life.

One that did not include her.

He lowered his mouth to hers, soft, intense. Tears

threatened to fall. With a sigh, he drew back, the desire in his eyes stealing her breath.

"The night falls, Breac Castle is secured, and we have supped. Come with me, I wish to make love to a woman who moves me as no other."

She moved him as no other. She doubted his feelings would ever be more, or for her, enough. "I love you," she whispered. Piercing green eyes stared at her, hard, hot, with an intensity she'd never seen. Silence spread, swirled around her.

She held her breath. Waited for those magical words, but his silence proclaimed the truth. Only in the privacy of the bedroom would he show her the depth he felt for her. Words he was incapable of saying—ever.

"Linet, I—"

"I am not asking for a vow in return. This night I wish to share your bed as well."

On a groan, Seathan lifted Linet in his arms. He cradled her against him, and headed toward the stairs.

The haze of morning light filtered through the chamber, nudging Seathan awake. The scent of their lovemaking was soft against the fresh spring breeze. A smile touched his face as he thought of the many times he and Linet had made love throughout the night. He might have initiated their love play last eve, but she'd quickly discovered and exploited his weaknesses as if a seasoned temptress.

Memories of her passion curled through his mind. What she made him feel had little to do with his needs and everything to do with a craving of his soul. She brought a fullness to his life that until he'd met her had never existed, not even with Iuliana, a woman whom he'd believed he'd loved. Now he understood what he'd felt for her paled in comparison to the emotions Linet inspired.

Aching to hold her, to smell the scent of her skin against his, to savor the smile that was uniquely hers, he rolled over and reached out.

His fingers slid through the tangle of sheets.

Seathan opened his eyes. A frown drew across his brow as he took in the empty swath of bed where she had lain, where her body had welcomed him, and where he'd taken her completely. He looked around the chamber.

Empty.

His heart stopped. Where was she?

The soft rustle of clothes had him turning toward the corner window. Blended within the shadows, Linet stared out the window as if transfixed by the dawning day.

"Linet?"

She started, slowly turned. A smile touched her mouth, but her lips held an edge of sadness.

Unease crept through him. "What is wrong?"

"I wish you to arrange an escort so that I may leave for the Highlands this day."

Confused, he shoved to his feet. "Why? This is your home. You are free to remain."

"My home?" A wisp of regret crept into her voice. "If this were truly my home, I would not have to be informed of what I am free or not free to do." He started to speak but she shook her head. "Unless I am imprisoned, I will go."

She was not making an ounce of sense. "I would never imprison you."

"Then you will let me leave?"

No! He wanted her to stay so he could go to her in the night, so she could forever share his dreams. But were his the wants of a selfish man? By keeping her at Breac Castle, he placed her in danger. Once King Edward learned he'd seized the Scottish stronghold, Longshanks would retaliate.

Neither could he forget the grief on her face as they'd buried Tearlach. Though she despised her brother, she held fond memories of their childhood, of loving the man before his soul had turned black.

No, he couldn't lose her. However wrong, however selfish, he didn't want her to leave. "Stay with me."

Linet watched him, lavender eyes so intense it was as if she looked straight to his soul. "Desire is but temporary. I need more."

Heart aching, Seathan walked over and cupped her face within his hands. "You said you loved me."

A tear slipped down her cheek. "Do not."

Then he understood the errant path where her thoughts had strayed. Seathan laughed, joy pouring through him.

Linet tried to break free. "Let me go."

He sobered. "And if I did, I would be a grand fool. I love you, Linet. Do you not realize that, you daft woman?"

She stopped struggling. "What?"

His heart swelled as if it would burst. "Never did I believe I would trust another woman, but you have taught me to trust, and more importantly, to love." He wiped a tear from her cheek. "I would rather live a day with you than endure a lifetime of living alone."

Tears flowed freely down her cheeks.

"I could not have received a finer present than to be blessed by the gift of you." He paused, needing her to understand. "I have wronged you, am unworthy of your love, but it changes naught. I love you. If you leave me, I shall never recover. You are my heart, my soul, and the woman I will always love. Stay with me, Linet. Be my wife."

Emotions tightened her throat as she stared at Seathan, at the man who made her complete. "When I freed you from the cell," she whispered, "I was furious Fulke dared to betray me, to steal away my right to choose a man I loved to wed. I swore then that never again would anyone, except myself, choose my destiny."

"Never would I take away your choice." Seathan pressed a soft kiss upon her lips. "I love you, Linet, for the woman you are. I demand not that you marry me. I want your love given freely or . . . not at all."

His words sifted through her as if a wish granted, an offering she'd never believed he'd bestow. The gemstone within her pocket softly warmed. She did not need to look to know it glowed, or to understand that however much he believed otherwise, magic existed.

"Kiss me, Seathan."

He hesitated. "You did not say whether you would be my wife."

"Did I not?" she replied with a smile, her heart full. "You are the man I love, the man I pledge my heart to, and the man who has taught me to believe that love is the greatest healer of them all."

"That still is not a yes."

Linet laughed, warmth and happiness erasing the lingering shadows in her heart. "Then, may I say . . . yes."

He swept her into his arms and claimed her mouth in a fierce kiss, his tongue demanding, taking, igniting heat in her very core. With a happiness she'd never believed possible, she poured her soul into the kiss.

Seathan may have claimed Breac Castle, but she had stolen this Scottish rebel's heart.

Read more about the rugged MacGruder family in
Diana Cosby's

HIS DESTINY,

coming in October 2011.

Scotland, July 1297

A woman's terrified scream rent the air.

Sir Patrik Cleary MacGruder whirled. Sweat from the grueling pace he'd maintained this summer morning soaked his skin as he scanned the gnarl of elm, ash, and fir.

"No. Do not touch me! Please!" a woman begged.

Men's crude laughter echoed nearby, rough, ugly, and thick with menace.

A muscle worked in Patrik's jaw as he touched the writ secured beneath his tunic. He must reach Bishop Wishart without delay.

Her next scream, raw with terror, pierced him as if a well-aimed sword. Nay, it struck deeper, into the pit of his soul, a dark vat where no weapon could reach.

Silence sheathed his steps as he wove through the woods toward the woman's desperate pleas. With Scottish soil crawling with the English bastards, only a fool would rush in alone to aid the lass. Yet, here he was.

"Look at her, she would be wanting us," a gruff English voice stated.

Another man's harsh laughter sounded nearby.

Bloody bastards! Patrik tamped down his fury and edged closer, scanning the forest for any sign of a trap.

Shadows flickered ahead.

He ducked behind a fallen tree. Pulse racing, he peered past the mossy ground and the tangle of weathered bark.

Caught between two English knights, a slender woman kicked and twisted to break free. Her chestnut hair, wild with the struggle, obscured her face.

Patrik's anger shoved up a notch.

"A fighter she is," a burly Englishman before her laughed. "And a good bedding she will be."

She lunged forward in an attempt to break free. "No!"

With a lewd smile, another knight reached out, ripped her gown. Swaths of flesh appeared beneath the flutter of cloth. He jerked the ruined garment free.

Naked, the woman fought harder. "No, I beg of you!"

Memories of watching his mother being raped scalded Patrik's mind. Darkness consumed him, a blackness so thick it smothered his soul. Hand trembling, he withdrew his blade, edged forward. They'd not touch the lass, or draw another breath. He scoured the area for any other men, then refocused on the knights.

Four of the bastards.

Odds he'd take.

Sword raised, Patrik sprang to his feet, sprang into the clearing. "Release the lass!"

The tattered dress sank to the ground as her closest attacker whirled, drawing his blade.

At the English knights' distraction, the woman tugged a hand free. Without hesitation, she whirled and kneed the other knight in the groin.

Face distorted in agony, the man dropped.

The woman clawed at another knight as Patrik charged, drove his sword to meet the closest knight's blade.

At the blow, the Englishman stumbled back.

Patrik slashed the knight's throat. At the spurt of blood, he spun to face the three remaining warriors. Fury pounding hot, he withdrew his dagger, hurled it at the nearest knight. His blade sank into his opponent's chest.

Shock and pain widened the man's eyes. Blood spewed from the wound. The man stepped toward him, crumpled.

The knight the woman had attacked cursed, staggered to his feet, outrage carved upon his face.

Nostrils flared, Patrik drove his sword into the Englishman's chest, then spun to face the final warrior. "The odds are even. As they were not when you tried to rape this woman."

"You will die for this," the Englishman spat.

Patrik arched a brow, scanned the knights sprawled

around them. "'Tis English blood that stains the earth."

"Once I carve your worthless arse, I will find the Scottish whore. Scum, the lot of you." The English knight angled his blade. "If she pleases me, mayhap I will allow her to live the night."

Patrik tamped down his fury. His opponent wanted him angry, wanted his thoughts blurred with reckless emotion. Nay, too many battles lay behind him to make such a critical error.

With a roar, his enemy drove forward.

Patrik dropped and rolled. Steel whooshed a hairsbreadth above his head.

Shock that he'd missed twisted to outrage upon the knight's face as he whirled.

Patrik shoved to his feet and swung. His blade met flesh, slashing the man's throat in a satisfying spurt of crimson.

Knees trembling, the knight sank to the ground, his words mutilated within a gurgle of blood.

"Die, you bastard," Patrik hissed. "Rot in Hades where one day your English king will join you!" Chest heaving, he ignored the groans of the dying men as he scoured the thick greenery for the lass. She'd run. Curse it!

Steel hissed against leather as Patrik secured his blade. He jerked his dagger free of the dying man, scooped up her tattered garment and followed the soft indents of earth that betrayed her passing.

With her screams of terror and the clash of blades, 'twould be but a matter of time before more of the English bastards arrived. He had to find the lass before they did. Given the graveness of his mission, the thought of abandoning her flickered to mind, a thought he abandoned just as quickly. As long as he breathed, never would English scum touch a Scottish woman he could protect.

Leaves rustled in the dense thicket ahead.

Patrik halted. He scanned his garb, grimaced. His tunic and trews splattered with the Englishmen's blood would not ease her fear.

"Lass," he called, keeping his voice soft as he listened for any sign of approaching men. "I know you are in there. And afraid."

Silence.

He stepped closer. "You know me not, but the woods are thick with English. More knights will come. We must go. Now."

A leaf shook. "How do I know I can trust you?" Her soft, trembling words held both courage and caution.

"I give you my word, that of a Scottish knight." He held out her tattered gown.

Long moments passed. He sensed her silent scrutiny, struggled to bank his impatience. His mission was crucial; the sooner he saw to her safety, the faster he could deliver the writ.

"Place the gown near the bush."

With slow steps, Patrik moved forward, laid the battered garment into the shadows as she'd asked.

"Move away."

He eased back.

A slender arm reached out, snatched the torn garb, then disappeared. Leaves shook. Hints of creamy skin against shadows slipped into view as she dressed.

He scanned their surroundings. "We must hurry."

The leaves stilled.

A fresh wind stirred, hinting at the warmth of the oncoming day, thick with the tension infusing the moment.

"Lass—"

The woman stood.

Patrik's breath left him in a rush. Though clad in a torn gown tied in hurried knots, her face marred by bruises from the knight's rough handling, she appeared as if crafted by the fey in the shifting light.

Nay, a paltry description for the beautiful woman who stood before him.

Thick chestnut hair with hints of bronze framed softly carved cheeks, a full mouth that would tempt a saint and emerald eyes that held naught but distrust. Her eyes. As if spellbound, he couldn't look away. They held him, mesmerized him, drew him as no other.

Embarrassed to catch himself staring, he cleared his throat. "Lass, I will not harm you," he said, keeping his words soft. "I swear it."

"Your name?"

The soft sweep of her burr wrapped around him like a dangerous luxury. He gave a brief bow. "Sir Patrik Cleary at your service." Regret touched him. Not Sir Patrik Cleary MacGruder, the latter a name he'd lost the right to speak.

In a nervous sweep, she took in his garb. "You are loyal to Scotland?"

The doubt in her voice he understood. "Aye."

"The English knights?" She shot a glance toward the spot where her captors had stripped her a short time before.

"They are dead."

If possible, her face paled further.

"They chose their fate," he stated, unapologetic.

She rubbed her thumb over her fingertips in a hesitant slide. "They did." Her breath trembled. "I thank you for rescuing me. Had you not . . ."

"Our worry is to leave. We must be as far away as possible before the English find their comrades slain."

"Of course." Nervous fingers tugged on a ragged tie as she assessed him.

What did she see? With the Englishman's blood staining his tunic, did she wonder if he was as merciless as the men who had tried to rape her? Did doubts crawl through her as to why he would come to her rescue?

"My name is Christina Moffat."

Her soft words erased his dark thoughts. A strange warmth touched him that after her terror of this day, she offered a sliver of trust. In this war-ravaged country, a name wrongly given could mean death.

He extended his hand toward her. "Come."

With hesitant steps, she moved from the brush. Dirt clung to her gown, the garment failing to hide the luxurious sweep of creamy skin, or the bruises left by brutal hands. She stared at Patrik's hand, then looked away.

He dropped his hand. "Never feel embarrassed. The shame is theirs. May they rot in Hades."

Thick chestnut lashes lifted. "They did not rape me."

Given mere moments more, they would have accomplished the deed, a fact they both knew. He remained silent, understood her battle against the terror clawing at her mind, allowed the lass to focus on her innocence retained.

"They have been slaughtered!" a man's voice roared nearby.

"Blast it!" Patrik caught her hand and pulled her with him. Sticks cracked beneath their feet, limbs whipped his body as he pushed her before him, then followed at a run.

"Their blood still runs," another man called. "Whoever killed them is nearby. Find them!"

A horse whinnied.

"They have mounts," Christina gasped as she leapt over a tumble of low brush.

He cleared the thicket, close on her heels. "Aye." And would easily catch up to them. Familiar with the land, he knew their only hope. Turning to the right, he led her through the tangle. "Hurry."

The leather of their flat-soled shoes slapped against earth as they ran. After several moments, the dense foliage of the forest gave way to a field dotted with tufts of fresh grass, brave buds of flowers and sweeps of heather.

Christina jerked her hand free.

Patrik whirled, his breaths coming fast. "We cannot stop."

She stared at the roll of hills leading to the formidable mountains to the north. "The brambles before us would not hide a field mouse."

"The English will be thinking that as well," he agreed. "But I know of a place to hide. Trust me."

Trust him?

Sir Patrik's piercing hazel eyes held hers. He was a warrior, from his muscled arms to his carved cheekbones and deep baritone voice. A man used to giving commands. A man many feared.

A man she, too, would be a fool to dismiss.

She turned in the direction they'd come and scoured the concealing woods. Shadows littered the dense foliage, providing numerous places where they could hide.

A shiver crept through her. Why was he exposing them? If anyone scanned the field, they would be seen. No, it was too late to question her decision. She'd committed herself to the journey long before this day.

She turned toward the handsome Scot, a man as intriguing as he was dangerous. A man who, if he learned the truth, that her real name was Emma Astyn, a woman acclaimed as one of England's top mercenaries—both known and hated by the Scots—would kill her.

Books by Bestselling Author
Fern Michaels

___The Jury	0-8217-7878-1	$6.99US/$9.99CAN
___Sweet Revenge	0-8217-7879-X	$6.99US/$9.99CAN
___Lethal Justice	0-8217-7880-3	$6.99US/$9.99CAN
___Free Fall	0-8217-7881-1	$6.99US/$9.99CAN
___Fool Me Once	0-8217-8071-9	$7.99US/$10.99CAN
___Vegas Rich	0-8217-8112-X	$7.99US/$10.99CAN
___Hide and Seek	1-4201-0184-6	$6.99US/$9.99CAN
___Hokus Pokus	1-4201-0185-4	$6.99US/$9.99CAN
___Fast Track	1-4201-0186-2	$6.99US/$9.99CAN
___Collateral Damage	1-4201-0187-0	$6.99US/$9.99CAN
___Final Justice	1-4201-0188-9	$6.99US/$9.99CAN
___Up Close and Personal	0-8217-7956-7	$7.99US/$9.99CAN
___Under the Radar	1-4201-0683-X	$6.99US/$9.99CAN
___Razor Sharp	1-4201-0684-8	$7.99US/$10.99CAN
___Yesterday	1-4201-1494-8	$5.99US/$6.99CAN
___Vanishing Act	1-4201-0685-6	$7.99US/$10.99CAN
___Sara's Song	1-4201-1493-X	$5.99US/$6.99CAN
___Deadly Deals	1-4201-0686-4	$7.99US/$10.99CAN
___Game Over	1-4201-0687-2	$7.99US/$10.99CAN
___Sins of Omission	1-4201-1153-1	$7.99US/$10.99CAN
___Sins of the Flesh	1-4201-1154-X	$7.99US/$10.99CAN
___Cross Roads	1-4201-1192-2	$7.99US/$10.99CAN

Available Wherever Books Are Sold!
Check out our website at www.kensingtonbooks.com

Romantic Suspense from
Lisa Jackson

See How She Dies	0-8217-7605-3	$6.99US/$9.99CAN
Final Scream	0-8217-7712-2	$7.99US/$10.99CAN
Wishes	0-8217-6309-1	$5.99US/$7.99CAN
Whispers	0-8217-7603-7	$6.99US/$9.99CAN
Twice Kissed	0-8217-6038-6	$5.99US/$7.99CAN
Unspoken	0-8217-6402-0	$6.50US/$8.50CAN
If She Only Knew	0-8217-6708-9	$6.50US/$8.50CAN
Hot Blooded	0-8217-6841-7	$6.99US/$9.99CAN
Cold Blooded	0-8217-6934-0	$6.99US/$9.99CAN
The Night Before	0-8217-6936-7	$6.99US/$9.99CAN
The Morning After	0-8217-7295-3	$6.99US/$9.99CAN
Deep Freeze	0-8217-7296-1	$7.99US/$10.99CAN
Fatal Burn	0-8217-7577-4	$7.99US/$10.99CAN
Shiver	0-8217-7578-2	$7.99US/$10.99CAN
Most Likely to Die	0-8217-7576-6	$7.99US/$10.99CAN
Absolute Fear	0-8217-7936-2	$7.99US/$9.49CAN
Almost Dead	0-8217-7579-0	$7.99US/$10.99CAN
Lost Souls	0-8217-7938-9	$7.99US/$10.99CAN
Left to Die	1-4201-0276-1	$7.99US/$10.99CAN
Wicked Game	1-4201-0338-5	$7.99US/$9.99CAN
Malice	0-8217-7940-0	$7.99US/$9.49CAN

Available Wherever Books Are Sold!
Visit our website at **www.kensingtonbooks.com**

More by Bestselling Author

Janet Dailey

Bring the Ring	0-8217-8016-6	$4.99US/$6.99CAN
Calder Promise	0-8217-7541-3	$7.99US/$10.99CAN
Calder Storm	0-8217-7543-X	$7.99US/$10.99CAN
A Capital Holiday	0-8217-7224-4	$6.99US/$8.99CAN
Crazy in Love	1-4201-0303-2	$4.99US/$5.99CAN
Eve's Christmas	0-8217-8017-4	$6.99US/$9.99CAN
Green Calder Grass	0-8217-7222-8	$7.99US/$10.99CAN
Happy Holidays	0-8217-7749-1	$6.99US/$9.99CAN
Let's Be Jolly	0-8217-7919-2	$6.99US/$9.99CAN
Lone Calder Star	0-8217-7542-1	$7.99US/$10.99CAN
Man of Mine	1-4201-0009-2	$4.99US/$6.99CAN
Mistletoe and Molly	1-4201-0041-6	$6.99US/$9.99CAN
Ranch Dressing	0-8217-8014-X	$4.99US/$6.99CAN
Scrooge Wore Spurs	0-8217-7225-2	$6.99US/$9.99CAN
Searching for Santa	1-4201-0306-7	$6.99US/$9.99CAN
Shifting Calder Wind	0-8217-7223-6	$7.99US/$10.99CAN
Something More	0-8217-7544-8	$7.99US/$9.99CAN
Stealing Kisses	1-4201-0304-0	$4.99US/$5.99CAN
Try to Resist Me	0-8217-8015-8	$4.99US/$6.99CAN
Wearing White	1-4201-0011-4	$4.99US/$6.99CAN
With This Kiss	1-4201-0010-6	$4.99US/$6.99CAN
Yes, I Do	1-4201-0305-9	$4.99US/$5.99CAN

Available Wherever Books Are Sold!

Check out our website at **www.kensingtonbooks.com**